AUTUMN FOOL

Copyright © 2007 Michael D'Emilio
All rights reserved
ISBN: 1-4196-6580-4
ISBN-13: 978-1-4196-6580-6
Library of Congress Control Number: 2007902866
Publisher: BookSurge, LLC
North Charleston, South Carolina

For more information or to order additional copies,
please visit: www.autumnfool.com.

AUTUMN FOOL

MICHAEL D'EMILIO

For my family

This story is dedicated to the memory of

Mattia P. D'Emilio
and
Karl J. Reinartz

They were warriors, and eventually brothers.

Prologue

European Theater of Operations
September, 1944

I can still smell that sky of impossible blue, blue like you never saw over Germany back then. A twist of oil smoke hung on the air, just a faint tang of sulfur and gasoline drizzling through the prop wash and reminding me of the job I had to do. The fear built slowly, like a static charge. It gathered strength from Flixton to the mainland, where the battles started. Those yellow Four-forty-sixth tail fins would bob outside my open window, bullet-holed and beautiful, flying so close it looked like you could just climb out and jump from wing to wing. I never got over the roar of it all. Sometimes during takeoff the other waist gunner, Van Orden, and I would spit gum wads down onto the English hedgerows. For a few minutes, we'd forget that we were also carrying things that wouldn't just bounce off a cow's ass or stick to some widow's bicycle tire. Anna told me later how she came to dread cloudless days. When the sky began to rumble and hum she would try to picture a rainstorm on the horizon, at least until the ack-ack started and the sirens wailed and she couldn't fool herself anymore. Four miles up, I pretended she didn't exist. She wasn't Adolf Hitler or Hermann Goering, just a girl like the ones I used to dance with back at the Pelican Club in Newark. Sixty years later I can imagine her peeling a potato and singing along with Ella Fitzgerald, struggling to sound American as our bombardiers zeroed their sights on her neighborhood. But not back then. I couldn't think about her then. A guy like me can't do that job with someone like Anna on his mind.

There was a picture of her husband on the living room wall, a serious young man in the field gray of the German infantry. Little innocuous swastika on his hat. Just a few lines on a little black button, banal and small, she said. But the more she stared, the hotter and more malignant it would become until what seemed like an afterthought was the only thing she could see. Behind that picture was a letter from a German officer. During a war, there are only a couple of reasons that guys with rank would write to the wives of foot soldiers. It's usually not good news. She had stopped looking at that picture long before September of Forty-four, but she just couldn't bring herself to take it down. Denial, maybe. Like singing to herself as the last seconds of quiet ticked into the first explosions on the edge of town. The machine gun on her rooftop would shake the apartment walls. She knew we were coming, but still she stood there and willed her voice to finish the song. That was Anna, a half-ton of audacity stuffed into a hundred pounds of pride.

Later that day, when she was halfway down the street and still in her apron, one of ours landed on the building across from her apartment and detonated. A three foot block of stone blew right through her living room wall, right through the spot where her husband's smile reflected the mortal sincerity of every soldier on every living room wall. Little bits of plaster sprayed into the drapes across the room. There was nothing left but sky where a door-sized piece of her wall used to be. It's strange to think that bricks and beams and lathe and undercoat and skim coat and paint — three layers of paint, three colors, three moods I never asked her about because I didn't want to picture her husband standing there saying "I'm tired of blue. Whattaya think? Beige?" — that all of it could come crashing into her living room, or that all of it was even there beneath the surface. Invisible layers between her and the war outside. Some things you just aren't meant to see.

When I woke up that morning, a crackling blue energy already filled the English dawn. No one had to tell me we were flying that day. Our B-24, the *Maggie Baby*, was assigned to the Purple Heart Corner of a formation of bombers headed up from the south and into the western Rhineland. Everybody figured there would be fighter planes and flak, lots of both. You don't just waltz into someone's backyard and light it up without an argument. Still, I always believed that Maggie was charmed, or at least bulletproof. She was named for our pilot's wife. It was something about that love, maybe, or damned blind luck, but up until that day we always made it back. I always kept the same rituals, same prayers. I ate my powdered eggs, smoked two or three Luckies as fast as I could — because eleven hours in an oxygen mask is just too damn long — and then crossed myself at the door and piled in. After that it was just me and Van

Orden sitting on our parachutes, not needing to talk because we had said it all twenty-four times before.

Over the Channel, I pressed my thumb to the cartridge just outside the ammo feedway, not for any mechanical reason but just because I always did. I rocked the gun on its base to make sure it was stable. Through the gun sight, I took aim at a patch of empty sky. There was a prayer I would say just before I fired off a few test rounds: "God, please guide my aim, and if I kill anybody please forgive me." Makes no sense. It reminds me of the stories I heard around the West Ward about the guys my brother Vin hung out with. They would all pull the trigger at the same time so no one could rat for the shooting. Everybody's guilty. I never wanted to kill anybody, but I figured if God helped me do it then he couldn't hold it against me. So I prayed. There was a dent in the metal frame of the waist window from a flak fragment that had ricocheted in and cut the bridge of my nose. Thing must have been the size of a baseball. If it was between my prayer and some German gunner's, I guess I won that coin flip. Twenty-four missions and just a cut on my nose. Not bad. So I kept praying.

On our twenty-fifth run, the first enemy contact didn't come until we had rumbled up through France and into Germany. Mönchengladbach was just a little bull's-eye on a map, but we were ready to give it the royal treatment. Our little Mustang friends peeled off with no Luftwaffe in sight, but then just like that four Messerschmidt 109s dropped down out of the sun and onto us. Our top turret gunner hollered into the radio: "Two bandits, one o'clock high!" They had stacked up, so he didn't know there were four. I heard the pah-pah-pah of their cannons before I felt the rounds pop our fuselage.

12

Wheeling, firing, my thumbs pinned the trigger as the gun moved like an extension of my wrists. A flash of silver. Five rounds. Ten. Gotcha! Belly-up, Kraut! He's bleeding smoke like a speared fish. Whoa, Jesus! Where'd they come from? Three more 109s. Wheel and rip. They're getting away. Who the hell is that screaming?

It was the top gunner. I called after him on the radio, but his voice just gurgled a little and then trailed off. I stood there, thumbs on the trigger, watching a small black dot emerge from the smoke of the plane I had just shot down. It mushroomed into a tiny parachute. I suppose I was disappointed at the time, but looking back I'm happy that pilot didn't die. And anyway, I'm not even sure he was the one who killed our top gunner. What a friggin' mess that gets to be, worrying about who got what justice. Lucky for me, I didn't have time think about it. A handful of 109s droned back in and cued another twitch-trigger symphony from our guns. My forearms were sore from squeezing the gun handles. The inside of my oxygen mask was wet from my breath against the cold rubber. The air in the plane was forty below. I reminded myself to breathe slowly, to relax my grip and feel the rhythm of the gun. The eyes see and the hands react, they taught us. Yeah, right. After twenty-five missions, the hands see.

Next to me and facing the opposite direction, Van Orden bucked against his machine gun. Between shots, I could hear him cursing through the radio squawk. Two 109s looped back in. He hammered at them until they crossed into my field and rolled to dive away. I knew then that we were headed into the flak field outside of Mönchengladbach. I turned to tap Van Orden on the shoulder and point this out, but just then a shell ripped a football-sized hole through the floor and smashed into a steel rib above our heads. Shrapnel sprayed everywhere. Van Orden turned around with a confused look on his face. His eyes rolled back as a smiling gash opened on the side of his neck. Black blood pumped from a nickel-sized hole in his leather helmet and streamed down into the fleece of his collar. I wondered what the hell was keeping him on his feet. He stood there for what felt like forever until finally his head lolled to one side. I caught him and laid him carefully onto the floor, but I could tell by his weight that he was already dead.

"We just lost Van Ord—" I tried to sound professional when I spoke into the radio that time, but my guts surged up and choked off my voice. Thank God I didn't puke into my oxygen mask.

"Roger that, Mateo," the pilot replied. "Okay, fellas, got to be even more alert now. Keep 'em off us, boys. We're moving in on the drop zone." Now *he* was a pro. He was older than all of us, and one hell of a pilot. He had never called me by my first name before. Always, it was "Albero," or "Jersey," but for some reason he chose that time to call me Mateo. It was all he needed to say. I had just lost two of my closest friends, yet with that single word he kept me from falling apart. The sound of my first name struck a filial chord, like somehow he was stepping in as a father to handle those complicated emotions for me, for all of us. At the same time, hearing my name reminded me of the other guys counting on me to do my job. Our pilot was not a pep-talk kind of guy, but he was a great motivator, a great leader in battle. He knew better than any of us what it took to get the job done, and he knew *us*, what was in our hearts and heads, probably better than we did ourselves. With that kind of credibility, a leader doesn't have to say very much at all.

14

Without it, his words don't matter anyway. He taught me more about leadership with that one word than anyone had before, or has since. Restraint can be a powerful thing.

As we approached the initial point of the final run, he lined us up behind the lead bomber. Flak exploded everywhere. I dragged Van Orden's body off to one side of the steel floor and tiptoed back between the smeared blood trail and the hundreds of spent shell casings on either side of it. A patchwork landscape flashed through the perforated floor, while deep staccato detonation echoed ahead and to the rear. I peeked out to see if our wings were still intact, but wind blast and shelling chased me back inside. Carrying eight souls, two corpses and four thousand pounds of explosives, the *Maggie Baby* bounced like the sky was full of boulders. Twenty-five thousand feet below, Mönchengladbach hunkered down, well aware of the work we intended to do. "Bombs away" buzzed in my ears. I could picture the bomb tails swimming as they fell, zucchini-striped and swollen with destructive potential. We jinked sharp left, then right as the formation began evasive maneuvers on its course back to Flixton. A single drop of blood traced a burgundy line across Van Orden's back. I closed my eyes.

Behind my clammy mask, I could taste the cigarettes waiting for me back in England. Those first drags after hours at altitude always made me lightheaded. Then I started thinking about the cigarettes that Van Orden and I had bought from some Irishman on a walkway by the Thames, how good they had tasted in the December mist. When I opened my eyes again, I saw that the blood that had pooled on his collar had seeped over and stained his whole shoulder. Someone in another plane hollered over the broadband: "Bogeys dead ahead!" He sounded like he couldn't believe what he was seeing. Seven German fighters were flying directly into the firing lanes of forty-six American B-24s. I watched one of the bombers on our wing take direct hits on two engines. One of his fans disintegrated as its motor housing was engulfed by a tulip of flame. Our pilot never budged off his line.

I chased the 109s with gunfire, but they had already circled way up high and headed back out ahead of us. Just when I thought they might have moved off for good, I felt the whole plane shake as they swung back and blasted away our cockpit glass. The pilot grunted into the radio and then went silent. The hundreds of shell casings on the floor started to roll forward as we nosed down into a dead-stick dive. Guys screamed over the radio about bailing out, but I didn't say a word. I don't know why I was so calm. I just clipped on my parachute and let the angle of the dive slide me forward to the bomb bay doors.

Ahead of me, our bombardier banged the lever to open the doors. Wind whipped in as we fell faster. The little ball turret gunner crabbed up from the front of the plane as the bombardier rolled out into the cold sky. When he fell, the bombardier smashed his right arm against the barrel of one of the belly guns and broke it mid-forearm. It flopped in the wind, like the only thing holding his hand on was his sleeve. My body tensed involuntarily, arms bent and tucked close to my sides. The ball gunner made it to the bomb doors, but then turned around and started to go back. He stopped and looked back at me with a weak grin.

"Forgot to turn off the power switches in the turret," he said. "I was gonna go turn 'em off." Tears gleamed in the little man's eyes.

"Force of habit." I squeezed his shoulder.

He shook his head, crouched and fell out of the door. Almost as an afterthought, I pulled off my glove and reached back for Van Orden's dog tags. The chain clumped in a sticky knot as I stuffed it into my pocket. When I hit the prop blast, I shut my eyes until the lift of the parachute told me I could open them again. I watched the *Maggie* arc down, but I couldn't watch as she sheared and screamed and broke in half. I mourn my friends, my crewmates, but I also mourn that ship. I can't explain it. We were her children.

A hint of moist soil wafted up through the scorch. I looked down at the city I had just helped to devastate. Fighting down panic, I forced myself to talk through the drill. Land someplace secluded. Hide the chute. Escape... Jesus, to where? I looked at the blood on my hand and felt fear begin to constrict my breathing. "Come on!" I shouted. Focus on the ground, look for landmarks. Entire blocks of the city were crushed beyond recognition. There. A park. What's that, a museum? Trees. Jesus, *Germany*. I thought about the silk map they gave us in England; it had most of Europe sectored off. I kept mine tucked next to a St. Christopher medallion, a Zippo lighter and a picture of my family. In that photo, Pop stood with one arm cocked behind him just like all the old Italian guys, like it was a rule that someone in Europe came up with when the camera was invented and everyone just followed along. There was Mama, next to Pop. And my sisters. Me. All standing on our stoop on Tenth Street in Newark. I wondered if I would ever see New Jersey again. Mönchengladbach drifted closer and closer. My God, we tore the crap out of that town.

Leaves and thin branches slapped at my face as I crashed through and snagged on a big oak limb about forty feet off the ground. I dug in my pocket for a knife. When I reached up to cut the parachute cords, the relative quiet of the moment made me realize how chaotic the previous hour had been. Our formation had moved on. Not too far away, massive fires made a sound like wind blowing. I caught the low whine of a distant siren. A few Germans were still taking potshots with their eighty-eights. The moment was framed with sounds, but to me it felt like utter silence. No machines roaring in my ears, no gun barking under my chin. No screaming. The stillness left me feeling even more alone. Suddenly, I didn't really want to come down from that tree. I knew that the bombs had stopped and that people would be out in the streets soon, but I kind of didn't care. It was so peaceful.

That's when I heard a small voice, singing. I shook my head to clear out the hallucination, but it was still there. Then I caught a glimpse of Anna through the leaves. My heart jumped, she was so beautiful. She was walking along a path about twenty yards away, wearing a kitchen apron and singing at full voice. In the middle of a city ripped by war, I couldn't believe what I was hearing. I thought maybe I had died, and that she was an angel coming to claim my soul. As she got closer, the muddy tears on her face made it clear that she was human — innocent and alone and forcing a smile through the same madness that had swept me up and left me dangling so far above the ground. She was wearing an apron and singing a song by Ella Fitzgerald. Doing a pretty spot-on imitation, too. I had to smile when I heard that broad Harlem "A" mixed up with the German "S" for "TH."

She even bounced a little between each step, trying to swing through the music.

I looked back up the path, wondering where she had come from. Beyond the park, her charcoal city glowed under heavy smoke. How bad is it out there that she has to walk in here? I thought of the girls I knew who sometimes danced and sang in Branch Brook Park. *Newark*. It hit me then, how utterly alone and far from home I really was. I squinted through the treetops for another snagged parachute. Up in the smudgy sky, there was no sign of our squadron. I told myself it was good, that at least they wouldn't drop on my location, but the icy knot in my gut knew better. Maybe that's why Anna's singing struck me so deeply. Her song — Ella's song — was the last thin connection I had to America. I wondered if anyone else had made it down safely, if the bombardier's arm felt as bad as it looked, if the little ball gunner was okay. It wasn't like I could just wander around calling their names. Jesus. I was a sitting duck. Watching her walk up the path, I felt ashamed to be worried about my own safety. Still, I knew I had to cut myself down before someone spotted my parachute and captured me.

As I reached up again with the knife, I heard a second noise on the ground. A man in a black Nazi coat darted from one side of the path to the other, oblivious to the presence of his enemy directly above him. His uniform was dirty and torn, and he had a thick scar on his cheek. He dragged his left foot a little but still moved quickly, as if he had long since learned to compensate. I watched him creep up behind her, cup his hand over her mouth and pull her down into the bushes. She bit his palm, then shrieked when he pulled it away. Her scream snapped me out of my shocked fugue. I sliced one of my parachute straps and let my weight swing me away from the heavy limb directly below. Through the trees, I watched her struggle frantically in the underbrush. She knocked the Nazi's hat off and grabbed a fistful of his white-blond hair. He batted her grip loose, but she clawed at his face again. After he pinned her hands, he reached down and started to fumble with his zipper.

That did it. Teeth grinding with rage, I cut the other strap. When my ribs slammed onto the limb below me, I clawed at the rough bark and held on, feet dangling free. There was a flash of silver where my knife landed. I hugged my way across to the trunk and shinned down to the ground. Knife. I found it, then looked for the Nazi. There, between the leaves. White-blond hair. Something inside of me felt dark and cold as I started up the path. Sprinting the last few yards, glaring at the scar that framed that predatory sneer, my eyes went black.

PART ONE: BLOOD

One

Newark, New Jersey
December, 1941

Less than a month away from Christmas, Nineteen Forty-one. I remember it like it was yesterday, walking my fingers through a streak of sunlight on the dining room table. God, I love that Jersey light. There's something it does on a cold, clear day, some way it plays across the red brick storefronts that washes the mundane out of everything. It shines through the bare treetops and down the long stretches of boulevard and reminds you that the West Ward sits on a hill above downtown Newark, and that this little bit of elevation puts you closer to something and not further away from something else. The sunrise coaxes the blue sky down for a visit, down to the pavement where you scuffed your hands that day you slipped and fell running home from school. Down to the sidewalk where a breakup crushed you between the hanging fog and the Sunday blues. Just when you thought maybe God forgot about you, that Jersey sunlight angles its way through the morning and even the trash has a poem to tell. People from other places might not notice, but Jersey people know what I mean. No one is denied redemption when the sun shines in New Jersey.

Nineteen years old. I was sitting at the dining room table, fingers grained black from a night on the job. Mama said scrub and I did, but that sooty fireground water soaks right through leather and finds its way into your fingerprints. It's humbling. That was the first lesson I learned as a fireman: "On your knees, boy!" It's not like you stride in, scoop up a frightened baby and walk out of a burning building. No, you crawl through the black smoky mess on your hands and knees, blind, wet and scared. You're either soaked or singed, and you better hope it's the first one. I watched the smoke trail up from my Lucky Strike and into that blessed morning as a little orange coal pumped under a hang of ash. It dropped onto the lace tablecloth, the first ash from the first cigarette of the first Sunday in December. Why I thought that, I don't know, but it's what I remember thinking. All this 'first Sunday' business they talk about in church puts it in your mind, I guess. I blew on the ash and it scattered.

That was a day for remembering the little things. For years, I walked around thinking everything changed on that day because that's what they told you — that our country would never be the same again. They get that stuff in your head and you believe it. Maybe it is true, maybe everything did change that day, but for me, looking back, it was the same then as it was the Sunday before and as it was the Sunday after. I crawled through a fire and dumped enough water on it to keep it from burning down the house next door. I made sure my buddy and I followed the hose line back out to the street. I knocked off my shift at six a.m., walked home, showered again, and slept a couple of hours. I sat at the table while the women took the children to church and Pop made his rounds for anisette and biscotti at every house on Tenth Street. Mama's unattended gravy filled the air with the scent of heaven. I stared as my hands relaxed in the light of God.

And the Japanese bombed Pearl Harbor.

But what the hell did I know? Nineteen years old. It's a damn big country we have, and all the Japanese bombs in the world wouldn't have made a ripple in my coffee from that far away. I lived my life between the lines that were laid out for me, sidewalks and sidelines and Sundays on Tenth Street. My house was full of the same superstitions as that of every other family on the block, traditions and habits that flowed from our southern Italian heritage and mingled like the flavors of the gravy that cooked on every stove. You trust God to bless your family, but you make sure you watch the butcher when he grinds the pork and veal for the meatballs. You go to church with the women until you are old enough to earn like a man. That morning, my big sister Carmela dragged our brother Vin along with her own kids to St. Antoninus again, even though at fourteen he was already hustling more pocket money and better confessional stories than people twice his age. I sat back in my chair and waited for them to return.

The corners of our pressed tin ceiling curved down to meet the wall. Across the span above me, individual plates had been stamped with a pattern and fabricated into one big sheet. I stared at the ceiling, seeing it but not thinking about it. There was a row of bedrooms along one side of the flat. Railroad, they called it. You could fire a shot into our front window and hit nothing but glass as it sailed through the living room and into the dining room, over my head, into the kitchen and out the back window. Carmela lived in an identical flat upstairs. Her son Mickey, the oldest of three boys, had just turned five. His favorite thing was to run and slide down the hardwood hallway into a throw-rug second base, squealing "DiMaggiooooooo!" The kid did that all afternoon. Pop would stir in his easy chair, look up from his *Il Progresso* and slap the wall with four sharp whacks that shook the crucifix by the door and reverberated through the upstairs. Carmela always ignored Pop and let Mickey keep running the bases. It was easier than singing him to sleep for an hour at night.

On the table in front of me lay a weathered copy of *Les Miserables*. Halfway through the twelve-hundred page translation, I had stopped seeing it as an athletic challenge and started to simply enjoy the story. The guys at the firehouse called it my "brick," but none of them even had a library card, so what did they know? Still, more often than not I listened to them. They were the older brothers I never had, and they lived the ideals that Hugo only wrote about. It all made sense to me back then — skipping the end of senior year to join the fire department, but also enjoying books that honor students struggled to finish. You worked, and *then* you played. I was the quarterback for two West Side High city championships and even made a couple of all-star teams. My grades were good, when I tried. But when the coaches from Fordham and Rutgers came around, I smiled and nodded and declined their invitations to apply. College was never an option. Instead, I stood in front of the bathroom mirror and buttoned a dark blue uniform shirt, staring at the fire department patch Mama had sewn onto the shoulder. I crouched to let her pin the brass "NFD" onto my collar. No letterman sweater would have made Pop smile that way. It was like that back then. You worked.

I took another drag, blew the smoke through the morning sunbeams and opened the book. My mind wandered back to the concrete horseshoe down on Bloomfield Avenue. City champions. Faded jerseys, ours white with dark green numbers, theirs white numbers on pale blue. My own voice barking cadence. The feel of the ball. The angry chuffing of linemen and beyond that, further away, the rush of the crowd. That was the sound of the running lane opening up, like when the surf rolls and breaks and you find yourself suddenly dry and alone on sand. All that sound just sucks you along. On the field, you get a quick glimpse of green. There's an odd, cool wind on your face as you pick up speed. Then comes that rapid-fire moment of freedom when you know, just know, that they aren't going to catch you. The blur of the sidelines. The sprint. The score. Such an odd sensation, how small the field is at that moment. It was on you in an instant, that bastard shifting goal line. You wonder if you'll ever remember how to shrink the field again, how to make third and five feel like wide open second and one, or first and ten, or whatever down it was when the walls parted and the hands lost their grip and the wind blew just enough to sail you through. It happens, but not nearly enough. And you never know when. So you just grind and gasp and bleed and keep that diamond moment in your mind so you'll know it when you see it again.

Touch. That was the other thing. You either had that on a given day, or you didn't. When you did, your fingers were safecracker fine and the ball stayed right on a thin little bead between your eyes and the receiver's hands. You didn't even have to throw it. It threw itself. You'd see a white blur separate from a light blue patch forty yards away and your hand would just reach through the tunnel and set that ball down between the elbows and the chest. On a dead run. If you really had it — touch, I mean — you even sped him up just a little. My God, sixty years later and I can still feel it in my wrist, my elbow, my hand. You're five, throwing a wadded-up rag to a kid on a vacant lot. Or you're twenty-eight, and you hit a grown man on the fly with a brand-new Wilson Duke. Or you're eighty-something and the page you just screwed up lands exactly where you wanted it to in the can across the room. Man, I'm telling you, your heart sings. You never knew the grace of God had a name, but it does. It's Touch.

I can't remember not loving the game of football. My friends grew up swinging broomsticks at tape wads, waiting for the decks of Yankee Stadium to explode when they connected with a game-winner. Me, I grew up dodging Redskins that looked like Buicks, up and down my very own Tenth Street Polo Grounds. The Giants were always a *football* team to me. I stubbed out my cigarette and glanced at the radio over in the living room. In a couple of hours, Tuffy Leemans was going to lead the Giants against the Brooklyn Dodgers in their final regular season game of Nineteen Forty-one, and I would listen as fifty thousand people cheered them into the championship playoffs. Nineteen and a working man, I still got excited for that moment when the radio announcer called the opening kickoff. I felt my own too-clean jersey, tight against my pads. I smelled the grass after the first good tackle, when you knew it was *on*.

Three hours at the center of the universe. Nothing else mattered.

I gave up on Victor Hugo and walked over to flip on the radio. Benny Goodman. Toe-tapper for sure, but I preferred Ellington. I believed Duke was a guy who had been there before. Where? Everywhere. He was confident, not frantic. His music let you know that it was damn hard to rattle him. And from the way he worked, you can be sure he knew the price of greatness.

My watch told me I had time for one more smoke and maybe a cup of coffee before my solitude ended and the family returned. Pop would shuffle back down Tenth Street, crust of biscotti in his hand. Mama would bustle in and check the gravy. At the stove, I lifted the coffee pot and stared at the black liquid as it rolled across the bottom of my cup. Out of habit, I glanced at Pop's seat when I sat down. My match flared and touched the end with the writing. I had the cigarette reversed, but it didn't matter because there wasn't any filter anyway. Pop had decided when I brought home my fire department patch that I could smoke at the table. "You have'a the good job," he had rumbled, waving me over with the back of his hand. "Sit, sit." Above all things, Work. There were no saints with soft hands. Pop said maybe ten words on a given day, so the fact that he had spent seven of them granting my newfound habit a place at the dining room table was a big deal. I played it off, nodding in detached silence as I set my ashtray down. Think of Duke, I reminded myself. Act like you've been there before. But I knew it was eating at my brother. Even Carmela gave me deference that day. Pop's respect was never given lightly, and never fully unless it was somehow connected to hard labor. I looked down at the cover of the book and imagined Jean Valjean busting up rocks in Toulon. Pop would've loved that guy.

On the side table, Pop's *garavone* squatted like an upside-down mushroom, gleaming in the sun. It was a clear sipping bottle, pinched at the neck. He would fill it with the red wine we made each fall and stored in wooden barrels in the cellar, then lift it to his lips with the hand that was missing an inch of index finger. His stump fit perfectly in the pinched notch. Hunkered at the end of the table like Vesuvius in an undershirt, his subterranean smolder cast a shadow under which all laughter might cease at the first rumble. Forearms hardened by a life of manual work. Finger severed at the second knuckle by a garment factory steam press, a casualty of the dangerous work left to immigrant hands. The story was repeated like a liturgy in our family. Without complaint, Pop had slid the crisp new shirt out of the press and wrapped it around his hand, then put on his hat and walked ten blocks to St. Michael's Hospital. When I was five years old and heard it for the first time, I asked if he had just left the severed finger in the steam press or if he had taken it with him. Carmela had slapped me hard on the top of the head. You don't question scripture, no matter how implausible.

For nineteen years, I bristled under Pop's dominion. My furtive rebellions were conducted in the angles between his linear perceptions. He was the patriarch. The impact of that role and of men like him rippled through the lives of every family on Tenth Street, washing back to the hazy coastline of old world tradition and returning again, its force redoubled. In the church confessional, women begged forgiveness for failing both their Lord and their master. Children spoke in whispers of the rock-handed impatience brought home by fathers laboring in soul-rending ambivalence, scratching for currency in a place that did not value ancient custom. Postponing modernity, families like ours throughout the West Ward huddled around these men and fanned the thin flame of reverence. Fashions change faster than hearts.

"Hey, Mat! Tell me about the fire!"

The door banged against the wall as Vin's demand cracked the rhythmic ease of an Ella blues. He was my little brother. Despite his wild streak, he had a touching reverence for some of the stories I told him. He mimicked my passion for swing music, feigning interest in every puff-cheeked drifter who so much as honked out Reveille in four-four time. His taste needed work, but his spirit was there. I used to pride myself on always having answers for the hundred questions he asked — even if they weren't always right. When we first heard "A-Train," his head snapped around as fast as mine did. That simple little piano riff told me it was Duke, but I had to fudge the title when Vin asked. He didn't care, or remember. He just sat there like me, head bobbing back and forth, fingers tapping quiet time with every other beat of the bass drum. When those horns rolled through, just gleaming with urbane sophistication, we were hooked. At nineteen, I knew two things for sure: Duke Ellington was the king of American music, and that music came from a place I just had to see.

Jazz music was the second of three great passions in my life. The first was football, and I'll get to the third later. Jazz, to me, is the finest work that Americans have ever done. It is the unifying beat of millions of disparate hearts, the one communal passion in three centuries of raucous individuality. It runs through the blood of this

land, animating and strengthening us, reminding us all
that no matter who we might hope or aspire or pretend
to be, we all carry the same dominant and recessive
strains of that thin little tune called Liberty. Black or
white, rich or poor, the tincture of freedom washes us all
with the same glowing hue. And jazz explains all of that.
Driven by the tempo of supreme talent, hands working
valves and sticks and keys, minds seeking and finding the
one true beat, jazz is America laid bare. It is ambition, but
also cooperation. It is the guiding example of how so
many people, with so little in common, can stand
together like brothers and love the same thing the same
way at the same time, not because it's better than us, but
because all of it, every little bit of it, *is* us.

My little brother understood that back then, but I
think he forgot about it as he got older. Bounding into
the living room and tearing at his collar of piety, he
wasn't necessarily conscious of what drove him. Neither
was I, all the time. But it was the same thing: that
American beat. There was that feeling of Okay, I'm home
again, but there was also that promise of what's Out
There, that dream of Big Time America. Ella's fecund
warmth and Ellington's rolling brass.

Vin wanted to hear about the house that had nearly
burned down around me the night before. I slapped the
seat next to mine. When he sat, I started to tell him in
hushed tones — in "don't alarm Mama" tones — about
the searing black inside the foyer, the glow that had
danced in the kitchen as I crawled closer, the explosion of
a flashover that sent me diving for the floor. I
embellished, pausing to let Carmela set the plates down,
watching to be sure that Mama didn't hear the part about
the beam that fell and snapped our big Irish lieutenant's

shinbone. I ducked to let Vin see the blisters on my ears, the scorched stubble where my hair used to curl at the ends. I finished the story as Mama set down a huge bowl of pasta and frowned at me for the astonished pallor on her younger son's face. Leaning back, I lit another one as Pop shuffled in, reveling in the privilege that work, dangerous work, had conferred upon me.

You can call it the sin of pride, and maybe I would have bought that at the time, but I don't see it that way now. The way I figure it, a guy has so few chances to feel his place in the world, to really see his impact on things. Let him enjoy it. Yeah, maybe that look on my face sparked something in Vin. Maybe all that stuff he did later came from thinking, Hey, *I* wanna be the big guy. Okay, maybe. But what the hell did I know about that? I used to talk to Vin about the Big Time, about "Slappin' Seventh Avenue with the Sole of My Shoe" like Ellington. I used to tell him about New York City, where men in long coats walked beautiful ladies down boulevards chromed with Cadillacs. Where granite was piled to the sky and cigarettes dangled from mouths untainted by accents and sloppy tomato gravy. Where they tipped their hats and whisked their dates onto dance floors. Every step pulsed with rhythm, no movement awkward or unrehearsed. Out there in Big Time America — a place we had never seen. It was just beyond the limits of what we knew, beyond Newark, where a lucky man had a job and a really lucky one had clean hands with all ten fingers.

"Padre, e figlio, e spirito santo..." My hand jumped to my forehead and darted around my torso to catch up with Pop's mercifully slow intonation of the Sign of the Cross. I prayed as I always did, for my family. I looked at Carmela, twenty-four and already the established matriarch of her own small brood. Her husband was in the South Pacific, on a Navy battleship docked where a small volcanic island had just met the lapping tide of history. His part of the prayer came a few hours too late. I looked at Federica, my younger sister, whose light spirit was as beautiful as her physical form. Sweet Rica, God save your delicate heart. And Mama, from whom her sons received the untamed Sicilian blood that would torture her cautious soul. And Pop. Always, Pop. And Vin, little Prince of Illusions. How many of those illusions came from me? From all my bullshit about Big Time America? Later on, while I was still dreaming about slapping Seventh Avenue, my brother Vin would land in and out of jail trying to steal his way there. Did my pride have something to do with that? I don't know, maybe. You'll have to hear the rest of the story, then you decide. It all started that day. December Seventh, Nineteen Forty-one. I didn't know it then, but on that day things were happening thousands of miles away that would change my life forever.

Two

Mönchengladbach, Germany
December 1941

I can see Anna now, smoothing her dress and staring
into the mirror at its clean white lines. Simple, elegant,
like everything else about her. Her eyes found the flowers
on the table behind her. The walls of the sitting room,
oaken and warm, were too close for her. They were
crowded with smiling photos of hearty German drinkers
at long tables. One was packed with soldiers in the dress
uniforms of the Third Reich. I know her smile faded
when she saw that. Picking at the seam that circled her
waist, her gloved fingers began to tremble. A single
teardrop darkened her bosom. She looked up. The mirror
blurred, but stubbornness and wedding day jitters helped
her fight off the melancholy. For now. The lace of her
handkerchief blended with her silken gauntlet as she
dabbed her cheeks dry and smoothed the makeup that
had begun to streak. Her hand stopped. For some reason
she thought of her mother, wishing just once to hear that
cautious, urgent murmur again. The walls moved in on
her. Her chest tightened as she struggled for air and

rushed to the window to breathe deeply of the dark winter chill. It did not steady her shaking hands. She was completely alone.

In a few minutes, a thin band of gold would encircle the third finger on her right hand. Her fiancée's booming voice echoed through the heavy door and around the back end of the restaurant. Another man bellowed back, equally loudly. German men, always puffing their chests and blowing hot air. Let one of them whisper to me, she said, and he will own my heart. Her cheeks flushed with shame. She had already promised her heart to a man who was anything but quiet.

Once there had been a quiet man: her father. She smiled at the crystals on the black window as she thought of his laughing eyes. Her pulse settled. He had loved to listen to her sing, and to watch her jitterbug across the room to raucous American music. His hands had earned his living, forming wood into the skeletal frameworks of houses and buildings as his mind and voice lay still. Evenings found him peaceful, exhausted from fingertips to toes but refreshed by time alone with his thoughts. Each day, the other carpenters chattered away as his own silence lent him the refuge in which he found his meditative rhythm. She had loved to watch him, high in his rafters and smiling patiently at the idle banter. But one November day in Nineteen Thirty-eight, when the conversation turned ugly, he broke his silence and paid dearly for it. There had been a week of violence in the streets of her country, violence against Jews. Everywhere, even on his work crew, the brownshirts had crowed about it. In the end, her father's caution had yielded to basic human outrage.

"Swine," he had declared. "You are swine."

For that, they hurled him from the roof. The courts ruled it an accident, but Anna knew better.

Early in Nineteen Forty-one, her mother joined him. Friends tried to comfort Anna with assurances that her mother had died of a broken heart, so deep was her love for Anna's father. But Anna believed her mother had died of fear and guilt — simple, selfish emotions made lethal by the sacrifice Anna's father had made.

One final, deep inhalation of the December night, another smoothing of the dress, then Anna took three unwavering steps to the door and jerked it open. Her bridesmaids gasped at the intensity in her eyes, but when Anna saw Karl her expression softened to concern. The skin on one of his cheekbones was blackened around a swollen gash. He fingered the wound and shrugged with a sheepish grin. She could not suppress a smile. He had a chest like an oaken barrel and thick, rawboned limbs that strained even the most perfectly tailored clothing. His army dress grays barely conformed to his awkward figure, and his bristling mop of hair nearly brushed the door frame above him. He seemed unkempt despite his best efforts to button up and comb down, as if his wild soul were unable to tolerate a polished exterior. But it was his voice that truly could not be contained. It roared from him at all but the most intimate moments, yielding only when he applied his entire will to the task of suppressing it.

Next to Karl, Anna felt safe and small. Part of her was no less alone in his presence than when they were apart, but she chose to ignore that feeling and to focus instead on the comfortable familiarity they shared. They had known one another for most of their lives. Their childhood relationship was rooted in a mutual passion for boundless exploration, but while his sense of adventure was entirely physical, hers was primarily spiritual and intellectual. Through adolescence and early adulthood, they had grown apart. She needed more than his raw instinct for freedom to hold her attention. She sought understanding, reflection. He wanted simply to keep roaming and playing. She grew restless. He struggled for control, for more than mere acquaintance. She edged away, then ran.

And then her father's death changed everything.

Before and after he died, there had been others; awkward young men who chased her beauty without considering what lay beneath. They were a series of snapshots, not companions. She barely remembered any of them, but each time she saw the Nazi flag she thought of one boy, and one lonely night. He had sat on the edge of her couch and leaned into a note on an old saxophone. Her hazel eyes, usually flecked with gold, were darkened by the weariness of grief and apathy. As she watched his pale cheeks redden with effort, she wondered what it was that drew such extremes of desire from some of the men she met. Her complexion was slightly olive, and her thick brown hair fell in long waves around the angles of her face — hardly the Aryan ideal. Her shoulders, as ever, were squared with haughty defiance. She was barely a hundred pounds, just a hair over five and a half feet tall, but she held herself as if she alone were responsible for the world around her, as if with a wave of her hand she could silence or mobilize those who stood nearby. Confidence. That's what it was. But she didn't know that, not back then.

They had come to her with music, at least the ones who took the time to learn what she loved. She was blessed with a voice that could reach into a man's soul. Her young heart was just beginning to grasp what it awoke in those shadows. They were drawn to her ethereal sweetness, but also to her steely resolve. At first, most of them would have been frustrated by their inability to solve the riddle of her. Then they would be angry, either at their own failure to possess her or at the absence within themselves of even a fraction of her self-assurance. On those rare occasions when she was greeted with a male personality that did not require the augmentation of her own, she had allowed herself to toy with the idea of real love. But in her heart, she held little hope for even the most promising advances. She had always felt that she could never truly fall for a German boy — even one with enough skill to mimic the simpler elements of a jazz tune on a saxophone.

With academic dispassion, she had studied the effete young musician on the couch across from her. He was sixteen, still undetected by the war machine ravaging her country's male population. Really just a little boy, she thought. Once again, she contented herself with the notion that true love was in some far-off place preparing itself for her. For now, at least there would be music. She had stared at the mantelpiece photo of her father, feeling that familiar tightness in her chest at the sight of her mother's Rosary beads hanging on the frame. Each morning when her mother passed that picture, she would make the Sign of the Cross. It was a gesture that made Anna rage at the sky. Why?! Why would You take him and leave her here with her hypocritical superstitions? Anna had never forgiven her mother for the relief on her face when she learned, after hearing the news of her husband's death, that all he had said was "Swine." Anna had wanted to grab her mother by the shoulders, to scream into her face: "He died defending you! And all you feel is relief? It would have been better if he *had* told them that your mother was a Jew!" But Anna had said no such thing. She knew she didn't have to.

Instead she had stared at the picture, missing her father with all of her heart and ignoring the feeble affections of those incapable of such love. She had not noticed when the blond boy stopped playing his saxophone. When his thin hand found hers, his eyes were wide with concern. She dismissed his empathy with a toss of her head, turning away to wipe the tears from her cheeks. But when she looked back at him, the words began to pour from her lips — at first merely the facts of the event without comment as to its cause, and then nearly, so nearly, more. But he cut in before she could reveal her grandmother's religious identity, blurting a story about his own uncle who had died in Poland. A brave man, the boy said. A proud lieutenant in the Waffen SS. Anna recoiled as he spoke. *SS!* A whirl of images swam through her mind. Old women dragged by the hair into the streets, their flimsy nightgowns torn open to the November air. Children wailing as fathers were beaten and houses burned. Everywhere, broken glass. Night after night of broken glass...

Two years later, at a safe remove from that terrifying evening, Anna stood in the hallway of the restaurant and shivered in her wedding dress as she recalled the conversation and the images it invoked. She looked at Karl, laughing with two other uniformed soldiers, and thought about the last time she had seen the blond boy. A few months after their date, she had waited by the side of a broad boulevard for a parade to end so she could cross the street. She looked up and saw that familiar, androgynous face marching with a troupe of Hitler Youth, blond hair cropped close, smooth cheeks flushed with pride. His young eyes had still seemed free of cruelty, yet he passed the Nazi flag with his arm outstretched to salute that broken crucifix floating in its sea of blood. He must have known what it stood for, she thought. Yet his face had been serene, untroubled.

Forcing the memory away, she brushed at one last tear and inhaled to her full height. At the end of the hallway, the man she was about to marry wore that same twisted symbol on his lapel. She closed her eyes, but the image lingered. Karl might not have chosen to wear the swastika, but it was there nonetheless. As the crowd in the main room fell silent, he looked back at her with love in his eyes. She kept her eyes on his, away from the uniform and focused on the soul who had no choice but to wear it. She felt cold. Somehow her legs found the strength to follow him down the aisle. Years later, that would be the last thing she remembered about that night.

As he watched his bride walk toward him, Karl felt the bruise around his eye begin to throb. He was grateful that the small gathering would be looking at her and not him. No one noticed the cuts on his right hand. No one knew how badly he had injured the man who had attacked him three nights earlier. He licked the cut on his lip, suddenly parched with anxiety. His eyes spoke his doubts. A woman like her, marrying me? She saw his fear and smiled to reassure him.

Karl Eisenstark was not a man given to worry or

introspection. He had risen fast in the German infantry through fearlessness and an instinctive awareness of even the smallest details of a combat situation. He fought without remorse, led without hesitation, and slept soundly at the end of it all. Anna knew there was no little voice in his heart that bemoaned the circumstance of his military service; he had accepted it as his only possible choice, other than death by firing squad. Still, she also knew that not even the tiniest part of him enjoyed anything about it, except perhaps the occasional friendships with other soldiers who, like him, despised the authoritarian government they had been forced to defend. He was intelligent enough to recognize the futility of his situation — the irreconcilable difference between who he was and what the Reich required him to be — but he gave it as little thought as he could and vowed only to survive.

Three nights earlier, he had been in good spirits at an encampment along the Rhine. There was talk of an offensive involving his regiment, but then there was always talk of that. A few times, the word "Russia" had been whispered around. He was unfazed. The dimming sky was crisp and clean, the enemy was miles away and he was headed home for three days' leave. He and two friends had found a dry, secluded patch of ground by the riverbank to sit and share some smoked landjäger and a small flask of schnapps that one had received from home. As Karl took a sip of the liqueur, a dark shape darted past him and pounced on the precious bundle of dried sausages. Before he could react, the dog had devoured most of the meat. Karl dropped the flask, grabbed two handfuls of fur and flung the dog high in the air. It grazed a tree trunk and landed awkwardly on a gnarled root, but immediately jumped back up and attacked. He barely got his forearm between the dog's teeth and his own throat. In one motion, he turned his body and used the dog's momentum to swing it out toward the freezing Rhine. Still clutching a piece of Karl's sleeve, the dog hit the black water and was quickly swept downstream.

"You!" The voice had come from the shadows behind the trees. Two soldiers in SS black stepped forward. Neither one outranked him, so Karl ignored them and picked at the gray flannel in the lacerations on his arm. "You there!" the man persisted. "Asshole! Look at me."

Karl smiled but did not look up. From his blind side, the other soldier swept a backhand across his face. The man was wearing a ring on the outside of his leather glove. Karl's friends edged closer, but when he shook his head they stopped.

"Who are you, the fucking Queen of England?" Karl growled. "Wearing a ring like that?" He licked his split lip.

"That was his dog," the man said as he straightened the ring and wiped it on his trousers.

"That was our landjäger," Karl shot back. He turned his attention to his shredded arm, but his awareness never strayed from his adversaries. The first punch came from the dog's owner, a wild right that Karl slipped easily. Karl countered with a tight jab that emptied the man's lungs. Before Karl could get his hands back up, the other man landed a ring-studded punch just below his eye. Karl ducked behind his upraised fists and flicked two quick lefts into the man's nose. He drove a right up through the man's chin, grunting at the crunch of breaking teeth. When the weight of the first man hit his shoulders, he ducked forward instinctively, bulled his neck to break the man's chokehold and flipped him onto his back. The soldier struggled once more for air. Karl straightened up and let his hands fall to his sides to signal that his point was proven; no more violence was necessary. But then he realized that these were not reasonable men. They were Waffen SS.

As the soldier on the ground recovered slowly, the one with the ring and the shattered sneer drew out a knife. Karl's friends stepped forward again, but again he motioned for them to stay back. Circling, Karl dodged one slash, then another. Without lowering his eyes, he studied the man's feet. When the blade flashed a third time, Karl slid past the weapon, stepped behind the man's forward leg and lowered his weight onto the extended knee. With a shriek, the man released the knife and crumpled to the ground. The entire movement happened so fast that Karl's friends wondered if it had been an accident. Karl picked up the knife, glanced at the death's head on its handle and tossed it into the river as its owner writhed on the ground. Turning to his other opponent, Karl waited patiently. The man closed his eyes and shook his head, then crawled over to his battered comrade. The latter roared at Karl with unintelligible rage. Karl waved him off, bent to pick up the flask and sat down with his friends as the SS troops limped away.

The next morning, Karl was awakened by the sound of screaming. It was a few seconds before he realized that he was hearing his own name.

"Eisenstark! Where is Eisenstark?!" The lieutenant's accent was Bavarian, his boots patent leather and barely worn. His pale hands and soft paunch emphasized the fact that his officer's commission had been the product of political largesse, not combat experience. "Eisenstark!!"

Karl slid backward out of his bedding and shrugged himself up to his full height. His chin was level with the top of the screeching Nazi's cap. "Ja, here I am," he mumbled, his salute anything but crisp. A beat too late, he added "Sir."

"Working class turd," the lieutenant spat. He peeled two sheets from a portfolio and slapped them across Karl's face. "Here, learn about Russia. It's where you will die." Karl took the papers, saluted and started to read them as he turned away. "Did I dismiss you?!" shrieked the lieutenant. "You do not turn your back on me! *I* turn first! Not you!!"

"Yes," Karl said, now fully awake. He held up the orders. The mission was to begin that afternoon. "Actually I —"

"You will listen to a commanding officer! Listen to me!!"

"Javoll," Karl said, "but —"

"Javoll, *Herr Leutnant!* Say it!!"

"Javoll, Herr Leutnant." He held up the papers. "But this is today."

The lieutenant's face flushed with rage. Karl didn't blink when the little officer cracked his riding crop against the side of his shiny boot. He stood still as the lieutenant began to pace back and forth, breathing loudly through his nose and occasionally pointing with his short whip. After a few turns, the pacing stopped. The lieutenant glanced around at the troops who were watching with groggy amusement.

"I am an *officer!*" he shrieked. He turned and jabbed a finger in Karl's face. "You! I'm going to make an example out of you. You arrogant dogs will show me respect!" Standing on tiptoe, he leaned close to Karl and let his voice drop to a snarl. "You think because you have been in battle that I do not have authority over you? Huh? Do you?"

Eyes lidded with indifference, Karl didn't seem to notice as the lieutenant stepped back and turned. When he whirled and lashed his riding crop at Karl's sleepy face, Karl dodged backward and to the side and let the whip sail harmlessly past. As the lieutenant stumbled, several of the soldiers behind him snorted to suppress their laughter. Karl remained still and impassive, his expression unchanged.

"You—!" The lieutenant choked, his face as red as the flag on the pole behind him. As if realizing for the first time that he had a sidearm, he broke off his breathless rant and fumbled at the clasp on his holster. He used both thumbs to cock the luger and then aimed it at Karl's forehead with one shaking hand. Karl did not flinch. His eyes remained fixed on the same spot they had held since the lieutenant started pacing, but his arms relaxed slightly and hung loose, ready to deflect the weapon. The lieutenant muttered as if his words were part of a long-standing inner monologue. "I should shoot you, you smug bastard. I should shoot you now."

"You will shoot no one."

The clear baritone of authority sent a flash of terror across the lieutenant's face. As the major strode between the troops, his junior officer holstered his weapon, saluted nervously and stood at attention. Gray hair at the major's temples reflected his forty-one years, but his athletic build had been kept lean by a long career of military discipline. He had served with courage in several campaigns along the western front during the First World War. His opposition to promoting unseasoned officers was widely known, and his disdain for politicians, if less outspoken, was every bit as vehement. He had commanded Karl's regiment in battle, and while Karl had little contact with him, he respected the evenhandedness of the major's leadership and the obvious intelligence of his tactics. The major put one hand on the lieutenant's shoulder and steered him to a spot where only Karl could hear their conversation.

"Herr Major," the lieutenant stammered, "this man's insubordination..."

"You mean his desire to go home and get married?"

"But..."

"You know as well as I that he has been granted leave."

"But he has upset the commandant of the Waffen SS." The lieutenant's eyes narrowed as his voice gained confidence. "He has made enemies in higher places than—"

With a look, the major cut him off. The lieutenant's eyes widened with fear again. Instead of cowering in political self-defense, the major stared down at him with aggressive contempt.

"This man will be transferred to the Twenty-first Panzer Division in El Agheila." The major waited for the lieutenant to comprehend what he was saying. "Libya," he added.

"Africa?" The lieutenant was astounded. "The Afrika Korps? But the commandant will see this as an even greater insult. General Rommel has gone out of his way to exclude the Waffen SS from... his campaigns... in..."

As the major raised one hand and pinched the lieutenant's collar, the smaller man sputtered to silence. The major studied the insignia, then raised his eyes and let them bore into the lieutenant's faltering gaze. After a few seconds, the lieutenant looked away.

"Perhaps one day, *Herr Leutnant*," the major said quietly, "Daddy will make your dreams come true. But for now, remember that you are *not* in the Waffen SS. I will expect to see Eisenstark's transfer papers on my desk in one hour."

The major returned the lieutenant's salute and walked back toward the rest of the troops, pausing only to speak to Karl.

"Don't drown any more dogs," he said. Karl straightened to attention as he acknowledged the order. "They are more valuable than some of our junior officers," the major whispered with a wink.

On the morning after the wedding, Karl packed his duffel slowly. Anna watched him, aware that the story he had told her reflected more than just the odd luck that had graced his military career thus far. He was trying, in his own way, to justify his participation in the war by reminding her that not all German soldiers held the same political beliefs. She wondered if his growing admiration for Rommel was rooted in the spiritual and physical distance that service in the Afrika Korps would place between him and the religious atrocities occurring in Germany and along the Eastern Front. Several times, he had emphasized his own — and Rommel's — distaste for the Waffen SS, as if she might find more room for him in her heart if she could believe that he was on her side. They had been married in a civil ceremony that made no mention of church or tradition, just as she had wanted. He was her husband. Yet he knew, instinctively, that she was holding something back. Part of him wanted her to share his enthusiasm for this new assignment, for the fresh start it gave him and for the remarkable leader he would be serving in Libya, but he understood that he would not get a hero's goodbye. Her heart was too wounded, her losses too great. She had never shared the secret of her mother's religious heritage with him, but he sensed that something deeper than ideology was fueling her bitterness toward the government.

There was more than a little energy in his step when he boarded the train that afternoon. Her complicated emotions were too much for him. He knew that he could withstand the searing terrain and the unorthodox tactics of desert warfare, but he was afraid of what lay below the surface of his new bride's polite smile. To be married to her — officially, irrevocably — was sufficient for him. To have experienced her physically was more than he had ever dreamed possible. But to linger in the shadow of her powerful heart and discover how little of it he actually owned was more than he could bear. Folding his slim hopes into one of the many bundles in his service bag, he packed himself up and shipped out. "One day," he had said to her, "this will all be over." She smiled, knowing that by "this" he did not really mean the war, but rather the dissonance in their relationship. She nodded as she kissed him goodbye and ended their first day of marriage with three little words that she knew were both merciful and untrue.

"Yes, it will."

Three

Newark
May 1943

The Number Six Crosstown used to stop at the corner of City Stadium and Bloomfield Avenue. That's where I got off that day. I ambled down toward Branch Brook Park, breathing in that warm-sidewalk smell that only happens when winter is truly over and the sun has had time to bake down into the concrete and draw out that sandy little whiff. Spring always takes its time coming to Jersey, but when it finally arrives you can't even force yourself to remember what winter felt like. It was one of those days. Dappled green leaves crowded me with kisses. Every skirt flashed before me like red to a bull. The Six had taken me down Roseville Avenue past manicured lawns and brick houses with crisp white columns. I used to wonder if I would ever live in a place like that, but when I thought about moving away from Tenth Street it left me with a lonely feeling. Maybe that's what was wrong with me. Ambition is all about getting out, moving up, being excited about a huge pile of nice stuff. But that really just bored the crap out of me. I wanted to see places and maybe do some things I never did, but I never got that aroused by having more things. All I needed — especially back then — was a radio, a book and a pack of smokes and I was as content as a flower in a field.

But you've got to do something in this life, and that's where pride finally caught up to me. It made me mad that I had more skills than other guys who were doing more. It was never about money or praise or any of that. It was this nagging feeling that God had dropped some really special things in my lap, but all I did was settle for the status quo. I was a fireman with a few old football trophies and a shelf full of books. When I died, what would they would say? "He threw a nice spiral. Liked to read. Didn't say much." Pride stabbed me when I thought about that. I squared my shoulders to the sidewalk and kept walking. In my pocket, I felt the letter from Thursday's mail. I was fit to serve, and the draft board said it was time. My physical was on Monday. I sized up the unlit cigarette pinched between my fingers. Chances are I won't even see action, I told myself. It's more likely that a burning building will fall on my head than some little Japanese guy will pop me with a bullet. But still, that letter made me aware of my own mortality. I had to take stock and then ask myself, is that all I was?

At the edge of the park, I notched the Lucky Strike in the corner of my mouth, cupped my hands around a match and leaned in for a light. I flipped the match out onto the grass and watched it die in a little puff of smoke. The night before, a wood-frame on Bergen Street had gone up so fast we nearly lost half the block. Early on, the word outside was that it had been a grease fire; one of the kids had tipped a coffee can full of fat drippings onto

an open burner. But then the story changed a little. I was
one of the first guys in. The scene flashed through my
mind as I walked across the grass to Vin's baseball game.
He was a junior, playing catcher for West Side High. I
angled for the crowd at one of the diamonds, but my
mind was still back in that kitchen on Bergen Street. I was
still crawling through the smoke, sliding my axe handle-
first ahead of me on the ground and hoping that it would
meet something soft, something human. I smiled as I had
the night before when it did.

I had found the last child in the house. I lifted him
onto my shoulder and retraced the line of the wall back
out of the apartment, passing a hose crew as they made
their way in. There was a lot of glass on the kitchen floor,
but from the outside you could see that only one window
was broken. I didn't stop to think about that at the time,
but in hindsight it made a lot of sense. When I got to the
front stoop, I stood up and carried the boy down to the
sidewalk. He was unconscious but breathing, his face and
chest badly burned. His mother was having a rough time
with the rest of the kids, and finally decided to herd them
off to a neighbor's house so they didn't have to watch
anymore. That side of Cleveland Junior High was a mixed
neighborhood. The hair on the boy's head was short and
curly. The skin on his little face — the part that was not
burned — was deep brown. I stood there under a
streetlight with him shivering in my arms for more than
half an hour until the ambulance finally arrived.

Our crews fought hard, but the kitchen and then the
whole house went up in the time I was standing outside
with the boy. We gave up and worked on the neighboring
houses so the whole block wouldn't burn. Grease fires
were notoriously hard, but a few of the guys on the

interior crew had observed that this fire was even faster than usual. I stood there listening to them speculate about arson until the owner of the building walked up. Mystery solved. We all knew who Benny Bells was.

"Friggin' shines," Benny said, as if to himself. He bit the side of his hand, playing like he was really angry. "Fryin' pork on an open flame with their little brats runnin' around. And there goes my building."

I was standing right there, three feet away, holding the little boy. Benny never even looked at him. A few other firefighters were there, too. Later on, we all agreed that it felt like he was rehearsing his story or maybe trying to get on record with us. Something like that. Most of us had seen him really mad, and this wasn't it. Everybody knew he was lying — even Benny. But it was his town, his little world. If you lived in it, you covered your wallet and hoped he didn't sniff it out. He was the size of my nephew, and the whole town shit its pants when he strolled by. Benedetto "Benny Bells" Corlese. Five feet square, with a temper twice his height. He rolled like an unexploded round through the streets of the West Ward, primed to bump into something, anything, that would set him off. Although no one actually saw it, people said he once hung a guy upside down in a church bell tower. The poor slob was crushed when they rang up morning mass. True or not, the story gave Benny a nickname and a reputation, which he used to keep the local ward bosses dancing at the end of his strings. One of them would eventually sign my brother's draft deferment when he turned eighteen.

I tried to forget about the little boy's face, but it stayed with me as I walked over to Vin's game. Such a little guy, to carry those scars around. Before then, Benny was more of a local curiosity than anything to me, but after that night I knew him for what he was. The last thing I heard him say as he waddled off was something about not wanting to pay the ambulance drivers' fees.

As I got closer to the baseball diamond, the images of the night before faded away. I spotted Vin near home plate and shuffled down the grassy slope to the field, watching my scarred black boots rustle in the shiny grass. A hint of steel peeked through one worn toe. I put my hand in my pocket and felt the draft notice again. Japan. Where the hell is that? And where is Germany? I tried to picture the pale green and pink countries on the maps in school. All I knew of Germany was what I had read in old novels about hearty outdoorsmen. That and the high-pitched screaming of their lunatic dictator on the radio. News broadcasts played that recording over blaring trumpets to highlight stories about the Nazis. Those people always sound like they're choking on something. How the hell could we let them take over the world? We'd never hear a decent song lyric again.

I leaned against the cyclone fence and watched my brother squat behind home plate to catch the pitches delivered by the lefthander on the mound. Vin was at that age where it was a struggle to control his gangling limbs. A drift of cigarette smoke caught his attention. He grinned through his battered catcher's mask and nodded over at me between pitches. The pitcher strode into his delivery, a three-quarter sidearm that every lefty I ever faced seemed to have. Vin swatted at the curveball with his fat leather glove, missing it completely.

"Good thing you don't have to use one of those to catch a football," I ragged.

He reached around his back with his 'meat hand' and

flipped me a sign no pitcher could misunderstand. When the inning ended, he tossed the mask to the opposing catcher, walked over to me and reluctantly accepted a hug and a kiss on the cheek. It was an old Italian custom, but I did it more to bug him than anything.

"How ya doin'?" I asked. I figured it was around the third or fourth inning.

"Winning three-two, top of the sixth," he answered.

"Jeez, I missed the whole game."

"You didn't miss much," he mumbled. "I'm o-fer. Can't time this kid up." The boy warming up on the mound looked lumpy and soft, his looping curveballs barely popping the catcher's glove.

"Looks like you ought to hit him a mile," I said.

"That's the problem."

Neither one of us could hit a breaking ball. I told him to wait on one and drive straight through it. He nodded at me as I bounced up the springy bleacher boards to a spot five rows back. I leaned my elbows on the bench behind me and watched Vin walk up to the plate with his usual swagger, an unconsciously wide, rolling walk, more awkward than proud. He looked like what he was, and what I had been; a football player who played baseball only because no one thought about anything else in the spring. Settling into his stance, he waited as the ball spun off the pitcher's hand and hung fat and slow in the air. At the last second, he uncoiled. A loud crack sent the ball towering into left field, just foul. After the outfielder retrieved the ball and relayed it in, Vin whiffed at two more spinning lobs and stalked back to the bench.

I hated to see him put his head down. It was a rare sight in October, but an unfortunately frequent one in May. After one more strikeout, West Side let two opposing players reach base before finally getting the third out to preserve the victory. They gathered for a recap and then dispersed. Walking back to the bus stop, Vin raved to me about both the win and his long foul ball. When we reached City Stadium, I looked up at the curved colonnade and thought about the crowds that used to roar when I got the football. The flag rippled in the breeze. America's pastime, huh? Then why do they play baseball in pastures and football in coliseums? Strange place, America. I was going off to fight for a country I barely understood. But how would life be without the war? I'd probably stay put in my little corner of Newark, babies crawling across the hardwood, kitchen filling with the scent of Sunday gravy. Jazz music on the radio. Me in my easy chair sneaking glances at the wife's ass, a book on my lap and a pack of Luckies on the end table. And that's what they'd write on my tombstone.

My ears went hot. That's not all there is! But what then? *What else are you gonna do?*

I stared up at the red stripes rolling back and forth past that blue square with its forty-eight stars. We walked around the perimeter of the stadium to Roseville Avenue and pulled up at the bus stop. My fist closed around the draft notice in my pocket. Jesus, Monday. One more weekend and that's it. I knew if I told Vin about it, he'd tell Rica. She'd tell Carmela, and neither one of them could keep a secret from Mama if their lives depended on it. So I decided to keep the news to myself for a while. Hell, I might even get 4-F'd. Why worry everyone now? The bus rolled up.

"Hey, Mat, I forgot to ask." Vin turned around as the doors opened in front of him. His eyes were narrow, but there was a childish innocence in his voice. "Carmela said you saved some little shine in a fire last night?"

"She did, huh?" I replied. "Just like that?"

"Yeah." He wouldn't look me in the eye. "Where was that, anyway? She said Bergen Street?"

The bus driver clicked a coin on the steel railing to let Vin know he was ready to leave without him. I turned Vin around by the shoulders and pushed him gently toward the steps. After he had stepped up, I dropped two coins into the driver's palm and sidestepped to the aisle. I reached up for a strap as the vehicle jerked into gear and caught Vin's arm before he fell backward.

"So tell me about it," Vin continued.

"First of all, ease up on the 'shine' stuff."

"Whattaya mean? He was a black kid, right?"

"Yeah, he was, but..." I looked around at the crowded bus. Faces were tight; people maintained a civil anonymity with those who were not from their own neighborhoods. Maybe this was not the place. I looked down at Vin. The boy's blistered face flashed across my mind. Then again, maybe it was.

"See Vin, it's kind of like music," I started. Vin frowned. "Not the fire, the other thing," I continued. "See, you love the music that Duke Ellington plays, right? 'A-Train,' all that?"

"Yeah," Vin mumbled, suspicious.

"Well, if he was sitting in that seat over there you might walk over and say 'Mr. Ellington, I really do love your music.' Right?"

"Maybe." He looked away. "I might be too nervous."

"You?" I grinned. "Yeah, right. Now, let's say you didn't know that was Duke Ellington sitting there."

He looked back at me. "Yeah?"

"Well, you might say 'There's a shine sitting in that

seat right there.' Right?"

"Not if it was Duke Ellington," he said warily, as if he was on to my game.

"Yeah, but you don't know that," I countered. "All you know is it's a black man."

"Well, then... I don't know, maybe." Vin scowled. "Forget it, I don't wanna hear about the fire."

"Hang on," I pressed. "So what changes when you know he's Duke Ellington? Or put it this way: Which one of you changes?" Vin stared out the window, ignoring me. "Him? You? What's different? Nothing, right? He's the same guy, same overcoat and hat. Just sitting there, minding his own."

"Like you oughta be," Vin shot back.

"See, I would say that *you* changed," I continued. "You saw him differently."

Vin's face was stony. The familiar landmarks of our neighborhood started to pass by the windows. He pushed past me as the bus slowed down, then stepped off and started walking without waiting for me. I caught up to him in front of the Estinziones' house and chucked his shoulder, but he shrugged away.

"What the hell do you care about a buncha shines, anyway?" he cried. "That's right, *shines*. Carmela didn't say that, *I* did. Not every goddamn thing I know comes from the two of you! *You*. You're what, a fireman? You got five bucks to your name and you talk about the big time? The hell with your big time!" His eyes filled with tears. "You ain't nothin' but a straight and a sucker! I got my own money! More than you. You save some little kid who ain't even supposed to be home and you think you can lecture me? *Va fongool!*"

My mouth fell open. I watched him run to the house

and stop on the porch to wipe his eyes so Pop couldn't see he had been crying. *"...who ain't even supposed to be home."* I felt sick. Vin was running with a fast crowd, but I had no idea he was in that deep. Sixteen years old. Christ. As I stood there, my safe little street began to blur and whirl around like some strange carnival ride. What had Vin done? Benny Bells' face flashed across my mind again. What bothered me the most was the way Vin's eyes had narrowed when he first asked me about the fire. I don't know why. There was plenty else to be concerned about; he could have been in real trouble. But there was a cold amusement on his face when he asked that question, something smarmy and dishonest, as if deep in his heart he believed that the truth was something silly and trite and that he was far too clever to be bothered with things like honor and kindness. It reminded me of the look I had seen on Benny's face as I stood beside him with the injured boy. Just a fraction of a glance out of the corner of his eye; one split second that revealed the empty character of the man. It was the flicker of humanity denied, the remnant of a soul long since sold. To see that look in my brother's eyes was more than I could bear. It nearly broke my heart.

That night, I didn't go home for dinner. I rolled in late, went to bed, and left early the next morning. Same thing the next day, and the next. I took my physical, accepted Mama's tear-stained St. Christopher medallion, ate a farewell dinner with my family and never once mentioned the conversation to Vin again. It was the most cowardly thing I have ever done, turning away from it — away from him. Vin stayed away from me, too. There was no part of me that was ready to see all the way through to the truth of it, and no part of him that wanted me to. I guess I figured that if I didn't know for sure that he had helped with the arson, even just as a lookout or whatever, then maybe he could still be my little brother. But I knew. Many times after that, I would think of those few days as the cause of everything that happened later between us. Nevermind Benny's money, or Vin's wild nature. Something arrogant and punitive within me still believes that I could have changed things, that it wasn't simply his destiny. That *I* failed. Say what you will, but in my heart I know I could have saved my little brother and I didn't.

Four

Mönchengladbach
September, 1944

White-blond hair. There were shadows across their
faces, but I could still make out the scar on his cheek.
That Nazi uniform. Ten yards away. She sees me. No, no,
I don't want to hurt you! I raised a finger to my lips.
Shhhh! My God, she's beautiful. I sprinted the last few
steps, driven by instinct, every fiber of muscle and blood
in me screaming Stop this! Stop him! The Nazi was biting
his lower lip, enjoying a private joke as he struggled with
his zipper. Anna's expression was as much nausea as
terror. At the last moment, he saw me and rolled onto his
back. I dove at him. He kicked my hand and sent the
knife flying. I drove my forearm into his chin and
blocked the slapping punches he threw. Struggling to see
what I was hitting, I tried to aim at his face and throat but
instead connected with his brow ridge and collarbone. My
heavy bomb coat deflected his blows, but it also slowed
my hands. He twisted and dodged away from my punches
and rolled the fight into the underbrush.

Pushing a half-turn further, I gained the top position again. My fist just missed his nose and connected with his brow, opening a small gash. I still remember the tiniest details, as if I had sensed them from outside of myself. Twigs and leaves. Dark earth. Musty wool. Foul German onion breath. Then everything went white when he popped me in the eye. "You little Kraut motherf—" I drove a forearm through his jaw. Blood. I did it again and again, pounding his thin, pale hands back into his face. His eyes widened, and one hand darted to his side. Gun! I whipped my hand back and knocked it away as he was bringing it up, then pinned his hands to the ground. I noticed the Nazi death's head on his lapel, the arrogance in his sneer. He glanced at Anna and smiled just a little. I felt the rage well up and nearly blind me. My fists flew wildly, angrily. I was aware that I was fighting badly, even stupidly, but I was too mad to care.

We rolled again. I pushed him away from the gun and gained enough separation to line up a decent punch. Chin. His eyes rolled. Bam-bam-bam broke his nose. Blood. I grabbed handfuls of his blond hair and slammed his head down on a knotty root, over and over, muttering about my friends who had died and innocent girls and everything else but all the time knowing that it was my own fear driving me. I banged his head down again and again. My blood howled. I looked at the death's head on his lapel. Horrified, I relaxed my arms. His neck was slack, his eyes closed. Slowly, I lowered his head and let it rest on the root. Blood started to seep down into the crevices in the gray bark. My mind reeled back to the *Maggie Baby*, to the confused look on Van Orden's face as he struggled to comprehend the gash in his neck, the blood in his eyes. I looked down. Is this another dead man? No! Did I kill him? *Please, no!* I looked at my bloody hands, then at the Nazi. Swastika. Red and black armband. Blood on my hands. And the howl, in my heart. I heard it. Blood on my hands. *But he was going to rape...* Blood. *But... I had to!* Blood. My mind roared with dissonance and confusion. Had I killed a man? I looked at the swastika on his arm. Am I no better than that?

"Stand up, Choe." The world blurred with tears. My eyes burned. Who's that? It was a man's voice, but shaky. Where am I? "You, American Choe, *steh auf.*"

I turned around. Both barrels of a trembling shotgun stared down at me. The old man's hands were palsied with fear. My first shreds of detached consciousness began to knit back together. Anna was speaking to the old man, and had been before he spoke to me. It's odd what you notice when you aren't really there. Her speaking voice was even more sensual than her singing voice. She spoke again. I could tell that she was pleading with him to spare my life. She had been attacked, and she had witnessed my horrifying brutality, yet she was able to rein herself in and project a tone of absolute reassurance. His trigger finger quivered involuntarily. I stared up into the twin chambers of my fate. But life is funny sometimes. There I was, facing my own death. After what I just did, you'd think I might be worried about damnation, or that I might see my life flash by, but I didn't think about any of that. All I could focus on was the fact that his gun sight was bent. The sliver of metal sticking up from the barrels of the gun was angled, off by about thirty degrees. The barrels themselves were edged with rust. I wanted to reach up and straighten that gun sight. Okay, there you go. Now fire away.

But whatever Anna was saying was working, because the gun barrels began to lower and the old man's face softened. When he pointed at the Nazi with his trigger hand, I realized that I was still straddling a man whose skull I had bashed in. I lurched backward and scrambled to my feet. When I looked at the old man again, his hand was back on the trigger and the gun was aimed at my heart. Anna spoke rapidly, reasoning at the speed of sound. Slowly, he lowered the gun again and patted her shoulder. There was kindness in his eyes. I followed his glance to her face. My God, is she beautiful! I could feel the bottom fall out of my stomach. I didn't know if it was love, or just plain sadness. I remember thinking, Somebody gets to look at her for the rest of his life, and it isn't me. It didn't seem fair. As she spoke, I studied the contours of her face, the color of her lips. Her petite body. That voice. I tried to deconstruct her, to find the element that did not fit, to seize on any detail that might someday help me forget the totality of her perfection — but there was no flaw. I looked at my hands, tainted first by the blood of a fallen comrade and then by a rage I could not control. I felt in my pocket for Van Orden's dog tags. I glanced at the man I had brutally beaten. For a second, I thought I saw his chest move.

No, I thought, he's probably dead. And my penance was instant. There she was, a German woman. The enemy. I couldn't have her, but I could think about her for the rest of my life. The whole thing was gauzy and surreal, like a dream you're not even sure you had. I stared at her. The old man walked out of my peripheral vision. She was talking, but I just stared, dreaming. Sleepwalking. Looking at the shining waves of dark hair that framed her face. When the sun found the flecks of gold in her eyes, I knew I would die in the presence of this woman, after either a lifetime of love or a mortal struggle for one more moment with her. Enemy or not. Her voice emerged from the muddled haze. She was giving me orders.

"Come on, you have to move now. Here, take off that heavy coat. You will change clothes with him. Put on his uniform. Do not worry about the old man, he will not come back. I told him you saved my life. When I said my name, he said he might have known my husband..." The word slammed into me. Husband! It tore through my flesh and muscle and bone and ripped into my heart. *Husband.* I wondered how it happened so fast, how I fell for her so instantly and to this day, fifty-nine years later, still have not forgotten the feeling. I went through the motions of escaping that park. I stripped down to my skivvies and buttoned on the Nazi's tight black evil as she rolled him into my sleeves and zipped him up. I jammed my head into the narrow hat and strode with an authority I did not feel. I looked down at the foreign insignia on my chest. I rested my hand on a Luger that I could never fire in my own defense because I was already dead and damned. Husband.

Anna scooped up a handful of dust, lifted my hat and dumped it on my head. She patted it all over, evenly.

"You are not fooling anyone with that black hair," she smiled. "Your eyes are blue, yes, but that hair... We will have to bleach it."

I nodded, oblivious to the notion of preserving myself. We passed through cratered streets, smoke and fire billowing everywhere. I walked behind her, watching her hips move beneath that apron. The Nazi must have looked out from under this same visor, seeing what I was seeing, lusting as I lusted. He had no right. But neither did I. I followed her down alleyways and across ruins of buildings. Smoke and fire were everywhere. A bed hung halfway out of a room that had only two walls. Its occupant might have woken up that morning to the scent of coffee, or frying eggs. Or maybe to the sound of our payload arriving. Sorry pal, I thought. Rude awakening, huh? I looked at my own bloody hands and tried to shake my head clear of the complicated emotions that roiled inside of me. We kept walking. A gaunt old man shuffled along, holding the hand of a thin little girl. She looked up at me with curious apprehension, her cheeks sunken with hunger. No, I thought, *she* can't be the enemy. Not her.

"Quickly," Anna whispered. "And stop looking at people. They will see in your eyes that you are not SS."

We rounded a corner. Anna stopped short and stared at a building that jutted from a flattened city block like an unbridged tooth. I think she was genuinely surprised. Whether it was because the whole block had been devastated or because her apartment had not, I don't know. Two corners of the building were shredded. Jagged bricks and wooden slats hung loose, bitten and torn by indirect impacts. There were several large holes in the front façade, but the walls still seemed straight and more or less plumb. We mounted the stoop and opened the front door into a pile of shattered glass. I followed her up the stairs. When she unlocked the apartment door and held it open, I heard another one click closed behind us. Anna's eyes followed my glance.

"My neighbor," she whispered. "Always with the nose in everyone's business."

She stepped through a narrow hallway and into the living room. Her shoulders tightened as she gasped in a funny little way, less scared than surprised. I followed her in and stopped short when I saw what she had seen. You can't imagine how strange it is to see someone's living room just end and open out into space. Only about eight feet of wall was missing, but it was enough. When she looked into the kitchen and saw the potato she had been peeling, she started to cry. In that instant, I snapped out of my mental haze. From then on I was wide awake and locked in on one thing: protecting her. After a long moment, I stepped up from behind and touched her shoulder as lightly as I could. She recoiled and raised her hands to protect herself, her eyes wide with horror and transfixed by the blood-spattered insignia on the uniform I was wearing. Then she recognized me and relaxed. When I took off the Nazi tunic and shirt she touched my arm, visibly relieved. I was thankful that only my clothing had been exiled from her good graces. She looked at me for a curious moment and then summoned the courage to survey the rest of her apartment. With the exception of two broken windows and the gaping hole in the living room wall, it wasn't that bad.

Then she looked up at the ceiling, suddenly frightened. An attic door hung open. It was scaled with the same pressed tin panels as my own dining room ceiling back in Newark. They spanned to the edges of the walls and wrapped down the rounded corners on all four sides. If the attic door were closed, it would have been impossible to distinguish it from the rest of the space around it.

Abruptly, she crossed to the dining room table and dragged a chair back to the spot below the broken door, then opened a closet and took out a small broom and a wooden coat hanger. She unscrewed the metal hook from the hanger and threaded it into a small hole in the end of the broom handle. Her movements were rapid, deliberate; she had done this many times before. When the handle-hook was ready, she stepped onto the chair and poked at a spot near the center of the door. A three-inch section of tin lifted inward, allowing her to slip in the hook and catch it on the door frame. She pulled the door halfway down but then suddenly froze, staring at the hole in the living room wall. The entire neighborhood could see her. Retracting the hook, she pushed the door up with the soft side of the broom. It fell once again and hung slightly open.

"Come, help me," she said firmly.

She went into the bedroom and emerged with a sheet. Taking a hammer and some small nails from the kitchen pantry, she moved the chair to the wall, climbed up and motioned for me to hold the sheet in place. As quietly as she could, she tapped the nails into the top corners. When the sheet billowed slightly in the breeze, we anchored its bottom corners with bricks from the rubble in the center of the room. She moved the chair back and opened the attic door again. A retractable stepladder allowed us access to the crawlspace above. I followed her up. She struck a match and lit one of several candles melted onto the wooden floor. In the flickering light, we could see that a heavy board had fallen and severed the rusted hook from the end of one of the springs. I tried to stretch the spring back through the metal eye, but it snapped and clattered against the door frame. A tiny noise caught Anna's attention. She pressed a finger to her lips and then scampered back down to the living room. She wadded the SS jacket, shirt and hat and tossed them up to me. After folding up the ladder, she reached for the broom. I finally heard the faint knocking at the front door.

"There is a bolt," she whispered. "There, by the edge. Lock it. And try to be silent."

I caught the door, pulled it closed and bolted it. At one end of the attic, a pile of bedding lay below a slatted square vent. The vent let in a tiny amount of light, but I did not dare crawl to it. I blew out the candle and flattened myself against the floor, pressing my ear to the wood. An old woman's greeting bore the sing-song tone of curiosity masquerading as concern. Anna's voice had a slight tremolo. Fear. Every instinct in me wanted to help her deal with this intrusion, but as excruciating as my passivity was, I reminded myself that it was only the beginning. In order to stay alive in this country, I would have to let her lead me. This was a place through which she had navigated many times before — one in which my own lack of familiarity would already have gotten me killed if not for her. The old woman's voice crossed directly beneath me, stopping for a moment as Anna slid away the bricks and lifted the sheet that covered the hole in the wall. At once, the woman began to chatter dramatically. She dissolved into sobs. Anna's tone was gentle and consoling, but firm and final in response to several declarative protests from the older woman. They moved back to the front door. It opened and closed. Several bolts clicked into place. I lay in silence and pictured Anna in the center of the room, still wearing her apron. Waiting. Listening.

Directly above me, an enormous thud was followed by two sets of crunching footsteps. A third walked more slowly in the opposite direction. I heard a scrape, then a short flow of light, tinkling sounds. Another scrape, another cascade. So familiar, but what is it? I listened. Scrape. That's a shovel. Cascade... into a bucket, being filled with...? I looked up at the black rafters, suddenly chilled. Those were shell casings. Directly above me on the roof, just a few feet away, was a German gun battery. It was just like the Krauts to tidy up a gun emplacement while the whole neighborhood was falling down around them. I gripped the Luger and pulled it from its holster. The man on shovel detail dragged his bucket closer. As I aimed at the noise, Van Orden's face flashed in front of me. My finger tightened on the trigger. One of the soldiers said something and the shovel guy laughed. I felt the blood on my hands. Glaring at the sound of scraping, I tried to picture the man above it. I zeroed my aim. Van Orden's blood was sticky between my fingers. Or was it the Nazi's? My trigger finger relaxed. Behind my head, a light tapping startled me away from the darkness. I unbolted the door and blinked into the sunlight, into her eyes of gold. I don't want to die.

It was my turn to put a finger to my lips. As she climbed to me, I holstered the weapon and pointed upward. She nodded.

"I told my next-door spy that a soldier helped me home and then left," she whispered. "She does not believe that you are gone. She said there is nothing wrong with a widow seeing a man after a year. Especially now, since..."

Widow! My face must've lit up the whole attic.

"What?" She was startled. "What is it?"

Light turned to heat. I was beet red and could not look her in the eye. At last, I brought my eyes back up. She was smiling with what seemed like affection. Or it could have been pity. I chose to see the former.

Leaning closer, I whispered: "What's your name?"

"Anna." Chin up slightly. Light in her eyes. Mischief. I feel that moment even now, fifty-nine years later. I feel it.

"I'm Mateo."

You wouldn't understand if you've never met her, but the sound of my name only fully made sense in the echo of hers. It was the first time in my life that I really knew who I was.

There was a name carved into the wood plank floor of the attic: "Simon Knuffmann, M-Gladbach, 1943." I carved my name next to it: "Mateo Albero, Newark, USA, 1944." An epitaph followed by a graffito. Later on, Anna spoke about the few desperate souls who had taken shelter in that space on their way out of Germany, about the loud tick of each second that death walked the rooftop while just a few feet away its quarry slept with one ear tuned to the turning of a key. She was as brave as anyone I have ever known. The next day, she went about the business of scrounging food at what was left of the local market, listening for news of downed American airmen and walking loudly on the stairs so suspicious ears could have their fill. There was talk of a man who had been attacked in the park and who remained unconscious. Some people insisted he was an American, but others claimed he was a German loner who had been dismissed from the military. I felt more relief than fear when I heard that all of the stories said he would pull through.

On the second day, Anna decided to bleach my hair so that I might look more convincing in the SS uniform. I lay back with my head in the sink. Amused, she smiled down at me as her fingers worked water through my scalp. But when she opened the bottle of peroxide, she let it hover over my head for a few long seconds and then capped it again. There were tears in her eyes.

"I cannot," she whispered.

At the time I thought maybe her reaction had something to do with the Nazi and her memories of the attack, but now I think maybe she was just a little confused about how to feel. She was a war widow with few illusions, but also a young woman sharing a dangerous infatuation with an enemy of her country. Over the next thirty-one hours, we reached for one another in ways that only the obsessed would understand. When we spoke, I memorized every detail of her. Each moment that I was in the attic, I sensed her passing below. She knew that I was watching from the shadows, and she took comfort in that. We reached, but we did not touch. Somehow, even between two people whose lives had entwined as quickly as ours had, the boundaries still held.

We tiptoed around the broken glass of her husband's picture frame until she finally brought herself to pick it up. I had seen the photograph on the floor when we first walked in. It lay half out of the frame, a letter tucked behind it. The picture was old. Karl's face was brave and innocent below a cap bearing that dirty little eagle and its button-sized swastika. She picked up the frame, shook out the glass and hastily tucked the letter behind the pressboard backing. It slipped sideways, protruding slightly from behind the photo as she set it on the shelf and turned away quickly. I thought about that letter a lot. Hell, I probably could have written it. "...he died defending his country with honor and courage..." In those letters, nobody ever gets shot five times in the back or dies sobbing in the mud, involuntarily shitting himself, comrades nowhere to be seen. In the minds of his survivors, he stands tall on a hill of victory as one clean and tragically premature bullet pierces his heart without spilling a drop. He dies in full dress, not the tattered remnants of five weeks afield. To the very end, he is certain of his mission and not riddled with questions about the life he will never have. He is military fiction, but I suppose there's kindness in that.

By the time we were ready to leave her apartment, I was desperate to go. The more my thoughts began to revolve around her, the more I sensed the ghost on that living room shelf. It was his house. Those were his layers of paint on that shattered wall — his choices. Nevermind that I was miles behind enemy lines, in the direct path of every Allied bomber and Kraut sniper in the E.T.O. That I could deal with. Somehow I knew I would think or run or fight my way out of all of that, and if I didn't then I would be dead and it wouldn't matter anyway. It was my heart that I was afraid of. We talked about the route we would take, walking our fingers over my airman's map and across the rough sketches that she had drawn for the people she had helped to escape. She wanted to get out of Germany almost as badly as I did. Both of her parents were dead, and her husband too. There was nothing left for her there. Between the two of us, I knew we could do it. It was the part that came after that had me worried. The goodbye.

On the day we decided to go, Anna made one last run into town for a few potatoes and whatever other supplies she could find. I had no idea what we might need. My idea of camping was to walk up South Orange Avenue to

the South Mountain Reservation with a few buddies and
run around pretending we were Indian braves. We were
never more than a quarter mile from civilization, which to
my nine-year-old mind was an ice cream float and a short
bus ride home. Waiting in that attic, I thought about
those days, how we walked anywhere we chose without a
second thought. Anna must have felt like that too, in her
own park. But suddenly now, even her apartment was no
longer secure. I wondered if I would ever see the West
Ward of Newark again. The shops. The churches. Little
old ladies walking to mass in the evening. Young mothers
pushing strollers. My own extended family of street
corner singers and sandlot heroes. Jazz. Football. I
pressed my eye to the slatted opening and squinted at the
wrecked city below, wondering how I would ever get out
of there, how I would ever return to the two original
loves in my life. I'll find a way, I vowed. A tiny knock on
the trap door reminded me that a third passion was
rapidly supplanting football and jazz. *We'll* find a way.

I slid the bolt and let the door drop a few inches.
Anna's brow was pinched with anxiety. She waved me
down. I watched her hurry between the rooms, pulling a
second wool dress over her first, then a sweater. She
stuffed a pillowcase with what food we had, which wasn't
much. She tossed me some old clothes and motioned
with impatience at the SS pants I still wore. As I fumbled
with the buttons, she hissed that I should hurry. I smiled
with the same amusement that I had in the park. Even —
or maybe especially — at her most vehement, she was
adorable.

"Mateo, please! There is no time."

Her eyes darted around, checking for last items. I
turned my back and struggled out of the black trousers,

relieved to button up a baggier pair. I cinched the belt and turned to the rough wool sweater that lay on the couch. She looked away quickly and resumed her preparations. I smiled again. She handed me a floppy hat and the sack full of food, then slipped the luger from its holster and extended its handle to me.

"You will need this too."

I froze. "'You?'"

"Please," she whispered. "It must be this way."

"Anna, I'm not leaving without—"

"Please!" Her eyes glistened. I stared at the gun in her shaking hand. Slowly, she lowered it. Her whole body seemed to deflate as her resolve wavered. I stepped closer and caught her in an embrace. "Mateo," she whispered. Her breath heaved and trembled into sobs. "You must go alone. I saw her talking to the soldiers at the market."

"'Her?'" The instant I asked, I knew the answer. The neighbor.

"There is something you should know," Anna whispered. "My grandmother. Her maiden name was Knuffmann." *Simon Knuffmann.* "She was Jewish." She glanced up at the attic door. "In this place, that is not something you want your neighbor to know."

"But how...?" I stammered. "You're still..."

"Alive?" She looked up at me. "I was raised a Catholic."

She said that she always suspected the old woman knew about her bloodline. Perhaps when she saw Anna with an SS soldier, it did not make sense to her. Maybe after that she started to listen to the stories in the market and put it all together. An American, next door. In that country, one secret was enough to get you killed. But two...

"That's all fine," I cut in, "but I'm not leaving you."

"Well at least go out first, so we are not seen together. They will be looking for two people."

Still hesitant, I nodded. At the window, I memorized the route to the cratered façade of the building she selected as a rendezvous point. I took the food, but tried to give the gun back. She refused, saying she wouldn't know how to use it anyway. Opening the door slightly, I looked across at its twin and wondered if a fearful ear was pressed to the other side. As quietly as I could, I made my way to the stairs, grateful that they were solidly constructed of stone and not the creaking wood from which almost every two-flat in the West Ward had been built. I rounded each landing, pistol aimed straight ahead, hugging the wall in the shadows, heart pounding. The image of Anna alone in her apartment helped to steady my nerves. I listened for the sound of jackboots from below, determined to kill anyone in a German uniform who tried to pass. Crunching through the broken glass in the foyer, I tucked the gun into the waist of my pants and glanced up and down the shattered sidewalk. I pulled the floppy hat low over my face. One deep breath, then out the door.

Remembering Anna's instructions, I shuffled with the stooped deliberation of a much older man. All of the young ones are fighting, she had said. I tried to stay out of the sightlines from the old woman's apartment and from the rooftop above, desperate to look back, to see who might be following my movements. But a German would not do that, so neither did I. Peering out from under the dark brim, I turned the corner. Halfway up the block, a small army truck careened through the rubble directly at me. My legs tensed to run, but I forced myself to maintain the slow gait and frail posture I had assumed. I kept my eyes on the ground as they passed within ten yards of me. They never slowed as they roared by. When they reached the corner, they turned and gunned the motor. I listened. Keep going, I prayed. The pitch of the engine dropped sharply as they downshifted and stopped — too soon to have passed the one building left on the block, Anna's building. I froze, lifting my eyes to scan the sidewalk. Only one other person was there to watch with surprise as I dropped the bag of food, straightened up and sprinted back in the direction from which I had come.

Four troops in standard gray piled out of the truck and ran for the door of Anna's building. I was vaguely aware of the possibility that a fifth had stayed behind to drive, but I didn't care. Working the Luger free, I glanced into the vehicle. It was empty. I took the stairs two at a time, listening to the footsteps above. One voice barked in German as they climbed. Backing into the shadows, I waited for the echoes to die down. A door banged open and then closed. Silence. I checked the gun, then set my jaw and flew up the stairs, letting speed and instinct take the place of fear. When I reached Anna's hallway, I locked in on her closed door and lowered my shoulder, accelerating into the impact and ripping my forearm through. The door slammed against the wall behind it and rebounded back against the splintered jamb. In the empty living room, I felt my throat tighten with anguish. Am I too late? Where are they? Above me, the familiar chuffing of the machine gun started to shake the walls. For the first time, I was conscious of the sirens that had been screaming as I ran. A distant rumble confirmed that the purpose of the soldiers' urgency was not Anna.

But where was she? I ran from room to room, whispering her name as loudly as I dared. Jogging to a stop in the center of the living room, I looked up at the unbroken stretch of ceiling. The damaged attic door had been bolted into place, which was only possible from the other side. I dragged the kitchen table into the room and stood on it to tap at the bumpy tin, first calling her name and then my own. The bolt scraped and the door slowly lowered. I caught her in my arms and held her tight as the first explosions shook the building. We did not speak, but each of us knew at that moment that we would not leave one another again. I looked at the huge block of stone in the middle of the room and shuddered at the thought of the force with which the city was once again being attacked. But it didn't matter. We had no choice but to leave — together.

Five

Western Germany and Belgium
Autumn, 1944

That threshold moment, when everything past is physically behind you and the balance of your time lies sprawled at your feet, can be rough for some people. It is an instant of mortality, a bare point on the continuum of life. Standing there, you become aware of both ends. To fulfill your birth, you must proceed toward your death. It is the paradox of our existence, although it rarely seems illogical until you're standing on the verge of something dangerous. You tell yourself you have no choice, and in reality you don't, but there are some who spend their lives turning away from those moments, who reach back for the regurgitated certainty of the past to avoid the unknown risks of the future. Anna was not one of those people. Peering out at the smoky haze, with all that was familiar crumbling around her, she was well aware of the magnitude of her decision. She paused, but she stepped across. Waiting and watching from the other side, I took her hand, half expecting the building behind her to implode without the force of her personality to hold it up.

We ran down the street, dodging in and out of one set of buildings as my airborne compatriots laid waste to another. I didn't know what to think about that. I looked up, wondering vaguely if anyone I knew was in the airships overhead. Dancing in and out of the shadows, I prayed that the drop zone was far enough away to keep us safe. The image of those who were under the bombs flashed in my mind, but I shut it out. This was war, after all. It was an attack on the enemy, no matter how confusing it was for me to be on the wrong side of it. The blasts started to get closer, louder. I picked up my pace. Anna stayed with me.

"There," she shouted. "That way." I followed her gesture and recognized the large park. "We will be safer there."

"How do you figure that? Last time, you—"

"Trust me." Her reply was curt; there was no time for debate. We headed for the trees. I couldn't help but think that the people most likely to know about me were those who lived closest to the park. Ahead and to the right, the edges of the city were being blasted away by snaking lines of bombs dropped from distant Liberators. Flak blotted the sky. I tried to gauge how many more ships might be in the formation, but it was impossible to see them all through the thickening smoke. At the edge of the park, Anna angled left and kept running. We crossed it at a jog, seeing no one. Throughout the wrecked streets on the other side, desolation unlike any I had ever seen lent the abandoned rubble an air of foreboding. If any people were there, they were underground. She stopped for a moment, confused by decimated landmarks, then pointed toward the west and kept going. We turned a corner. At the far end of the street, a small child stood crying by the side of a smoldering foundation. Rigid with emotion, she waved her tiny hands at her sides, her piercing wail barely audible above the reverberating echoes. Without hesitation, Anna ran to the girl and stooped to comfort her. I looked around as Anna crooned in quiet German, unable to let my eyes focus on the tear-streaked three-year-old face.

I tensed as a figure stepped out from behind a jagged wall. It was an elderly woman. She froze when she saw me, then smiled with relief as her gaze shifted to the little girl. Her hands drifted to her mouth as the tears came. She called out something in German as she hurried to the girl. *Renate... Renate!* Anna smiled at the woman and lifted the girl up to her for a trembling hug. As she set the girl back down, Anna asked the woman a question in German, gesturing at the broken buildings that flanked us.

"Hindenburgstrasse," the woman replied.

Nodding, Anna thanked her and laid her palm against the girl's face. "*Wiederseh'n, Renate. Du bist jetzt sicher.*" As we continued down the street, I asked her what she had said. "I lied," she said. "I told her she was safe now."

We moved on in silence, occasionally stopping to pick landmarks from the jagged smolder. After a while, I noticed that the bombing had stopped. Here and there, people peeked from behind doors and made their cautious way out to the street. Behind us and to the right, fires raged in the swath cut by the B-24s. Gradually, the tight city buildings opened into suburban neighborhoods, and then to farmland. I don't know how long we walked that first day. A single-lane road wound through fields interspersed with stands of trees. When the treetops stood black against the dimming sky, I thought about the food I had left on the sidewalk. A charred shell of a halftrack reminded me that I was in a combat area. The harsh pang of duty straightened my back. It occurred to me that in my hundred glances at Anna, in all of the countless brushes with her hand, her shoulder, her hair — in every little detail over which I had allowed myself first to muse and then to obsess — I had lost all thought of the dangers facing us. Stateless and serene, we had declared an armistice of our own.

The edges of our fingers touched again as we stepped off the road. We angled for the woods. On the next arm swing we touched again, deliberately. On the third, our hands caught and held. I felt the blood surge in my body, awakening a fierce, reckless anticipation. The scent of the grass rose from our footsteps and assaulted my senses with its irrelevance. Trees rustled in the dusky breeze, taunting me for attention. Wild hunger opened an ache in my chest and left me hollow and preoccupied, deaf to the sounds of enemy territory, blind to the markers of safe passage. Every shred of my consciousness was focused on her warm hand. I didn't think about the farmhouse, the wooden pickets, the rounded barn. I ignored the movement of livestock along the edges of the field, and completely missed the shadowy arc of a sprinting animal. Suddenly, not three feet away, the night air broke with the point-blank staccato of barking. We were running before we were fully aware of it. The dog yapped at our heels until we crashed through the underbrush, and didn't stop howling until we were well into the woods. When I realized that the dog had stopped chasing us, I turned back and stared at a vertical rectangle of yellow light in the center of the darkened farmhouse.

Heavy shutters covered all but the narrowest slivers of window, rendering the house invisible in the dark. The British bombed at night. "Light discipline" was what we called it. I remembered the black half-moons painted on the tops of car headlights back home, thousands of miles from the closest enemy bombers and yet still not far enough away to mollify cautious minds. A heavy-set man backed up the farmhouse stairs and into the lighted doorway. He had been standing on the lawn, but I didn't see him. I looked up at the sliver of moon still low in the dusky sky and realized why it was so dark. The dog slipped through the door as the man edged backward into the house. He leaned a shotgun against the jamb and closed the door. I reached for Anna, motioning for her to stay close and remain silent. We eased back against a thick tree, our eyes riveted by the hair-thin glow at the bottom of the door. My hand found the butt of the Luger tucked in my belt.

"Hungry?" I asked.

Anna nodded. It had been hours. As my eyes adjusted to the country night, I was able to discern the small outbuildings that stood on the property. Off to one side, a chicken coop gurgled with muted clucks. I stared at the door again, conscious of the shotgun on the other side. Screw it, I thought. He'll never hit me. Gauging the distance to the chicken coop, I lifted the pistol from my belt and held it out to Anna. She stared at it for a long time before she accepted it with both of her hands. I touched the hair alongside her face, wishing I could kiss her before I left. Without a word, I slipped away toward the sound of the roosting hens. Inching silently toward the little structure, I listened for sounds from the house. The low coop wall was made of brick, above which was a small, tightly tiled roof. It was quiet inside. I edged to the tiny door and felt for the latch, glancing back at the house in one final moment of caution. The small metal lever creaked slightly and opened to an odd rustle of feathers and low clucks. I crouched and stepped inside.

A squall of cackles erupted as I grabbed the neck of the nearest bird. Fighting to corral its wild wings, I held my face away from the chicken's claws and scrambled back into the cool night air. The bird relented as I tucked it tightly under my arm and sprinted for the woods. Behind me, an enormous blast split the darkness and sent a spray of dirt across my feet. I cut left and right in Red Grange serpentine as the farmer emptied the second barrel. A guttural mix of German epithets and frantic barking trailed me into the woods. I knew he was reloading. Ahead and to the left, the crack of a pistol guided me to Anna and stopped the farmer in his tracks. I followed the sound of her movement through the brush as a third blast echoed behind us. The fourth erupted from the same place and spattered against the branches to my right. He was firing, but not following. The light wriggle of the chicken reminded me that I was not carrying a football, but my feet danced between the trees with the muscle memory of a dash through scrimmage. Anna had a head start, but I quickly caught her and maintained her pace as we put distance between ourselves and the gunshots.

Deep in the woods at last, we slowed to a jog and then a walk. She looked away as I broke the chicken's neck with the quick snapping motion I had seen a hundred times in the poultry markets on Fourteenth Avenue. Some of the butchers used a knife, stuffing the birds into long tin funnels where they bled out, but Mama preferred the cleaner method. Wishing I had kept my knife, I looked around for a sheltered place to strip the bird. Anna tapped my shoulder and motioned to her right. We fought through tangled underbrush to a tiny clearing at the base of a huge tree. I set the chicken down and swept away dried leaves and twigs, then set about the gruesome business of plucking it clean, gutting it and peeling off its skin. We used my Zippo to light a tiny fire, and then tore off strips of chicken to roast on the ends of sticks. After we had eaten, we smothered the fire with dirt and buried the feathers along with the rest of the chicken. Bone-tired and groggy, we stood and trudged away from the place where the scent of our meal might linger. After a half hour, we arrived at the edge of a low ridge and nestled down into the underbrush. Wrapped in my arms, Anna fell into a fitful sleep. I lay there for a long time with the scent of her hair pressed against my face, feeling too overwhelmed by the sensations of the day to doze off.

The grind of metal jolted my eyes open. Above us, thin-fingered branches spread black against the pale gray dawn. A deep rumble of engines rose from the valley below. Anna's quiet body tensed as she awoke and turned to me with panicked eyes. Gradually, her face relaxed as her mind worked through the memory of the previous night. Suddenly conscious of the noise in the valley, she tried to sit up. I gently pressed her shoulder and motioned for her to stay down. In the distance, the triangulation of sounds gave me a rough idea of how far away the convoy was. It went on and on. I pictured armored vehicles stretched to the horizon, no more than a quarter mile away. There would be peripheral scouts, but they would have worked in advance of the column and had most likely already passed us. I lifted my head a few inches and wagged it back and forth, listening for the sound of boots. Shadows told me that the sun was rising to my left, the direction from which the column had come. East. They could only be German. By the time the sound of machinery drifted away to the right, the sun had risen completely. We sat up slowly and peered out of the bushes. A muddy road passed within a few hundred yards of our position, deeply plowed by the treads of tanks and trucks. I saw the piebald gray of a Panzer bringing up the rear, trailed by a handful of soldiers on foot. Ahead of them, the long line of armor disappeared over a distant hill.

"What's that way?" I whispered. "West."

"Belgium," Anna answered.

The Siegfried Line. I was suddenly aware of how far behind enemy lines I really was. Mönchengladbach had seemed surreal to me, so far beyond my comprehension as to preclude any thought of escape. But we had been briefed about the Siegfried Line. Unlike Mönchengladbach, it was a place that American troops expected to see shortly — a fortified border in Western Germany that Hitler believed was impenetrable. Our generals didn't agree with him. Anna pointed at the hilltop over which the last of the German platoons had marched.

"That is where we must go," she whispered.

Haike Ludwig owned a small farm outside of Liege that the Belgian underground used as a refuge for people fleeing the Third Reich. That and the fact that Haike was as dense and powerful as a plow horse were all I knew about the woman who was to help save my life. I'd like to tell you that I single-handedly fought my way out of Germany, charging through troop encampments with a dagger between my teeth and a lovely damsel in my arms, but the simple truth is that Anna and I relied on a series of priests and partisans to shelter us and keep us stocked with food as we walked through the long autumn nights. We slipped through a well-mapped break in the Siegfried Line one rainy midnight and never looked back. The last thing I wanted to do was fight a German patrol with my bare hands, and firing the luger would have brought the whole place down on us. So we took our time, picked our spots and walked as light as ghosts. I'm not saying it was easy — my heart was in my ears most of the way — but it wasn't any big heroic thing, either. You've got to ask Audie Murphy for stuff like that.

There is a lot of beautiful land in Belgium. Places you wish you had a camera. But every time I started to get carried away goldbricking and forgetting the circumstances that put me there, I would see another town that had been blasted by tank fire or piled high with sandbags. War never lets you forget. I was traipsing across the Old World like a tourist with a girlfriend, but I was still a soldier. My friends were still up there gunning with everything they had. So I tried to button it down and remember the mission. But she had those eyes, that smile. I held her as we slept out in the cold, dreaming of nothing but the subtle curves of her skin hidden beneath so many layers of woolen formality, yet right there in my arms. Out of respect, perhaps for the memories that haunted her or maybe to preserve that fairytale moment when the war would finally go away and leave us alone, I played the gentleman. She slept with her back to me, and I never forced it. We waited for that first kiss, burning with it but letting it build to its own time and place. Maybe I let that justify things — you know, hiding out and enjoying a break after a year of military discipline. I was getting back to duty, just slowly. Besides, I had flown my twenty-five missions. The Army Air Force was finished with me anyway.

On the last afternoon in October, the skies opened up and a cold rain streamed down. It rained so hard that my shoes began to fill up with water. We stepped out of the woods and into a pasture that overlooked a small cluster of farmhouses and buildings, the largest of which was our destination: an old stone church. Sloshing across the muddy field, we angled for the front doors of the church and the warm space within. But when I grabbed the wrought iron handle, something told me not to open the door. I don't know what it was — maybe I heard something. Anna nudged me, but I just stood there and shook my head. I motioned for her to follow and trudged around the corner to a tall window. Inside, two pews of German soldiers sat watching a nervous old priest perform a wedding ceremony for one of their young comrades. I had to laugh. What is it about beautiful women? They pick the ugliest guys sometimes. Maybe that's what people would say about Anna if they saw me with her, I don't know. At the altar, a German private with a face like the ass end of a Thanksgiving turkey was in the midst of marrying an absolute knockout.

Anna stared up at me with wide eyes. Despite the fact that we had almost barged into a Nazi wedding, I was more annoyed by the rain than anything else. It all seemed like borrowed time anyway. I had it all worked out in case they captured us; I would confess to kidnapping her and forcing her to help me escape. She would show them her papers, tell them her house had been destroyed and eventually make her way to Haike's farm. This was a scenario that part of me had long since accepted as inevitable, even though we had come so far. I was just determined to savor every moment I had with Anna until that day when the dream ended and I had to face the reality of my life again. Life without her. Inside the church, we could hear the loud old priest with one blind eye as he blessed the mismatched lovers and droned on and on. Anna said he was talking about the "garden of wedded life" or something. He kept repeating one word — "Himmel" — so I asked Anna what it meant. When she told me that was German for "Heaven," I nearly laughed out loud. Those Nazi Catholics were all trying to get to a place with the same name as a Jewish halfback from Weequahic High who had gained a hundred yards on us in the Newark city championship game.

The priest raised his arms over the couple in one final blessing and sent them on their way. The soldiers stood and filed toward the back of the church, where a row of rifles leaned against the wall. We scrambled around to the other side of the building and ducked under some bushes, pressing our faces into the mud at the base of the stone wall and barely breathing until we were sure the last of them had moved off. Dusk was settling, but the rain would not let up. Although the ground was soaked, the bushes and the eaves of the church were keeping us relatively dry so we decided to wait until it was completely dark before emerging from our hiding spot. When the old priest opened the door, his one working eye looked us up and down and concluded that we must bathe and change our clothes immediately. Anna's face was streaked with loam, but even at her mud-soaked worst she was breathtaking. It's almost as if the dirtier she got, the more her natural beauty shone through. I felt a pang of jealousy as the old man's cloudy eye took its liberties with her. Fifty years in a cassock, half-blind and probably senile, and I'm even worried about him. I had lost all perspective.

We spent a comfortable evening in the church wine cellar, although we did not dare partake of the sacramental drink. In the morning, Anna charmed our aged host while I sat listening to her sultry German, content to simply hear the sound of her voice and not needing to know exactly what she was saying. With a kind, albeit conspiratorial smile, he sent us on our way in our old clothes, which had been washed and fire-dried by a nun whose face we never saw. Anna kissed the old man on the cheek and thanked him again as we left. He shook my hand without ever looking away from her face. I doubt he even realized that I was an American — I could have been Mandarin Chinese for all he knew.

Carefully, we made our way past the little town and into the woods at the far side. After a few hours of walking we emerged at another clearing, a broad field laden with crops that were ready for harvest. I had no idea what it was. Anna guessed that it was barley, but she was as urban and clueless as I was. Anyway, we agreed that we couldn't eat it, so we moved on. In the distance, a few thin lines of smoke rose from the place she said was Liege. The small city was an Allied stronghold — the end of the line. Near the house on the other side of the pasture, a huge woman stood working a water pump. Two goats played by the door of a barn. The woman looked up as we waded through the fields. She squinted at Anna and broke into a wide grin when recognition dawned on her, then she dropped her bucket and lumbered toward us. Part of me wondered if Anna would survive the impact, but Haike was gentle as she lifted her small friend into her arms. She could easily have lifted me that way too, but opted for a handshake instead. I smiled with gratitude and nodded politely as she jabbered at me in German. Still holding my hand, her smile faded when she realized I didn't understand what she was saying. She glanced at Anna with panicked annoyance, and scanned the perimeter of her fields as she hustled us toward the large barn.

"*Anna, er ist Amerikaner?*" Haike jabbed a thumb at me. "*Und* auch *Jude?*" An American *and* a Jew? Anna shook her head at the latter question and offered a quick explanation. I sensed the fear in Haike's voice, but I was more interested in the little ways in which her German sounded different than Anna's — and very much like the old priest's. Thinking about things like that had helped preoccupy my mind during the more harrowing moments of the journey. It had become a habit for me to distance myself from the broader reality and narrow down my thoughts to the tiniest safe detail I could find. There was hope in the little things that still existed despite the war that raged around them. We had arrived at a place I never expected to see. I could feel relief and sadness well up inside me and nearly bring tears to my eyes. Truth be told, I had not completely reconciled myself to being captured after all.

Inside the barn, Haike gestured up at the hayloft and nudged us up a wooden ladder. She walked to the door and peeked out. After a long silence, finally satisfied that we had not been followed, she turned to Anna and whispered up to her. Waving us back from the edge of the loft, she latched the door and carried her water bucket back to the house. I stretched out in the warm hay and let myself relax. Anna sat up, picking nervously at a thread on the hem of her coat. I tapped her shoulder and pointed out the open window. Through the sulfurous clouds in the west, the setting sun had painted the sky a reddish orange. She lay back on my shoulder. We watched as the wispy canvas was washed with deepening shades of fire. Just before the color began to fade, she turned and pressed her lips to mine. There were tears on her cheeks as she pulled me closer, holding onto our blessed solitude as tightly as I was. The deep blue heavens drifted to black. Across the muddy yard, the last lighted window in Haike's house went dark. In that no-man's land between the armies of our two countries, it was as if the last of our personal boundaries had finally been swept away. Anna and I were finally, completely, alone.

Her warm skin against my hands felt like the fulfillment of destiny, like the acceptance of roles for which we had been created. Our bodies came together for the first time as if through an ancient rhythm, as if she were the missing element of my anatomy, and I of hers. Deep inside both of us, an odd tension eased as our bare legs entwined and her breasts met my pounding chest. Our physical distance had always been unnatural, yet somehow necessary, if only to emphasize the absolute harmony of our union when it finally happened. Without effort, we found one another and pressed close, joined more through instinct than conscious action. We made love as if the very notion of love itself was balanced on the delicate symmetry of our desire — and yet we didn't think at all. It was all as simple and self-evident as the beating of our own hearts. After we had exhausted ourselves, we lay back and covered up with the layers of clothing strewn in the hay. She fell asleep in my arms. I drifted off with a prayer on my lips, not one of contrition, but of thanks. What had visited my life was less an occasion of sin than a moment of grace. No matter the condition, or the complication, love had found me. I was grateful for that.

I awoke suddenly, fitfully. After weeks of attention to the noises around me, I was used to this feeling. But everything was quiet. I watched Anna sleep, curled beside me. She had awakened during the night and put her dress back on. The black ribbon from her hair still lay on the hay, so I picked it up and tied it around my wrist. I don't know why I did that — for luck maybe, or maybe just to make the memory of her more tangible. Outside, the sun was rising behind the barn. Trees that had faded into the previous night's dusk were now awash with the gold of sunrise. I lay back and buried my face in the scent of Anna's hair, sensing in myself a desire that was beginning to rob me of all rational thought. Beyond the trees to the west lay salvation — contact with American forces, safe passage, home. Newark. I could feel the dark miles that lay between me and my family. We were continents and oceans apart, yet somehow the distance comforted me. They were far enough away from the wreckage of Germany and Europe to escape its stain. But they were also a world away from the place I knew my heart would remain. Anna and I had not talked about our destination, whether it lay in the neutral safety outside of Germany, or further away and more permanently secured. Like her, I didn't want to face the end of the road, no matter where it lay.

From a distance, an odd whistling broke my reverie. At the last moment, I realized what it was and threw myself across Anna's body. The shell ripped through the peak of the roof and exploded, its force driven by the flat arc of its trajectory as it blasted chunks of tile and heavy timber out across the adjacent field. Splinters rained down from the shattered eaves, a shower of wood and burning lead that cascaded around and onto my back. Fifty little daggers seared my shoulder blades. The impact shocked Anna from her sleep. I pushed myself up and looked at the fire burning in the hay around us. There was a second whistle. I dove back down onto her, muffling her screams as the shell took out the far corner of the barn and rocked the rest of the structure. The familiar pinch of flame bit my ears. Instinct or maybe training set me in motion. I took her hand, crawled with her to the ladder and tested its stability before guiding her down the rungs. We edged to the door and peered out. A handful of soldiers were walking through the mist toward the barn. The profile of their helmets filled me with relief. I pushed open the door, wincing at the shards embedded in my shoulders.

"Hands up, Kraut!" The point man leveled his rifle at me. His New York accent made me smile.

"C'mon, Sarge," chided one of the troops. "He ain't got but one weapon, and judgin' from the look of things he already shot that load."

For the first time, I realized that I was stark naked in the middle of the barnyard. I glanced at Anna, who seemed relieved to have put on some clothes.

"Kraut's a Kraut," growled the sergeant. "He's just lucky I ain't greased him already."

"Easy, Brooklyn," I called out. "I'm U.S."

He remained alert, unconvinced. He grunted the password challenge: "Flash!"

"Thunder," I replied, as calmly as I could. "Albero, Mateo. Sergeant. Three-two-seven-six-seven-two-one-fiver. Four-forty-sixth Bomb Group, Seven-oh-fourth squadron." I grinned. "And Joe DiMaggio is the greatest ballplayer alive."

"Give this guy something to wear already," the sergeant barked, waving at one of the privates who pulled off his jacket and tossed it to me. I wrapped it around my waist. "We got some reports of Kraut soldiers hiding in a barn around here," he continued.

"We saw a column of 'em headed this way," I confirmed. "That was back in Germany, east of Siegfried."

"Jesus," the sergeant muttered, "you were that far east? Bomber, you said? Where'd you go down?"

"Mönchengladbach."

"What's back there? Whatta ya see?"

"They're strong along the Siegfried Line, but gappy. We didn't have too much trouble walking right by them."

I looked back at Anna again. She was staring with horror at my lacerated back. I had already forgotten about having covered her up, but she had not. Those wounds would have been on her chest and face. The sergeant asked a few more questions about gun placements and troop strength. I told him what I could. He waved over a medic, who dragged me to the water pump and started washing out the splinters as I stared at Anna. Behind us, Haike Ludwig came barreling out of the house, screaming at the soldiers in a strange Flemish dialect that even Anna didn't understand. She waved both arms at her burning barn. Two of the troops leveled their rifles at her, believing that she was too big to be a woman. I quickly vouched for her. They dropped their aim, but they never took their eyes off her. She was several inches taller than a couple of them, and she had a wild look on her face. When she saw Anna, she realized the insignificance of the property damage compared to what could have been lost. Falling silent, she walked over and embraced her petite friend.

"Jesus Christ!" I screamed. A flame shot through my torso.

I whirled around, fist cocked involuntarily. The medic grinned with pride. Between his bloodied fingers, a three-inch metal shard dangled like a prized fish. He turned to toss it away, but I stopped him. When he dropped it onto my palm, I closed my fist around it. Anna walked up to me with a bundle of clothing that Haike had given her, so I stepped into Herr Ludwig's old pants and then pulled on a pair of dung-spattered boots. The medic picked at my back. Bored of watching the fire and satisfied that there were no enemy soldiers hiding in the house, the patrol moved off to secure a perimeter around the property, leaving me, Anna and the sadistic doctor. In a few minutes, the medic was satisfied that he had found every painful fragment, so he administered the coup de grace. I clenched every muscle in my back when the sulfa powder hit my open wounds. He patted a few bandages into place, winked and walked away. I muttered my thanks through gritted teeth.

Anna glanced around at the soldiers stationed near the far corners of the pasture and looked back at me. After a moment, I broke eye contact with her and hollered after the medic. He nodded at my question and produced a pencil and a piece of paper from his pack. Walking back to Anna, I wrote as fast as I could. There were two addresses on the paper I handed to her — one in Flixton, England and one in Newark, New Jersey. She nodded, tears at the corners of her eyes. My back tightened with pain as we embraced, but I didn't let go. Separation would be far more agonizing. As the troops moved off into the woods, I heard a Brooklyn voice bellowing my name back across the fields. I waved with one hand and kept the other around Anna as his echo faded into the crackling rush of the barn fire. The forces of war tugged from every direction, but in the mist and smoke of that Belgian morning Anna and I clung to one another for as long as we could. For all we knew, it was all we had.

Six

Aliceville, Alabama
December, 1944

Karl Eisenstark was wary. It had become second
nature to doubt his surroundings, and to see almost every
person, no matter how familiar, as an enemy. To him,
every task or activity was a trap, every landmark
impermanent. He had been in the prison kitchen every
morning for the past several weeks, yet he still did not
trust his mind to know what it was seeing. For nineteen
months he had been a man without a past, struggling to
recall anything prior to the blinding heat of that morning
in Tunisia when he had awakened to the sound of
American voices, his shirt torn open and one half of his
round dog tag broken off as if he were a corpse left to rot
in the merciless sun. He could remember rolling onto his
side, struggling to his knees, reaching for his rifle. He
could still see the empty slot where his ammunition
cartridge had been. His pockets had been turned inside
out, his Afrika Korps belt stripped. *They left me for dead*, he
realized. The sudden rage that had gripped him at that

moment had never truly faded in the months since then. He had clenched his half dog tag in his fist, then struggled to read and comprehend the name stamped on it. *Eisenstark, Karl J. Oberfeldwebel...* Technical Sergeant? On his arms, tattered insignia confirmed that he had held that rank for quite a while, but he had no recollection of having been promoted — or of anything else. He had ripped the tag from his neck and roared his frustration as he hurled it over the side of the hill. Had he not done that, the Americans might very well have passed him by.

That was in May of Forty-three. More than a year and a half later, he still could not remember his life before that day. With a humid West Alabama breeze wafting into the window, he stood over a counter dusted with flour and pressed a wooden rolling pin into a large mound of dough, working the heavy cylinder back and forth until the pliant material had flattened into a broad sheet. He used two small tin outlines to cut the dough into shapes: Christmas trees and wreaths. Peeling the excess from around the cookies, he painted melted butter onto them and slid the tray into the oven. The one officer he had grudgingly come to trust, Werner Sauerbrun, busied himself sweeping the other end of the kitchen and murdering the only American song he knew, "Jingle Bells." Werner was one of very few men in the compound above the rank of lieutenant who despised the Nazi mentality with as much passion as Karl did. When the enlisted men had been moved out of Aliceville in July, Werner had lost many of the allies he had cultivated in his opposition to the hard-core Nazi element. But none of the Nazis were brave enough to challenge Karl, so through a friendship he had developed with an American

M.P. named O'Malley, Werner arranged to draw the same assignments as his large, surly friend.

Werner could count on the fingers of one hand the times he had made Karl laugh in the past year. Sadly, he was certain that those had been the only moments of levity for Karl since his capture in Tunisia. He watched as Karl stood in silence at the other end of the kitchen, his vacant stare suddenly darkened by a moment of acute pain. With both hands, Karl clutched at his head and leaned forward onto the counter. In the next instant, he stood and stared back at the oven, tears in his disbelieving eyes. He looked at Werner, then slumped down onto a chair. Werner pulled his own chair over and sat down, waiting patiently for his friend to recover. After a long silence, Karl focused on Werner and forced a rattling whisper from his throat.

"Her name was Anna."

The kitchen had begun to fill with the warm aroma of cookies. Werner cocked an eyebrow and glanced from Karl's glassy eyes to the oven, then back again. Karl nodded. Rocking back in his chair, Werner bellowed with laughter.

"All this time in the dark," Werner cried, "and one batch of Christmas cookies snaps you out of it?"

Karl frowned, but then let his face relax into an embarrassed smirk. He began to laugh along with Werner, but his amusement was hesitant and distracted, as if he were watching his own memories as they rushed back into his conscious mind. Gradually, he fell silent again.

"I am from Mönchengladbach..." Karl began. He told Werner that he had been in a battle on Djebel Sidi Mansour, a scrubby hill in Tunisia. The images flooded back, and Karl described them as fast as they came. Sharp edges of grass scraped his cheek as he pressed his face into the pebbled earth. An artillery shell shook the hillside, sending cascades of rock and dirt onto his thin platoon. Choked by dust, he clawed up the hill. *Zeee-whump* bullet impacts crept closer, kicking sprays of soil across his arms and legs. On his right and left, men struggled for the cover of the ridgeline. The American attack seemed to come from every direction, a thousand muzzles trained on the backs of their heads. Only dumb luck and bad shooting kept his brains from being blown out of his eye socket like the unlucky soul crawling next to him. Above, just yards away, he saw nothing but sky past a jagged shelf. "Please," he had prayed, even though he did not believe there was a God to hear him. "This time let it end!" Twice before he had rolled over ledges that promised salvation, only to reveal another hundred feet of sheer hell. It was instinct more than faith that drove him on, his seared throat burning with each breath.

Werner's eyes widened; he had never heard more than two terse sentences in a row from Karl, and now Karl could not talk fast enough. Werner had heard about those last battles in Tunisia, but never with this sort of candor. It was as if Karl was experiencing it all again as he spoke.

The African sun beat down. Sand exploded into his eyes as the whine of a bullet died beside his right ear. Blinded, he clawed the last few feet, rolled up and over the ledge and gasped for air. He blinked the grit from his eyes. There was an odd stability; at last he had reached flat ground. Four minutes on that hillside had felt like a year. He scrambled for an outcropping of rock. Just yards from cover, a rushing roar exploded behind him with enough force to torque the ground and throw him head over heels. In his last waking instant, he hit the rock wall upside down and started to slide toward the loose sand below. Then darkness. After a while, there were voices. First German and then American. He knew the latter to be the enemy, but he did not know himself to be anything at all.

For years, he had been hoping for an honorable end to his military service. His pride would not allow him to desert, or to drop his rifle and surrender to an enemy that had not defeated him. He had been passed from the moral putrefaction of Nazi Germany to the sun-bleached wasteland of Libya, where he was burned clean by the pure heat of desert warfare. Mercifully, North Africa had provided distraction. The flavor of the Mediterranean coast, a hint of burning grass mingled with fetid humanity and the sharp spice of exotic food. Palm trees swaying past bleached white arches. The odd articulation of a camel's legs, and the mercantile smile of its ageless, leather-faced rider. But there had been other preoccupations as well. Lice and fleas in every article of clothing scrounged to fill short supplies. The paper-strewn aftermath of battle as the pockets of the dead were turned inside out, their contents scattered by greedy survivors. Bomb-shattered mosques. Trucks burned and buried up to the door handles by drifts of sand. Ornate German gravestones placed in the meager shade of the ephedra and the tamarisk.

Karl pulled up his sleeve to reveal the twisted bite scars on his arm. He told Werner the story of the SS dog, and of the man who had transferred him to Africa. He concluded that the major was right; Rommel had orchestrated a tactical war against a military opponent — a campaign that Karl believed had been an honorable struggle. He had watched the Luftwaffe hammer the fortress at Tobruk, the last major victory for the Afrika Korps. Huge fountains of sand had risen from the bombs, sending guns and men twisting high into the air. He had charged through lanes carved in a dense field of British mines, exhilarated each time a shell from a Matilda tank had roared overhead. He had personally watched Rommel ride as a conqueror into Tobruk, to survey the devastation and to appraise the wounded dignity on the faces of the British prisoners. Those prisoners would be avenged at El Alamein just seven months later, when the stark light of parachute flares would illuminate the smoldering remains of Rommel's defeated Korps. Karl had fled Alamein with the survivors, up the coast road to Fuka and then on through the Sirte wasteland and into Tunisia where at last his war had ended on Sidi Mansour, a bald *djebel* looming above the corpses of those whose faith and Fatherland had betrayed them.

As the memories settled in his mind, Karl stopped talking. He thought about those first waking moments in Tunisia, when he had blinked up at the American riflemen and realized that his service to the Reich was over. When they asked him his name, he had glared up at them in silent confusion and tried to remember the words on his dog tag. "Benny Goodman," he muttered at last. It was the first thing he could think of, one of the only American names he knew. They had smiled — he remembered that. Americans were always smiling, all the way from the Bizerte waterfront to the prison kitchen in Alabama where the warm waft of butter cookies had penetrated the veil around his mind and connected with a memory from his childhood. Sitting across from Werner, he let his thoughts wander through the emerging details of his youth, through his years in school, his months in army training, and his last days in Germany before fate surged in and swept him away to the Sahara. There had been one constant, one dream that tied it all together: Anna. Now that he had a past against which to compare his present circumstance, his choice was clear. Werner nodded as Karl concluded that he could not live in Germany again. America was a special place. He had not known this before, had not seen it for what it was. But now he did. And he would take her there.

"She is my wife," Karl whispered. "I must go back. I must go back for Anna."

Seven

West Texas
September, 1945

The Army said to me, "Son, go on home and teach them boys what you learned. Help 'em shoot down some Jap Zeroes." I didn't argue. But then again, I didn't know that when they said "home" they meant the Texas prairie, which to a city kid like me was about as much like home as the far side of the moon. It was better than Germany, I guess, although I spent most of my time in Germany with Anna, and most of my time in Texas with rattlesnakes and rednecks. Thank God for rattlesnakes. Thank God for football, too. They played a lot of it down there; pickup games, high school, college, what have you. Four kids and a balled-up rag were a football game in West Texas — same as Tenth Street, I guess. Playing out there on the baked clay, under sun so hot it made me wonder what I had done to piss off the Almighty, I actually managed to forget about Anna for a few hours at a time. There were enough of us with real game experience to field two pretty good sides. We even scrounged equipment and talked about challenging the local college team, although that never actually happened while I was there. Still, it was enough. For sixty minutes at a time, I felt like I was finally home.

It was nearly a year after I left Belgium when the letter came, a thick envelope with a Newark postmark. Rica's flowery handwriting and misspellings made me smile. I sat down on my bunk, tore open the brown paper and worked the letter free. A second envelope fell onto my lap, still unopened. It was strange to see my own name drawn with the squiggled precision of European penmanship. I looked at the return address. "Haike Ludwig... Belgium." My hands shook as I carefully split the paper at the crease. *Anna!* Suddenly, a cold feeling crossed over me. "Haike Ludwig...?" I fumbled to flatten the paper, scanning phrases as quickly as I could. *Anna has asked me to inform you that she is well... she left a few weeks ago... regrets that she cannot contact you now... sends her love...*

After a year of thinking about her, willing myself to forget and yet remembering, hoping... After a year of wondering what must have happened, this was how she reached out to me? One polite page from a friend of a friend? What I did not recall until much later was that Haike could barely speak English, much less write it. The letter was in Anna's own hand.

Emotions that had simmered for twelve months finally boiled over. Barely able to breathe, I watched two drops fall from my eyes and run down the onionskin page. Remembering where I was, surrounded by soldiers and teammates, I fought it all back. Two tears were all she got. I crushed the letter down to a golf-sized ball and pelted it against a garbage can. Suddenly I was grateful that we had a football game scheduled that day. I craved the release of violence, the tangible collisions that might lend expression to the wild pain in my heart. If I could not have her, I would hate her — and I would let that hate drive me like a missile into everything around me. Still too raw for mature expression, what I felt would have to find its voice in the managed mayhem between the sidelines. Two hours later, still burning, I sat on a wooden bench and tied my cleats slowly, deliberately, tightly. I stared at the worn leather helmet at my feet. Someone slapped my back and I turned around a little too angrily.

"Whoa, pal, it's only a base game," drawled our defensive captain, Charlie Shapiro. "Not like we're taking on A&M or somethin'." Chiz was a lineman from upper-class Baltimore whose college career had landed him on the pages of *Life* magazine. He was expected to move on to the violent obscurity of the N.F.L., but instead had been drafted and sent to Africa on bomb runs with the Eighth Air Force. Winding down his active service, he had been rotated back to a stateside training assignment at gunnery school — as had I. Despite the difference in our upbringing we became good friends, drawn together by a shared love of jazz music and football, and a common distaste for the windblown netherworld of the southwest. He was the first friend I ever had who went to college. After three games on the base football team, he had started harping at me to try for a scholarship of my own. I had chuckled at the idea of telling Pop I wanted to go to college, but I said nothing about my deep regret at not having a team or a league waiting for me back home.

Shapiro shot me a quizzical look. "You okay?"

"Yeah bud," I mumbled. "Copasetic."

"Awright then," he said as he walked on, stopping only to add one more thought. "Leave it on the field, man. Whatever it is, spend it out there."

I nodded as I picked up my helmet and filed out with the rest of the squad. Without ceremony or fanfare, our kicker lined up and booted the ball. The game was on. From my position at defensive halfback, I glared into the backfield as the quarterback barked calls to the far ends of his line. He could have whispered them and still been audible. With the exception of a small sideline gathering of the injured and the curious, twenty-two players and one referee were the only souls within a quarter-mile. Around us, an almost lunar stillness was broken only by shots from the firing range and the occasional airplane landing or taking off. The prairie wind was asleep. The arid blue sky stretched further and brighter than any I had ever seen. Weathered goalposts were the only structures between us and the barracks squatting on the horizon a half-mile away. The first two plays were sweeps to the other side. I found myself chasing the action. Thoughts of Anna only compounded my frustration. Where was she?

That's not the sort of thing you want kicking around in your head during a football game, but it was on my mind that day. When the next play came right at me, I hurled myself into the space between two blockers and crashed into the fullback's churning knees with my shoulder and head. I stood up dazed and sore, yet thankful. We stopped them once more, and they punted. On offense I played quarterback, which for that team was more like a running back than a passer. Again I threw my body around with reckless abandon, and again I felt the catharsis of impact. The more I spent of myself, the greater was my peace of mind. As the game went on, Anna faded from my consciousness. Some situations required strategy and others brute force, but none allowed for thoughts of her. We were tied at ten apiece near the end of the fourth quarter. Backed down to our own fifteen yard line, exhausted from the heat and the struggle of the game, our defense tried to dig in and make one last stand. The offense ran a play to my side again. The lead blocker, a big Arkansas fullback whose jersey was stained with tobacco juice, drove his shoulder into my chest and ran me toward the sideline. I watched the halfback slip by to the inside, just out of reach. He gained eight yards before one of our linebackers ran him down. Furious, I stalked back to the huddle.

Shapiro fell in beside me. "Don't worry about it," he said.

"They're gonna pass, Chiz," I muttered.

"How d'ya figure?"

"First down, everyone geared up for the run." I glanced back at our opponents' huddle. "I would."

With an amused look on his face, Shapiro called the defense and we broke the huddle. I glanced at their fullback. He was grinning at me, a mocking leer punctuated by gapped teeth and tobacco drool. I nodded with sarcastic enthusiasm and made a kissing mouth at him. Enraged, he took his stance, slamming his fist to the ground and glaring straight ahead. Just before the play started, he leaned slightly toward my side of the field. As the ball reached the quarterback's hands, the halfback and fullback moved my way, the fullback way out in front and steaming at me with rage in his eyes. Still holding the ball, the quarterback turned and watched the halfback. I let my eyes linger on a spot well to the outside of where the halfback really was, and pretended to chase it. The fullback charged. At the last second I dodged to the inside and let him rush past, befuddled and out of control. I darted to where the halfback waited for the pass. The quarterback realized too late that I would beat his man to the ball. I intercepted it on a dead run and sprinted for daylight. The quarterback was five strides back and losing ground when I reached the far end zone.

There were no cheering fans, no witnesses to our triumph except the blue Texas sky and maybe a couple of lizards out in the scrub. I stood panting in the heat and waited for the happy mob that trailed the play. It was as fine a moment as I had ever known on a football field. Looking down at the scuffed old ball, I began to understand how to deal with the pain of losing Anna. Every day without her had been a slow torture, but for those few hours in the heat of battle, playing the game for which my instincts had been created, I was able to forget. The first of my teammates arrived. I ducked under their slaps and smiled along with them. Someone mentioned the cold beer at the local roadhouse and everyone cheered even louder. It would taste good after a game like that. Two lines formed and the teams filed past one another to shake hands. Still holding the ball, I brought up the rear and looked for the fullback I had hoodwinked. When he was a few paces away, he saw me and peeled away from the line.

"Hey, no hard feelings!" I called after him. "Nice game, pal."

"Go to hell, wop," he drawled.

I froze, wanting to drill the ball into the back of his head. It was Nineteen Forty-five. We had fought and won a war against totalitarian bigots, and yet this rube was still throwing around slurs. Although you had to figure people like that would learn slowly, I was still surprised. The southwest was a hard place, but it had welcomed all of us back from the war with an equal measure of gratitude. All of *us*. I looked around at the sunburned faces of the players, realizing for the first time what was so strange about that place. Everyone I had ever seen there was white. The fullback spat a cheekful of brown juice and shouted another insult over his shoulder. I raised the football and took aim at his skull. From behind me, someone knocked the ball out of my hand.

"Welcome to Tay-hass," Shapiro drawled, catching the ball and tossing it up in the air again. He slapped his arm across my shoulder and steered me toward the barracks. "So you would have called that pass, huh?"

"Yeah, but I would have completed it."

I grinned and took the ball back. We savored the exhaustion of a hard-fought win as we walked back to the barracks. On my same bench again, I looked across and saw the wadded letter on the floor beside the garbage bin. I walked over, picked it up and flipped it into the can. *Goodbye, Anna.*

A few of my teammates were in the showers discussing that night's social options. In reality, there was only one, a shitkicker dive just a mile up the road. Guys just liked to give it a little build-up, I guess. We used to do the same thing with the local pub back in Flixton as we rode our bicycles into town. The English girls were cordial and proper at first, but after a couple of drinks some of them would shed their pretenses. In time, we could identify them at a glance, even before they had ordered a drink. Feet parallel or perpendicular? The latter opened the knee and thigh, and sometimes the mind as well. Fumbling with her necklace or hair? Pupils dilated? By the time they got to such overt signs as touching an arm or leaning in for a light, some guys were already rehearsing their post-coital goodbyes. But after I met Anna, the whole mating ritual lost its allure. Between service points and a Purple Heart that I wasn't even sure I deserved, I had qualified for a stateside assignment. I left Europe in Forty-five hoping to forget about her, but even the brown-skinned beauties on our stopover in the Azores couldn't lure my heart away.

As I showered and joked with my teammates, I couldn't keep from thinking about that letter. She had given me the brush-off — had her friend do it, no less. Time to take the hint. That night, I vowed, I would begin anew. Find some pretty little thing and let her smile away the memory of Anna. I willed her out of my mind and focused once more on the world around me. Somebody's spot-on impression of Frank Sinatra echoed from the showers. Sacrilege though it is, I was never really crazy about his music. Yeah, he's an Italian kid from Jersey, I know, but I always thought he sounded a little flat-footed and straight-ahead, like someone who stares at you without blinking. Hell of a singer, for sure, but sometimes you just want him to maybe relax a little. Lose control, get it a little wrong. Maybe he's just too perfect, I don't know. You could say that about Johnny Hartman too, I guess, but somehow he didn't strike you as a guy who would bust you across the mouth if you flubbed the words to one of his songs.

Still, I found myself singing along as I pulled on my dress browns. Where I'm from, Sinatra is like church. You take it for granted that everybody knows the words. Maybe I overlooked him a little, kind of the way you find faults in your own family that you'd never see in outsiders. When you think about a world without fathers and brothers and doo-be-doo-be-doos, it makes you sad. But while they're there, you get on them for things that you know are picayune. You can't help yourself. Still humming, I walked over to the mirror and opened a can of pomade, knowing that my lacquered black hair would incite some hillbilly to pick on me and almost hoping that it would happen. Homesickness is a weird little thing. A sort of pissed-off Jersey pride took over as I stood there singing a song I didn't even like that much, and greasing my hair like one of the wiseguys who screwed up my brother's life. I growled at the mirror. What, I ain't *American* enough for you? Wop, huh? Hey, up yours, redneck! Deep down, I knew this wasn't really about Texas or Newark or any of that. It was all about the woman I loved being God-knows-where, not wanting me and not giving enough of a damn to tell me that herself. I knew I could either feel sorry about that or do something to make things better. What I loved about football was that it was always so easy to see the right choice. In the rest of life, my vision wasn't quite as clear.

Shapiro slapped my shoulder as I put on my garrison cap. Five of us piled into his fin-tailed Chevrolet and blasted out into the mesquite night, Bob Wills and the Texas Playboys on the radio fiddling like hell to catch a beat. They did, too. Even through his goofy cat-calls and bandleader posturing, Bob Wills knew how to make it swing. I decided to cut Texas a break, to admit to myself that there were places in this big country where people maybe just did things differently. We're all just after the same old Saturday night hang, looking for that sweet roll across green felt, that Count Basie corner-pocket moment when the shot goes in and the room feels good. I forgot about the pain in my ribs and the ache in my heart. Whatever she was doing, I hoped Anna was finding the same kind of moment herself. I loved her, but life had to go on.

The roadhouse leaned into the night like a weathered drunk, its dark corners littered with sawdust and melancholy. My teammates and I drank heartily, laughing and rehashing the play-by-play until at last the myth of the game got legs of its own and we could let it go. There's nothing like winning, even if no one sees it but you. The girls laughed at our exaggerations, letting us believe our own tall tales long enough to preserve the brittle confidence they needed to see in us. We seduced ourselves, men and women conjuring aspects of one another that coaxed along our own dreams as alcohol smoothed out the inconvenient details of reality. We danced ourselves into alignment, shifting partners until we settled on the one who best fit the fantasy. For me, it was a curvy blond whose face radiated a down-home sweetness that could never throw a hard look or a nasty word. Her heart seemed as golden as her hair. Dancing with her, I felt the grime of the city streets in my blood. She did too, but what shamed me excited her. I was not worthy of her purity, and we both knew it.

Beer and perfume swirled in my addled mind. She wore a light cotton dress, a floral print. Her waist was narrow, her hips strong. I knew virtually nothing about her. She loosened my tie and undid a few buttons on my shirt. We sat down at the bar, she in my airman's cap snapping off salutes to my teammates. I was preoccupied with the next round of drinks. As I reached across to pick up two glasses of beer, I felt the ring I wore around my neck swing out and back like a pendulum. I had taken the shard of metal that had lodged in my back when the GIs shelled Haike Ludwig's barn, and pounded it into a rough circle. It hung on the black ribbon that I took from Anna's hair.

"You Yankee boys sure are diff'rent," she giggled. "Wearin' jewelry and all." She reached out and flicked the ring with her fingernail.

I felt the heat rise in my face, suddenly angry that she had dared to touch something so precious to me. But in the next instant, I realized that it was my own fault. I had put both of us in that situation. I could feel Anna's eyes on me, laughing her jaunty laugh and challenging me to be a better man. Just like that, the spell of the bar was broken. The neon lost its hazy magic. The twang on the jukebox grated my nerves. I noticed the makeup dusted on the girl's cheeks, the smear of rouge that I had mistaken for the pink of desire. Flaxen enchantment revealed itself to be juvenile flirtation. She was probably eighteen, doe-eyed and incapable of the dialogue that I had supplied for her. Her coy smile had reflected incomprehension, not seduction. I smiled, took my cap back and handed her a beer. As I stood to leave, the room swayed around me. I was drunk.

"What's a matter?" she slurred.

I smiled again and kissed her cheek goodbye.

"What'd I say?" she called after me. "Hey, where ya goin'?"

The night air cooled my face as the light wooden door slapped closed behind me. In the distance, I could see a few lights burning in the barracks. I squeezed the shard ring in my palm until its sharp edge bit the skin. Solitude felt like an indictment. I winced at the stiffness in my legs, suddenly aware of the lonely mile that lay before me. Shuffling up the dusty road, I wondered how long it would take to rid myself of the memory of Anna. How many dances? How many false starts before that kind of love would grace my life again? The stars crowded down on me, so many more than I had ever seen in my life. I could never get used to the night sky out in the country, far away from city lights. It wasn't black and comfortable, but sharp and full of jagged bits of glassy light. A vague recollection of a Lenten sermon crept across my mind, something the priest had said about seeing God clearly and that not being a comfortable thing. My drunken mind couldn't piece it together, so after a while I stopped trying. I heard a car door slam back at the bar. I glanced over my shoulder and realized that I had already covered almost half the distance to the base.

Headlights veered onto my path as the engine grew louder. That's not Shapiro's car, I said out loud. I looked back just in time to dive out of the way as a pickup truck roared past. It ground to a stop and blew gravel from its wheels as it turned back. I was still on my hands and knees on the shoulder of the road, staring at the lights bearing down on me, feeling the adrenaline rise and begin to clear my mind. I was ready to spring out of the way again, but the truck crunched to a stop at the edge of the road. Two men threw open the doors. In the interior light I caught a glimpse of blond hair and floral print. I was on my feet before their boot heels hit the blacktop. They were in civilian clothes. One wore a straw Stetson and the other carried a baseball bat.

"Car trouble, fellas?" I gestured at the pickup. "Looks like your steering is a little off. Brakes work fine, though."

"Damn greasy bastard!" The one in the hat had been driving. His tone was murderous. "You made my sister cry."

"What'd you say to her?" The bat man didn't sound as irate as his friend. I was thankful for that.

"Nothing," I answered. "I just had to go."

"What, she ain't good enough for you?" The girl's brother wore his Stetson low over his eyes.

"Good enough, maybe. Old enough, no."

"'Maybe?!'" He took a step forward. "Whatta ya mean by that?"

The man with the bat stood where he was. I had a chance against one of them — unarmed. Both together and one with a bat did not present good odds.

"Listen," I said, "it was a misunderstanding. If you feel like you have to do something about that, then do it."

"The only misunderstanding was that Yankee bastards like you ain't supposed to talk to nice girls like her," growled the guy with the bat. I realized that his quarrel with me was more ideological than personal. Screw him.

"You wanna put that bat down and fight, I'm ready," I said to him. "But if it takes two of you shitkickers and a Louisville slugger to beat me, well then you're a bigger bunch of pussies than I thought."

The wooden clank of the bat against the pavement preceded his first reckless punch. In the glare of the headlights, I didn't pick it up right away and it caught the side of my forehead. I drove a fist up through his chin and heard his teeth click together, but he didn't even blink. His second punch landed on my ribs and drove the air out of me. I pulled my elbow tight to that spot and swung with my other fist, but I never saw where it went. An explosion at the back of my head was the last thing I remember. I don't know how long I lay there. When I woke up on that sandy ground, the shock of being outdoors — and not in my bunk — was overwhelming. I scrambled to my hands and knees, blinded by the sticky knot of pain at the base of my skull. The lights of the roadhouse shone through the darkness. In the other direction lay the low barracks. My forehead stung a little; I remembered the first guy's glancing punch. Except for sore ribs, I didn't feel any other damage. They may have suckered me with a baseball bat, but at least they were good enough not to kick me when I was down.

As I trudged back to the barracks, I grew angrier and more frustrated. The whole night had laid bare my weakness and vulnerability. But after a while, the anger faded. When I reached the barracks I was more depressed than anything. Everyone was still out drinking, so the room was empty. I sat down on my bunk, feeling a roil of emotions. *Anna.* I wanted to scream her name out loud. Instead, I walked over to my foot locker, took out a cigar box and opened it on the bed. Under a couple of letters from home, I found a folding knife and clicked it open. I knew what I had to do. The blade gleamed in the barracks light. *This is it. Once and for all, this will resolve everything. Do it!* I raised my other hand, twisting it for a better cutting angle. As the blade bit and grabbed, I pressed with my thumb. It sliced in and ground against something harder: graphite. With four flicks of the wrist, my pencil was sharpened. I took out a piece of paper and laid it on the cigar box.

Dear Anna, I wrote. *It has been more than a year since I saw you in Belgium, and I love you just as much today as I did when I left...*

Eight

Outside of Liege, Belgium
September, 1945

It was six o'clock in the morning in Belgium — not
yet midnight in Texas. Anna was on her back screaming
into the darkness, barely conscious and yet fully aware of
the agony between her thighs. She tried to force her mind
to a place of peace and comfort, but the next rushing stab
brought her right back to the farmhouse, and to the
stinking heat of old bedclothes and country sweat. She let
her eyes open slightly, just a squint, and saw the old
farmer staring down at her. His eyes were wide, as if he
had never before seen a woman in the position that Anna
had been forced to assume. She opened her mouth and
bellowed at the top of her lungs, but the pain did not fade.
Closing her eyes tightly again, she let the room go black.
It had to be endured, she told herself. She'd been through
worse.

December, Forty-four had been brutal. Wild battles
had raged in the hills around them. Legions of iron-clad
vehicles had crashed through lines of men worn ragged

from months of fighting. Planes had strafed in and out and bombed when they could. The snow was dappled red with blood. Bodies were frozen in mad contortions, reaching up through the drifts that had fallen around them. On the far end of the property, Haike was still finding thawed chunks of arms and legs as late as March. The odd shoe. Somebody's helmet. A piece of unexploded ordinance. Everywhere lay the detritus of war, washed back and forth by a border that finally stopped shifting in May, Nineteen Forty-five. Then everyone was told to celebrate, that the war had ended. Victory in Europe. Anna smiled grimly and kept to her routine. She was too far from town to catch up the revelry, and too far from her dreams to have faith in a peaceful future.

And now this. She could have killed Haike for letting the old man into the house. His coarse advances had amused Anna; she had swatted him away. But for Haike, the mere presence of a man had been rife with novelty and promise. She had given herself over, charmed by his meager flattery, awed by the tart smell of his bare body. Anna had lain quietly in the adjacent room, fighting back nausea as their rustic grunting reached its crescendo night after night. In the morning, Anna would sit at the kitchen table as he emerged from the bedroom and grinned through his stubbly beard, breath stinking of sleep, teeth angled and stained by a lifetime of neglect. Anna would nod and ignore him. He would frown and depart. Part of the routine. But now this.

In the last few weeks, she had not slept much. Her body seemed to be resisting the notion, or perhaps it was her mind. One of Haike's friends had passed along a rumor that Karl was still alive. Anna had shut out the message almost instantly, guarding herself against both hope and history, but it had weighed on her like the rest of the dank atmosphere of the house. Gradually, it all caught up to her. A caged panic had driven her to pack up and leave, but she had not gotten very far when the instinct for safe haven overwhelmed her. She went back. For months after the armistice, she had endured the daily reminders of Haike's abject lack of taste and remained on the farm. The old man had grown bolder, more familiar. As spring warmed the countryside, he had begun not to dress himself completely before leaving the bedroom. Anna was repulsed, but Haike laughed. One day, she had chuckled, he will walk out wearing nothing at all, and *then* you will understand. Anna had wanted to slap her for placing that image in her mind. The physical presence of a man was something that had long since grown distasteful to her. I'd like to tell you it had nothing to do with me, but it did. Just not in the way you'd think.

A sharp, pinching cramp gripped her abdomen. She wailed, the anger draining from her voice and yielding to desperation. When would it end? She thought she heard Haike's rasping laugh at the far side of the room, and opened her eyes again. Once again, the old man's face appeared. "Get out!" she screamed, lashing out at him with every bit of strength left in her. "Ooooooooout!!"

Something inside her seemed to slip loose and gush from between her legs. She felt as if she would break in half, vaguely aware of the splash of fluid on the rough wooden floor. The pain eased. When she opened her eyes, it was to watch the door close behind the old man. Haike's strong hand felt cool against her forehead. She placed a cold, wet cloth on Anna's lips and squeezed, letting the fresh water trickle into Anna's parched mouth. Unable to sit up completely, Anna rolled to one side and scanned the room with desperate, wild fear. She heard Haike's voice, but did not register her words. Listening, she caught them the second time.

"It's good," Haike whispered. "He's good. Here." She turned her large body and let Anna see the tiny bundle she was holding against her breast. Between the folds of a soft blanket, a shining pink face emerged and two blue eyes peeked back at her. "Your son," Haike said, handing the baby to Anna.

My son, she thought. My son. A hazy shadow closed in around the beautiful little face as Anna reached for him. She wrapped her arms around his tiny body as the last bit of tension faded from her mind. Mother and child curled together and let the waking world move on without them. Soon there will be real peace, Anna thought. And it will feel like this.

PART TWO: LIGHT

Nine

Newark
July, 1946

Like many virtuoso jazz musicians, Jeremiah Walker
was highly competitive. By Nineteen Forty-four, when he
was celebrated in the Newark Evening News as the
second coming of Charlie Parker, Jeremiah knew there
wasn't another saxophonist in town who could keep up
with his tempo or match his unique phrasing. A few years
earlier, he and his horn had found their way to the
Pelican Club on Tenth and South Orange, one of the
reddest embers in Newark's hotbed of jazz. It was a
simple storefront bar with a small seating area and a tiny
stage, and in it his late-night jam sessions took on an
almost subversive quality. To him, the ethnic variations
of the West Ward were nothing more than shadows on a
drift of snow. It took an act of will to step off the High
Street bus and feign indifference to the glares and
muttered curses as he limped to the bar on his polio-
withered leg. Even later, with the halo of celebrity
lighting his way, he still hated that half-block walk. On

125

the July night in Nineteen Forty-six when I returned from Texas, I watched him bob past the window of the Pelican and duck inside. He nodded at the young proprietor, Henry Izzo, and endured several patronizing handshakes from unfamiliar faces as he sidestepped toward the stage. I set down my glass of rye, pushed away from the bar and stood in his path, refusing to move when he mumbled "'Scuse me" without looking up. He raised his lids in mild indignation.

"Well, goddamn!" His surprise was genuine. I had not changed out of my uniform since arriving in Newark. Jeremiah appraised the two ribbons on my chest and nodded with an ironic smirk. "General Mateo back from the war. Well, goddamn."

"Sergeant, anyway," I said, knowing that the correction wouldn't have any effect on my instant nickname. I extended my hand. "How you doin', Jeremiah?"

"Not bad, General, not bad." His handshake was firm, not loose and cursory as it had been for the strangers. "How you?"

"Can't complain, and ain't—"

"—no one gonna listen no-how." His face broke into a huge grin as he finished his own canned response.

I nodded at his right leg. "Bad pin kept you stateside, huh?"

"Mama used to tell me the Lord works in mysterious ways." He shook his head and smirked again, this time at the white faces in the club. "She was damn right about that one." He looked back at the drummer and the bassist who were beginning to warm up. "Listen, I gotta..."

"I know, pal. Get in there and blow."

126

"Solid, General. We'll sit up later and talk it through."
He stuck out his hand again, nodding sideways at my
stripes. "Solid."

I took my glass from the bar as Jeremiah made his
way to the stage. He was lean and wiry-strong, with a
presence that commanded respect from men twice his
size. Leaning into the first phrases of a beat rife with
post-war swagger, he seemed determined to drive the
new sound of be-bop deep into the Benny Goodman
sensibilities of the world around him. From the middle of
a group of friends, I watched as he lured them first with a
few catchy notes, then a flashy sequence, and finally a
blistering solo that left them stomping for more. He was
a master showman. I recognized the techniques I had
watched him work out years earlier in impromptu
sessions on that very stage. "Let 'em fear you," he would
say, "and then let 'em hear you." He understood the
challenge that his music presented to the uninitiated, and
he knew the only way some people would be able to get it
was through the aggressive charisma of the front man. As
the room filled with sound and customers, I began to see
the logic of what he had said.

A loud bawl of a laugh broke the moment for those
closest to the bar. The bartender, Giordano Pietro,
jumped at the sound. Gio was a sculptor and an ex-
Marine from Izzo's old outfit. Unlike Izzo, he had been
overseas. His hands shook with the echoes of
Guadalcanal, a trembling that he could only ease by
working with soft clay until its beauty obscured the
images in his mind. Gio was ready when the second laugh
erupted. This time, I recognized it. I turned and saw my
brother Vin for the first time in three years. He was only
nineteen, but he looked about thirty. I would guess he

weighed two-eighty, which was a lot for a guy who was not quite five foot ten. Someone tapped my shoulder. It was Izzo, away from his post as keeper of the cover charge. For him to step away just as the dimes were turning into quarters, something had to be weighing on his mind. He motioned back at Vin and shook his head, caution in his eyes. I smiled and slapped his heavy shoulder, nodding in mellow acknowledgement.

"I know, Iz," I said. "Don't worry, no trouble from me tonight."

"You ain't the one I'm worried about," he grumbled as he started back through the crowd.

I watched Vin make his way to the other end of the bar, working the crowd like a man with diplomatic immunity. He was all smiles and sharkskin, a bloated caricature of the eager kid I used to know. A carbon copy of him trailed in his wake, sweating through a matching gangster collar and trying to act as tough as my brother really was. Izzo watched the two wiseguys for a few seconds, then turned and walked back to me, his expression suddenly lighter.

"Hey Mat," he said. "Bunch of us are starting a semi-pro team this fall. Couple of old West Side guys. We could use a good quarterback. You wanna—"

"Hell yes!" I blurted out, startling my friends. Reining in, I remembered the other reason I had come to the bar. "But only if you give me a job."

Izzo smiled at my presumption and nodded as he walked back to the door. He had been an All-State lineman at West Side before enlisting in the Marines. When his father passed away, he had taken on both the Pelican Club and a family hardship deferment that spared him from the meat grinder of Guadalcanal, and possibly also from the vast hillside cemetery on Oahu where so many of his and Pietro's friends would later be laid to rest. Instead, Izzo spent the war mixing drinks for a straggling crowd of retirees and 4-Fs, his warrior's heart wracked with guilt.

In the twenty-four hours since I arrived in Newark, images from my past had flickered around me like a spool-worn matinee. It was strange to be home, belly full of Mama's macaroni, the buzz of a family dinner still ringing in my ears. The Pelican was the same old place, but maybe just a little more shipshape now that the younger Izzo was in charge. Jeremiah Walker was famous in a local sort of way, but still blowing those same fat little Armstrongs through his horn. My family's flat was a block from the bar, a one-cigarette walk if you took it slow. Pop was asleep on his chair, *Il Progresso* tented on his tomato-stained belly. Mama was puttering, worry lines on her forehead and rosary in her hand. Rica and Angela and *DiMaggioooo* Mickey were there, the latter now three years bigger and slowed slightly by the weight of home cooking. West Side High was just up the avenue. My old firehouse was a few blocks away. I sipped my drink, listening to the voices, the music, the sameness. It was very loud, yet it was all so quiet. Mid-brain, habitual quiet. Nothing-ever-changes quiet. The places I had been for the last two years were already slipping into the haze of dreams. England. Germany. Even Texas. I thought of Anna. Was any of it real?

One thing was different. Sitting at dinner, after the hugs and the tell-us-abouts and the showing of photos and medals, but not scars, I had looked across the table at an empty chair. I started to joke about it, but stopped with my finger aimed at the empty seat when Mama began to cry. Pop shot me a look, so I dropped my aim and changed the subject. It was only now, watching my brother flash a cup-sized roll of cash at the bar, that I understood how much had changed. Mano Nero, Cosa Nostra, Mafia — in my family, those were curiosities, not career options. We always knew where the line was drawn: across the threshold of our front door. Other people did those things, people who lived on the other side of that line. People outside the family.

At that moment, my brother looked up at me. Three years and thousands of miles vanished in an instant of recognition, in the little-kid curiosity that played across his expression. *Who's that, Mat? Ellington, Vin.* I couldn't look away. I was still clinging to an image of my brother that was fading even before I left for the war. Young as he was in Forty-three, Vin had already chosen a path that none of us could divert. Still, I couldn't believe that the kid I saw buried under that mountain of vanity was all bad. He nodded at me in an off-hand way, like he would to a stranger. His eyes lidded with indifference, and his attention rolled back to his cronies at the bar. That was it. Maybe Pop had drummed him out of the family, but I hadn't done anything to him. Still, he turned his back. For three years I had watched friends and enemies die, but nothing had prepared me for that moment of loss. My brother's youth — his innocence — was gone. Stolen. Pop's rage echoed in my own heart. I had never killed willingly, but if Benny Bells had walked in at that moment, I would have sliced his throat without a second thought.

For twenty years, I had watched Benny stroll through our neighborhood and take what he wanted. A free apple. A choice prosciutto. A bag of cash. Vin laughed loudly again, exaggerating a joke that no one else found quite so funny. It was Benny's kind of laugh, one that invites everyone else to share in it as long as they understand that the joke's on them. With a tight smile, Pietro waved off Vin's money as he handed over a bottle of anisette. Izzo watched from the door, knowing the game and maybe feeling a little relieved at Vin's small-time instincts. A bottle of liqueur was cheaper than a third of the gate receipts. But he knew as well as I did that Benny's lessons would sink in one day and the tithe would be steeper. Vin was on his way up, making a name. He poured shots for a few people around him, then drained his own and chased it with a swig straight from the bottle. Onstage, Walker dipped his horn in a casual salute to a white girl wearing a sailor's dixie cup hat. She blushed as she danced across to her Navy man, glancing back at Jeremiah with a coy smile as she went. Anger flushed Vin's face when he noticed the exchange. Someone handed me a wide glass of rye. Izzo sat by the door and took it all in, his ears tuned to the clicking of tumblers and the trouble they could unlock.

Two more rounds softened my mood. The music rolled around the room, a living ocean of sound that lifted and swayed everyone it touched. The crowd glowed with the everlasting modern, the feeling that time and fortune would forever smile on our brave America. We had set the world free. Now it was time for peace and prosperity. Amnesia. I wanted it all. I smiled at a rose-cheeked lass from the Irish side of South Orange Avenue. Hypnotized by the sensual movement of her ruddy lips and the blue sky dancing in her eyes, I didn't notice that the music had stopped. As we spoke, she brushed my chest with her fingertips. I leaned close for a whisper. For a brief moment, the world got small again. But over the quiet of our conversation, a rising of voices drew my attention. I looked up as Vin jabbed a finger in Jeremiah's chest. Jeremiah was shaking his head, hands raised in protest of my brother's drunken accusations. My gut tightened with shame as I watched Vin shove my crippled friend to the floor and stand over him like a man at a urinal. Vin said one more word, one too many: "Nigger."

My feet found the openings in the crowd and propelled me toward him. I slammed my shoulder into his soft belly, driving him through two barstools and onto the floor. With my elbow, I pressed the side of his face against the floor. I tried to tell him that he ought to be ashamed of himself, but all I could work through my gritted teeth was a series of curses. An impact on the side of my skull sent a shower of glass and sticky ooze down my neck; he had smashed his anisette bottle on my head. Dazed, I managed to pin the hand that held the jagged bottleneck. Behind me, a metallic click gave me a sick feeling in my stomach. I turned around, knowing that I would see Vin's corpulent protégé but not expecting the pistol to be quite so close to my face. Vin's wrist worked free of my grip. I turned to block the slash of glass, but instead of swinging it up at my face he tucked the point low against my abdomen and pressed until it pierced my skin. I froze. The look in Vin's eyes made me realize that in the next instant I might be watching my intestines spill onto the floor. Izzo's voice broke the standoff. He reminded us that we were brothers, that this was not necessary, that all should be forgiven. I nodded, slowly relaxing the arm that pressed against Vin's face. Vin maintained pressure against the glass as I stood up, as if to say "Screw you."

A circle of blood appeared on my uniform shirt. Bits of glass bit into the area around the growing lump on my head. A mouse was already forming under Vin's left eye. We stood facing one another warily until his friend tapped his shoulder, nodding at the door. My brother knew that the Pelican Club was really more my turf than his, so perhaps it was old habit that compelled him to turn and leave. As the door closed behind him, I wondered if Benny Bells would later correct that breach of gangster etiquette. *You don't leave. The other guy, he leaves. Never you.* I took the towel that Pietro held out and pressed it to the small puncture above my hip. Jeremiah patted my shoulder as he shuffled past, mumbling his thanks so softly that I could sense his frustration at not having defended himself. It would have been a fatal mistake to do so, and we both knew it. Still, pride is pride.

I looked around for the warm Irish smile that had enchanted me, but when I saw the girl the smile was gone. She tensed visibly as I approached, looking back at a young man who looked like her brother. I kept my eyes on her face, avoiding any hint of confrontation with the rest of the group. With as sheepish a shrug as I could muster, I apologized for the disruption in our conversation. Half thinking she might respect someone who stood up for the little guy, I was shocked at the venom in her blush. She was morbidly ashamed that I had singled her out as the friend to whom I returned. Her brother whispered and she nodded as she turned to follow him. Still feigning humility, I quietly asked her what he had said.

"He said 'they're all hotheads,'" she replied.

"They?"

"Italians," she hissed as she walked away.

My face burned. Suddenly exhausted, I realized what a mess I had made. My head throbbed and stung as blood seeped into the rag I clutched at my side. Behind me, Izzo started to sweep up the broken glass. One of my friends handed me my jacket and cap. I looked around at the wide eyes, some politely averted and others staring with amusement or disgust, then I shuffled toward the door, drained and defeated, stopping only to offer Izzo some help with the cleanup. He shook his head at my feeble apology, grumbling that he had it covered and that I should just go home. At the threshold, I winced when my stiff hatband crushed glass fragments into my scalp. The closing door muffled the mellow notes that Jeremiah once again sent out over the crowd. I lifted a cigarette from my pocket and stared at the stark white line it made against my dark fist, but then I thought about Izzo's football team and decided to toss it into the gutter along with the rest of the pack. The taste of stale rye and blood would have to suffice. I checked up and down the block to see if Vin and his friend were lingering on the sidewalk. To my relief, I saw nothing but nighttime, and no one but me.

Somewhere, Anna would soon see the light of a new day. For me, the wait would be longer.

If you have drunk to excess, you probably know about that moment of waking shame in which your fully-restored conscience bares its claws and excoriates you for the hazy offenses committed in its absence. For anyone raised in the Catholic tradition, the feeling is particularly acute. The instinct to apologize is overwhelming. Out of habit, the Catholic will seek an arbiter of conduct, a rule against which the required penance can be gauged. Down deep, you want to know that everything will be okay, that nothing was broken that cannot be fixed. Deeper still, perhaps unconsciously so, you want to understand that thing that drives you to crush your judgment between the polished mahogany bar and the bottom of your next-to-last drink. But that comes later. First, it's all about having the courage to leave the dark comfort behind your eyelids, to face the light of day and to view the trail of wreckage that leads from the state-of-grace blindness of the night before to the clammy pillow where all of your demons are dancing in the morning sun.

The first voice I heard the next morning was Mama's. Still in my uniform, I listened to her muted paean as she worked a heavy iron skillet and bemoaned the evil that had possessed her sons. She was talking to Rica and blaming herself for our downfall. Christ, I thought, still hiding behind closed eyes. It was easier to wake up in the Ardennes with German troops two hundred yards away than to imagine the scourge of my adolescence in the kitchen cooking frittata. Mama's voice stopped suddenly. When Rica giggled, I knew I was screwed. Pop's rough hand shook my shoulder and slapped the side of my head. He muttered something in Italian as I bit back a scream of agony. My head felt like there was a hatchet embedded in it. I suddenly realized what Pop was saying: "*Vetro?*" Glass? It all came rushing back. I sat up too suddenly, queasy from the effort but certain that it was the best way to avoid the compounded sins of ignorance, violence *and* sloth. Too late, I realized that it was exactly the wrong thing to do.

"Madonna mia!" Pop bellowed. "What did you, get shot? *Jesuchristo*, the blood! On the couch!"

Pop grabbed me by the front of my shirt with one fist and lifted me to a standing position. A grapefruit-sized stain darkened the upholstery where I had slept. Mama rushed into the living room and gasped in horror through the pickets of her upraised fingers. She lifted the end of my uniform shirt, indifferent to the fact that it had clotted to my skin. I yelped. She squinted at the freshly opened gash and determined that it was not a mortal wound. After slapping me across the head, she gently lifted the sofa cushion and hustled it into the kitchen for emergency cleaning. Rica stood on tiptoe and examined my crusted scalp. Thank God for her. Without Rica, I would have lived and died convinced that my family was incapable of producing a single thing of beauty. She parted my hair until she found the lacerations, and then she gingerly assessed the cut in my side. After she had located a wet towel and a pair of tweezers, she sat me down at the dining room table and picked glass from my head as I dabbed at my abdomen. Pop grunted at me in broken English, wagging his finger in my face and threatening to kick me out of the house like my "no-good brother."

I stared at my knees, tensing occasionally when the tweezers grazed a raw spot but maintaining a stoic silence. Pop settled into his chair and snapped open his paper, occasionally glaring at me until he lost himself in the familiar rhythm of his native language. Mama muttered in the kitchen as she worked at the stain. Rica decided that it was safe to whisper a question. Confused, I asked her to repeat it, which she did in a barely audible tone.

"Do you still love her?"

"Well," I said softly, "she's a pain in the ass, but she is my mother."

"Not her, idiot," Rica snapped. "The Belgian girl. Do you love her?"

"Belgian...?"

"Hakey Ludwig. You know, the letter."

"Haike...?"

My face flushed, both with embarrassment and excitement. If I said Anna's name, would it mean that she was real again? Not just some distant dream? And if I didn't, would she fade into memory, as I knew she would have to sooner or later?

"No," I mumbled, "not her."

"Yeah, okay."

Rica set the tweezers down and brushed my hair back into place over the spot she had cleaned. She looked up at the ceiling where Carmela's heels clicked against the hardwood floor of her apartment.

"'Mela got out of here," she reminded me, "but us, we're stuck for now. So you might want to trust me a little more."

I stared at my younger sister. It had not occurred to me at dinner that she had grown so much in three years. There was a deep sobriety in her eyes, a level gaze that she had not possessed in her adolescence. I sat back and reached into my pocket for the cigarettes that were no longer there. With a deep breath, I faced a future devoid of yet another comfortable delusion.

"Her name was Anna," I said. "But it's over now."

Ten

Mönchengladbach
July, 1946

The door swung freely on its hinges, no lock or latch impeding its arc. Karl ran his hand up the jamb until he reached the thick splinters where I had broken the bolt through the frame. He stepped into his own living room, stopping short when he saw the wall that had been blown open and the huge block of stone in the middle of the room. Crossing the room, he peered out and recognized the same heavy brown blocks in the pile across the street. His huge frame nearly filled the hole in the wall. From where he stood, he could see most of his ruined neighborhood. People in that corner of Mönchengladbach had cleared away much of the rubble and stacked the reusable materials. He turned back to the room and looked around at the vestiges of his old life, some crushed and others spared by serendipitous fate. Beer steins from Düsseldorf and Braunschweig, still intact. Books on the far shelf, half of them tossed to the floor and damaged by water. A tight rack of American jazz records, many of them cracked or chipped at the edges.

He focused on his own picture, and then on the paper tucked in behind it. Pinching the corner, he worked the letter free of the frame and frowned at the Reichstag eagle stamped on the sheet. The page settled lightly into his shaking hands, yet its gravity drove him down to the dusty couch. Tears blurred the text as he read in silent confusion. *Killed in action.* He bunched the paper in his fist and struggled to stand. Empty and alone, nothing but remnants and wreckage scattered before him, he sagged back down again. Dust rose from the couch to his clenched knuckles as he pressed them to his forehead. He had nowhere to go.

It seemed to Karl as if he had been facing the same moment again and again, as if some lesson had not been clear and so he was forced to relive the experience until it was. Abandonment. Loss. Brief, incomplete redemption. He searched his memory for a consistent message, for the note in all of it that he had been missing. At least that's what I would have done. All of us have felt the darkness spin us around at times, but only some of us ever really try to decipher it. Maybe he didn't. It takes a degree of faith to believe that life is not just repetitive suffering, that it is more than just a series of meaningless trials. I need to believe that. I need to know that there is a greater composition, that even the coldest moments have meaning in a larger orchestration. I wonder if Karl felt that way, at that precise moment. I wonder if he had any faith at all.

He squinted through the dusty living room. The setting sun cast a spectral gloaming across the tattered space. At the west end of the apartment, a window allowed the day's last light to filter in. He had planned a future with Anna. A kitchen filled the warm glow of baked bread. Babies. Grandchildren... An old, familiar tension stirred within him. He knew she did not see things the same way. They were barely married when he left for Libya. Hers was not the spirit of the *hausfrau*, content to dwell in the shadow of a male ego and conjure the trappings of long-lost youth. And yet he had almost convinced himself that time and dependence might persuade her to love that life. Karl looked around and realized the totality of the devastation his life had endured. Wind and rain had weathered his furniture. Except for a few knick-knacks, his possessions were missing or destroyed. His wife was gone, too. A tiny voice whispered shame into his ear. Is that all she is to you? Just another thing you have lost?

Cold fear gagged his pathos. Anna was gone. He stood and ran into the bedroom, then bolted to the living room, then ducked into the bathroom. Nothing, not a trace. As he walked back into the living room, he looked up and saw the attic door hanging open. Confused, he unfolded the ladder and climbed up. At the far end, a pile of bedding lay in the slatted light. He crawled to it. Old candles had been melted onto the floor. Beside them lay a box of matches. Pinching one in his large, unpracticed fingers, he fumbled to light it and snapped it in half. More gently, he lit the next one and touched it to a candle. A few letters scratched into the floor caught his eye. He broke the candle free from its melted roots and passed it over the names carved into the wood. "Simon Knuffmann, M-Gladbach, 1943." And next to that: "Mateo Albero, Newark, USA, 1944."

"USA?" United States? Karl slumped back, rocked by the idea of an American in his own attic. Jealous anger straightened his spine. She always talked about America.

He glanced at the bedding, which only agitated him more. My imprint was probably still there. Thrashing at the blankets, he accidentally snuffed out the candle and left himself in darkness. It was a short grope back to the attic door, then down the ladder and into the living room to pace and rage.

"You bastards take three years of my life, destroy my home, and now this?" he fumed. "Sleeping under my own roof? Because my wife let you in?!"

His anger focused itself on the only intruder available, the massive block of stone. In two strides he was standing over it. He slapped his palms against its sides and squatted into the weight. Roaring into the dim light, he slowly lifted it from the floor. Three more strides to the broken wall and "Rrrwwwaaahhh!" the block tumbled out into the dusk and hit the sidewalk like a detonation. Down the street an elderly couple ducked involuntarily, their old terrors awakened by the explosive reverberation.

Karl stared down at the split stone, snorting with unsatisfied bloodlust, my name echoing through his consciousness. Life had moved on without him. For all he knew, Anna was in America by now. Gradually his rage ebbed, replaced by mild jealousy. America. He had planned to take her there. This place, this apartment, this city — it was not his anymore. On the train back to Mönchengladbach, he had rehearsed his brief speech in English, a language she had learned and he had disdained. "We will go in America," he had mumbled, pretending to hold her hand as he argued with his own destiny. "We will in the United States live." The other passengers had smiled with kind confusion. Karl had blushed and fallen silent, daydreaming once again about the plan that he and Werner had worked out. Werner's friend, the American

MP named O'Malley, was willing to sponsor Werner so that they could start a foundry in New York. Werner would sponsor Karl with a job. Karl would bring Anna to America.

He sagged to the floor amid the furniture, papers and books. The fatigue of his journey and the grief of his abortive homecoming swept over him. He slept. When he awoke, the summer sun was glancing through the open wall. A tickle against his face surprised him at first. What is this place? The panels of pressed tin above lent the first semblance of familiarity to his surroundings. He rolled over and sat up. There was a piece of paper stuck to his face. Out of curiosity, he smoothed it out and glanced at the words and images drawn in Anna's careful hand. Belgium? Karl read some more, then sat upright. It was a map. He jumped up and ran to the apartment across the hall. The old woman was evasive, engrained with deep suspicion from a decade of totalitarian bullying. Karl's gruff interrogation yielded few clues at first. An SS officer? With olive skin and black hair? Anna would not tolerate the former, nor would the SS allow the latter. Believing that she was lying, Karl pressed her for the truth. When she broke down and cried, he turned abruptly to leave.

"Ludwig," she sobbed.

Karl froze, hearing a name he had read only minutes before.

"I heard her say the name Ludwig. Perhaps that was his name?"

Karl brought the map forward and pointed to the name "Haike Ludwig" written in Anna's hand. Fascinated, the woman began to talk through the mystery with Karl, gradually lending depth and shape to his impression of Anna's last days in the apartment. With tears in his eyes, he hugged the old woman and hurried inside to retrieve his duffel bag. A quick glance around the apartment turned up little of value to his new mission. His attention lingered on the phonograph records; he decided to salvage the unbroken ones. The last thing he focused on was the letter. He bunched it into his pocket and turned to go, pausing for a final look at the picture from which the naïve face of his youth stared back at him. Across the dead air of the living room, he tried to close the gap of years and to regain for a moment the burly innocence of the manchild in the field gray hat. A small spider of white gradually emerged from the black insignia. As he stared at the swastika, ghastly memories and abandoned dreams whirled in his mind, draining the hope that seconds earlier had lit his eyes. *Killed in action.* Lifeless and alone, he shuffled through the door without bothering to pull it closed. It would be many miles before he spoke again, many black nights and brutal escapes as he tracked the footsteps of his wife's liberation.

Eleven

Outside of Liege, Belgium
August, 1946

"Yes, Nineteen Forty-four," Anna lied. "Late October — probably the Twenty-third."

"Probably?" The old man looked up from the heavy wedding book and raised his eyebrows above the thin gold rims that perched slightly askew on his purple nose. One iris was shot through with milky white. His other eye fixed her in an amused stare. "You do not remember your wedding day?"

"Ach, the war," Anna exhaled, "and so much was going on. I remember that it was raining very hard that day. We were frightened. Forgive me, Father. The Germans... I was so frightened."

"But you are German, no?"

"Yes, Father, but... he was not. We sheltered with you... on our way to Liege. I remember the prayers you said for us during the ceremony. That beautiful homily about marriage being a garden..."

The priest lay both hands on the pages of the book and looked up at Anna. His face was kind, serene even, but she knew his mind was chewing on the discrepancies in her story. In her arms, the tiny boy gurgled and tried to form the German word for "Mommy." It came out more like "*Mmmmussshi*," but the priest smiled anyway and tickled his little cheek.

"A year is a long time to wait for his baptism," the priest scolded gently. Anna opened her mouth to protest, but he cut her off. "I know, I know. The war..." He closed his eyes, then opened them again and looked up at a picture of St. Hubert standing next to a stag with a crucifix hovering between its antlers. He nodded slightly, as if seconding a decision that Hubert had made for him, and then looked back at Anna. "You are both Catholic," he murmured, more in confirmation than inquiry. "And he is alive? The father?" He raised his eyebrows again and peered over the tops of his glasses. "Your husband?"

"He is in America," Anna said softly. "Yes."

"And who will be the godparents?"

"They are outside," Anna replied. She winced ever so slightly at the thought of Haike and the old farmer standing in the baptistery. They were Catholics, and decent people, but hardly the most presentable accomplices she could have rounded up.

"Very well," the priest said. "Bring them in."

"Yes, Father," Anna whispered gratefully. "Thank you, Father." Anna bowed and turned for the door. "Oh, and if I could trouble you for one more thing?"

The priest looked up once again.

"The marriage certificate? You know, the one I lost in the fire?" Anna crossed her fingers again under the baby's blanket. Although God could see the gesture, she was fairly certain the half-blind priest was not perceptive enough to pick it up. "Could I ask you for a replacement?"

"Yes, yes," he mumbled, closing the thick book of handwritten names and dates that he had long since lost the ability to see. He opened a drawer and fumbled around for a long time before finally emerging with a pen, a bottle of ink, and a parchment form with gilded scrollwork at its corners. "What was that name?"

"Albero," Anna began. "A-l-b..."

Twelve

Newark
August, 1946

My first day on the job at the Pelican Club was spent in quiet penance for my fight with Vin, cleaning toilets and mopping floors. I suppose it was my frustration at not having heard from Anna that had made my temper so short. I wasn't sleeping too well. Little things made me jump. It wasn't until much later that I thought it might have been the war, maybe battle fatigue or something. At the time, I was just mad at the world for being so big that I couldn't reach Anna, and so small that I couldn't get away from people like Benny Bells. Izzo and I didn't talk about the fight, but late that afternoon the tone changed and all was forgiven. He took a phone call and went out for a few minutes. When he strolled back in, he had a white bakery box in one hand and a football in the other. He was singing in that corny tone he saved for times when the tree of fortune shook loose a few apples for him. I looked up from my mop just in time to catch the football. He set the box down on the bar.

"Whassat, cannoli?" I asked as I reached for the box. Izzo slapped my hand away. "What gives?" I asked.

"That's for Mary." He smiled, but an edge of nervous anger gleamed in his eyes.

"She finally quit crossing her arms and let you near those big—"

"Easy, pal! That's my future wife you're talkin' about."

"Hey, I said *arms*." I tossed the football up in the air and caught it. "God help her. When is that again?"

"Two weeks, he answered. "The Tenth."

Izzo took the ball back and tried to twirl it in a spiral, but it popped loose and nearly knocked the box off the bar. I caught the carom and spun it sideways on the end of my finger, moving it away from his swatting hands and slapping the ends to keep it spinning. After a few seconds, I let the ball settle into my palm, faded back a couple of steps and pump-faked a pass at the cannoli.

"Come on, Iz. She won't miss just one."

A flash of panic crossed Izzo's face as he pushed the box further away from me. I dismissed his rather extreme reaction as new-groom jitters, but it stuck in my mind. He asked if I remembered what happened in August every year. I didn't. He nodded at the football. "Yep, that's right." His grin was genuine this time. Henry Izzo simply loved the game of football, maybe even more than I did. He definitely loved practice more. "Two-a-days."

The team met the next day. It was technically still July, but close enough. Of the guys assembled for that first session, only Izzo and two 4-Fs had not gone overseas. Every man there shared the same feeling of regret at no longer being part of a fighting unit or a football team — especially Izzo, who still had not buried the ghosts of his fallen Marine Corps brothers. I knew the first practice would just be a big haggle for position and status, so I hung back and let the rest of them puff their chests. One wiseguy in street shoes announced that *he* was the quarterback, news that I received with a broad smile. A few guys had played in college before shipping out; one was even a starting end at Fordham for two years. Izzo had also rounded up a handful of our old West Side teammates, so I spent a few minutes catching up with them and tossing the ball around. Out of the corner of my eye, I saw a figure standing at the edge of the park. I waved off the next pass and walked over to where the man was standing. Walker had told me Johnny Mack was a "ringer," but I was not expecting someone quite so imposing. His crushing handshake and stone-faced stare made me think he was the sort of player you wanted on your side of the ball, and one you kept an eye on when he was on the other side.

"Newark Eagles, huh?" I asked.

Mack nodded as we walked back to the rest of the team. After three seasons with the local Negro League baseball team, he had been drafted into the Army. He had amassed enough combat distinction as a Sergeant with the Seven-sixty-first tank battalion in France and Germany to qualify for a Silver Star, but a year later he still had not received a single official decoration from the Army — and he wasn't holding his breath. Mack wasn't a bitter man. He just used experiences like that one to free his mind of any doubt about the nature of the society in which he lived. He hung back as I walked into the group that gathered around Izzo. I waved him in.

"Guys, this is John Mack," I announced. "Iz, this is the guy Jeremiah told us about."

Izzo flashed a salesman's smile and extended his hand. God bless him, all he cared about was winning football games. He knew a talented musician when he heard one, and he knew a ballplayer at a glance. Izzo was no more racially progressive in his outlook than the rest of the guys. He just recognized when people of any extraction might be useful to him. His big horsey grin reminded me of the moment that he had first told me about the team. I wondered if it was friendship or my two city championships that had made him greet me like a long-lost brother. Mack edged back out of the circle, preferring to stand alone as Izzo made the introductions. It was a moment that came to define John Mack for me. Facing thirty pairs of eyes — some hateful, some overly friendly, but all slightly ill at ease — he was as peaceful and impassive as he would have been if he were all alone on that field. Conscious only of those judgments rendered with absolute objectivity, he dismissed the approval and rejection of others as merely an extension of opinions they already held. Mack was a true stoic. I immediately held him in the highest regard. He intended to let his work on the field speak for him. He neither expected friendship nor trusted it when it was too readily offered.

Izzo led the team through calisthenics, which irritated some of the alpha types who felt that they should have been named captain on the first day. In the last row, I smiled to myself and let the gamesmanship go on without me. A few places over, Mack noted my amusement with a slight nod. Sometimes you know a leader by what he chooses *not* to do.

When Izzo lined us up for sprints, I realized the wisdom of having quit smoking when I did. My stamina was generally good, but with a few weeks away from cigarettes my lungs were that much stronger. Mack and I finished all of the sprints at the head of the pack. As we lined up for the last one, I looked over and gestured at the goal line to challenge him. He nodded. We set ourselves for Izzo's call. Mack got a better start, but I caught him in a couple of steps and held the pace until his longer stride won back the lead. He crossed the goal line a half-yard ahead of me, grinning broadly at the familiar joy of competition. Everyone else lagged us by at least three yards. The loudmouth who had declared himself quarterback brought up the rear, slipping along in his loafers and doubling over with exhaustion as he crossed the end line.

A pencil and paper circulated through the group. Everyone was asked to write down his name, telephone number and position of choice. A couple of guys didn't write anything, including my rival in the street shoes. Izzo had told me to expect some attrition after the workout he had planned, but I was pleased that the list was as long as it was. Practice was called for six the next morning and the group dispersed. With a nod, Mack turned and walked toward a sedan parked at the east side of the field. I glanced at the paper. His precise block lettering confirmed my growing sense of optimism; this rag-tag group had the makings of a team. Izzo and I strolled over to South Orange Avenue. Behind us, the setting sun raised a fiery curtain through the carbonized haze to the west. Dusk glowed down the broad boulevard. The vaulted façade of St. Antoninus Church took on a golden hue, silencing Izzo's chatter about players and positions and leaving him to gape at the clean lines of stone and stained-glass windows. We walked two blocks out of our way to stand and stare at the strange light on the church.

"Wow," he whispered, "I hope it looks like that when..." His voice faded, then revived. "Mary'd love that."

Nodding in silent agreement, I began to see how deeply he loved her. Marriage was something none of us took lightly. With the full weight of Church and Family resting squarely on that decision, it was a wonder anybody did it. But watching Izzo, I began to understand. He was raised in the same Roman Catholic tradition as I had been, measured against the same unreasonable images of perfection and laden with the same responsibilities to sacrament and society. Yet staring at that granite edifice, he didn't see tons of expectation piled on top of bedrock consequence. Instead he saw only the light that played through the colored glass and waited to warm his bride's smile. His faith was simple. He sought no rapture, and gained little grace. "Catholic" was a word on his birth certificate, a mode of identification that was not open to interpretation. Likewise, to him marriage was a marker on a map he did not draw, and did not question.

It was hard for me to see it the same way. I couldn't fathom the concept of marriage without Anna. I recalled my first glimpse of her extraordinary beauty, when the note of her voice touched a memory in me that could not have come from this lifetime. There was something peaceful in that sound, something certain. To be near her was to abdicate my own mortality, to reach past the bondage of the flesh to a weightless commingling of souls. It felt like the absence of burden. I watched the sunset creep like fire toward the rose-shaped window high on the church wall. It made me think of the tongues of flame on that Belgian barn, and then suddenly of the distance between myself and Anna. My chest felt hollow and cold. Please tell me, I prayed in silence, why You brought her to me if You only meant to take her away? But Heaven was silent, no rumble of acknowledgement, no cackle of disdain. I would have to solve the riddle of Anna — and of my own faith — for myself.

Two weeks later on a hot August afternoon, Henry Izzo waited at the altar for Mary Scartavilli. I stood a few feet away, sweating into a rented tuxedo and enjoying the view. So many faces. In the front row, Benny Bells sat next to Izzo's mother and murmured in her ear, working his venom charm as his eyes darted back and forth with the vigilance of a practiced liar. There were huge sprays of flowers on either side of the altar, even though the Izzos could not afford such extravagance. When I looked back at the front row, Benny was still whispering to Mrs. Izzo, but he was staring at me. The ice in his eyes sent a chill through my blood. Instinct told me to look away but instead I glared back, defiant. His neck went red above his gangster collar. He locked into the confrontation, at least until Mrs. Izzo noticed the look on his face and recoiled with fear. She seemed confused, as if his silken words couldn't possibly have come from such a murderous little mug. Instantly suave, Benny smiled at her and waved the back of a dismissive hand in my direction. But her smile was nervous; Benny's spell was broken.

In his humble grave at Holy Sepulcher Cemetery, Izzo's father must have been turning over at the notion of Benny Bells sitting beside his wife on his son's wedding day. Henry Senior had made it his mission to resist the corrupting influence of organized crime, paying only what was required to keep the local syndicate at bay and accepting none of the patronage that was routinely offered. His public neutrality masked a deep hatred of men like Benny Bells. In the Izzos' apartment above the bar, I had listened to him rail to his family about the prejudice that mobsters brought down on *all* Italians, honest or not. It was never clear to me who he hated more, mafia hoods or *Medigan* snobs. According to him, the Anglo-Americans — Medigans — had it in for us, and the Italian wiseguys just made it easier for them to justify their bigotry. He sounded a lot like my Pop. They were working guys, with no time or patience for people who didn't work. And wiseguys didn't work. Still, Henry Senior had smiled and handed over free shots of whiskey and anisette when they rapped their knuckles on his bar, just as he knew his son would do years later. What he didn't know was that Henry Junior had watched all of this with a weather eye for opportunity. Junior was tough and gung-ho, but he was not the idealist that his father was.

The organ played the first bouncy notes of the wedding march as a bustle of white lace appeared at the back door. Everyone turned to watch the bride take her first tentative steps into the church. I heard Izzo's breath catch in his throat. Mary looked down at the threshold, trying to keep her dress from bunching under her delicate white shoes. When she looked up at the congregation with wide, hopeful eyes, I saw a side of her that I had never recognized before. I felt like I was peering into her childhood, as if God had allowed me a glimpse of the vulnerable soul of a little girl so that I might better appreciate the significance of the vows she would make as a woman.

Mary stepped carefully to the communion rail. The ceremony began. Altar boys scurried to light candles and incense. Everywhere there were expectant looks from family and friends, most of which were lost on Izzo and his bride in their own moment of contemplation. Kneeling and standing beside them as they moved from communion to commitment, I thought of Anna. I wondered how her wedding to Karl had been; if she had blushed beneath her veil, if she had answered with the same halting self-consciousness as Mary, struggling to overcome the bashful awareness of her own projected and echoing voice. No, Anna would have been bold. But would she have been sure? And if she had loved Karl enough to make those vows, what could be left for me? How many of her dreams had died with him? Then it hit me again: she didn't want me. She had turned away, had ignored my letters and forgotten my name. My dreams were dead, not hers.

A thousand miles away from my wandering consciousness, the bride and groom exchanged their vows. Relief and happiness crossed Mary's face. Staring at his ring, Izzo seemed truly at ease. *The absence of burden.* The weight of doubt was gone for both of them. They looked into one another's eyes, and with that everything around them vanished. Their first kiss as man and wife happened spontaneously, and ended only when applause broke in to remind them of where they were. Izzo grinned as he swept his bride down the aisle and out into the bright sunshine. For them, a lifetime together had begun. I walked to the door beside Mary's sister, aware of her earthy beauty shrouded beneath layers of makeup and puffed silk. Benny glared at me as I passed. I tried to ignore him, and to forget about the life into which he had drawn my brother. I focused on the joy of the moment, the glass I would raise well into the night, the scent of the woman on my arm. It was a good night for a party. Gangsters and dead dreams could wait.

Outside, Mary's sister dropped my arm and ran to hug her new brother-in-law. I stood alone on the edge of the crowd, suddenly aware of my own inconsequence. It occurred to me, at the periphery of someone else's glorious day, how little my life really mattered. I felt free. People say they have nothing to lose, and sometimes they mean it, but just then I *knew* it. I was a footnote in a larger story, a son of the laboring masses and a near-miss casualty of a war that had sent greater souls to an untimely end. I always believed I was lucky, but maybe it wasn't luck at all. Maybe there's only so much fate to go around. You want to think that your life is worthy of deliberation and judgment, that your death and salvation are matters of the utmost import within the moral scheme of things. But maybe not. I watched a good man's life end in a plane above Germany, and I watched a lesser man's wedding dreams come true. Van Orden dies, Izzo thrives. Henry Senior goes, Benny Bells stays. I have to believe there is a thread of logic that runs through our capricious existence — one that ties chaos to order, and whim to fate — but I can't see it. And maybe it can't see me. Maybe I am so tiny in the eyes of the Almighty that it really doesn't matter what I do. That's what I was thinking that day. I know a little better than that now, but in the fifty-eight years since I stood and watched the

Izzos get married, very few things have happened to make me think that I am any more important than I thought I was then. They're still married, and I still have very few illusions about the relative significance of my life.

But then again, war plays with your head. Some of what I was thinking back then was maybe amplified a little by the echoes of combat. We had it better than the guys on the ground, for sure, but it's still about risk, about laying it out there day after day, about being ready for it *not* to work out, for the ship *not* to be bulletproof, for the flak fragment *not* to miss. Maybe I was ready, maybe I wasn't. I couldn't tell you for sure. But what I can say is that I got a lot more used to the idea of it, of living and maybe dying that way, than I thought I could. When you're first there, all you can think about is getting back home. You magnify the good things. Married guys make starlets out of average wives. Fathers fall asleep with their kids' names on their lips. Home pulls at you something awful. But then for some guys it fades a little, and maybe that's better. Maybe for them coming home was something fresh and new. What's strange is that when you finally do get home, you start thinking about going back. The corner store you dreamed about seems quiet and small. People don't talk the same way they did in your dreams. It's all moving to some other beat, something you left behind when you first shipped out, something maybe you can't ever reconnect with. You try, because you know in your head that you're home, but your heart makes it tough. At least for me it did, probably because of Anna, but maybe not. Maybe it was something else. I don't know.

I watched Mary's sister toss her hair and glance back at me as she laughed with her friend. She leaned on one leg, bending her other knee and opening her thigh beneath her long dress. When she looked at me again, she smiled in a way that stirred that ancient instinct in my blood. I let my glance drift down and then away. On some level I was amused at my own simplicity; chemical lust just danced me around on its puppet strings. I wanted to be a better man, but hey, if she's gonna smile like that... What the hell was her name again? I pinched my lip and struggled to recall. Suddenly, I felt silly. I looked around for the rest of the bridal party, not ready to abandon my solitude yet knowing that if I stood there much longer the only name I would be able to remember or think of or say out loud would be Anna's. Mary's sister shifted to the other leg, her breasts bouncing slightly with the movement. "Rosemarie!" I said out loud, smiling triumphantly. I think she might have heard me because she giggled. Her friends did too. Hey, whatever. If life wanted to keep moving me around and changing the scenery, I would just enjoy the dance. Nothing to lose.

A shoulder bumped my ribs, hard. I turned around, half expecting to see another long-lost teammate. The little black coals of Benny's eyes were the first thing I noticed, then the sweat beads on his forehead and cheeks. He looked even smaller up close, as if his shiny tuxedo had compressed his greasy bulk into an even denser and more explosive form. His grin was a leer.

"Rosemarie, huh?" he rasped. "Nice tits. She make you forget the German girl. What'ser name... Ann? Anna?"

"Shut the fu—!" I stopped myself, finger poised to jab at his face.

Benny turned every word into a profanity, but not that one. Not her name. I couldn't allow it. I sensed people's eyes on me and lowered my hand. Benny pinched my elbow. His fat little fingers were surprisingly strong. One of his soldiers lumbered after him as he steered me away from the church and toward the school building. I glanced down at the cornerstone, conscious of the deferential placement of my eyes. "...Anno Domini 1924." I forced myself to read the letters carved into the stone so that I could calm down before looking at him again. I wanted to punch his fat little face until he gagged on his own blood, but I knew he wanted me thinking that. He had played on my temper for a reason. But if Benny had something to say to me I would need to hear it with a cool mind.

"Nice tux," I muttered. Friggin' midget penguin.

"Your brother..." Benny bit the side of his hand to demonstrate his anger, but I could tell from his cold eyes that he was exaggerating his emotions. He rubbed his fingers against his thumb, as if the very word 'money' were too dear for him to share aloud. People like him seemed to feel greed in their viscera. He looked even smaller and more repulsive as his face pursed with avarice.

"Vin's been light the past two weeks," Benny continued. "He's diggin' a hole."

"Why you tellin' me?" My question was sincere. I had no idea why this was any of my business.

"This bar, Izzo's place," he said, his eyes darting across the wedding party. "Whatta you know about it?"

I was suddenly conscious of the fact that I was standing with Benny Bells, talking to him as if the conversation were a part of my normal routine, as if it were not a strange thing to be chatting with a gangster in front of half the neighborhood. I looked back to see if my father was still among the well-wishers gathered around the bridal party. "He's over there," Benny said, pointing directly at Pop. I know there was fear in my eyes when I turned back to Benny. Damn it, I know it. But I was shocked that the little bastard had read my mind. He leaned forward slightly. When he spoke again his irises were dead black, like a shark's.

"Now whattaya know about the bar?"

"Nothing," I shrugged. "I work there. That's it."

"Vin got anything goin' on there?"

"Besides a big tab?" I forced a chuckle. "No."

"Who owns it?"

"The old lady, I guess."

I was pretty sure of that. If Benny didn't already know that, he wouldn't have worked her so hard in the church. Besides, Henry Senior was too smart to leave his life's work to the whim of his opportunistic son.

"I want you to do a little checkin' for me," Benny muttered. "Listen around, tell me what you hear. I got a feeling..."

"No," I said flatly.

Benny's eyes widened slightly. It was not a word he heard every day. He turned to his minion and gestured at me with mock appreciation. "This guy, huh? Setta balls on him!" Without missing a beat, Benny backhanded the very items he was celebrating. I didn't even see it coming. A wave of nauseating heat sent spasms up through my abdomen and made me feel like I would either vomit or double over, or both. Benny leaned in again.

"I'll string you and your piece o' shit brother up if I hear he's using my vig payments for some side thing I ain't part of."

Benny Bells tapped his associate on the arm and gestured at the street, sending the man shuffling off in the direction of a black Cadillac at the opposite curb. I gasped for enough air to speak, but before I could protest he jabbed an index finger into the precise spot in my side that the broken bottleneck had pierced. The shock caused me to twist involuntarily, a spastic reaction that was first embarrassing and then infuriating. I clenched my right fist, but held it back. He raised his finger to my face.

"This is *my* city," he rasped. "Mine."

There was a flicker of desperation in his eyes, as if he badly needed to believe what he was saying. But in an instant it was gone, and once again he projected a dismissive indifference. His attitude seemed to imply that things like family, love and loyalty were merely quaint distractions. It was the look of one for whom the world held no surprise, no wonder, no joy — merely profits and victims. Vin had mimicked it with surprising effectiveness, but for him it had seemed more like a suicide of the soul, a palpable loss. With Benny, there was no sense of anything missing that had ever been there before. He turned and walked through the crowd, waving with the reserved formality of a man more obligated than interested. I stood there, keenly aware of how wrong I had been just moments before, and of how much I did have to lose. Watching that empty little man cross the street and slide into his limousine, I thanked God that the war had not burned away every last shred of innocence in me. It would be a struggle to protect what was sacred in my life from people like him. I knew that the strength to succeed would have to be built on the scraps of benevolence that still remained in my heart.

Thirteen

German Border, Southeast of Aachen
October, 1946

The tight wooden chamber felt like a coffin, but to Karl the sensation was not altogether unpleasant. He knew he could always push the boards aside, and that the light hay above would yield easily to end his temporary confinement. Stretched flat in the wagon, bumping along as the horses clip-clipped with a breezy morning pace toward the Belgian border, Karl felt safe. Invisible. It was a strange feeling for a man who forever sensed other people's eyes on him. His size seemed to draw attention wherever he went, even more so now that the country was occupied. The British troops who patrolled Mönchengladbach and its outlying regions knew they had little to fear from conquered Germans, but their fingers slipped nervously to the triggers of their rifles when Karl passed by. He refused to smile at them or to set them at ease in any way, even though he considered them a welcome change from the Nazis. Too many of his friends had lost their lives to British bayonets in Egypt and Libya.

Too many good men, sons and fathers. And too many of his own bullets had found their way into English bodies. He had killed in anger, in revenge. Perhaps in time he would be able to put it aside, but not just yet.

The light thumping of hooves on dried dirt yielded abruptly to the metallic clash of horseshoes against cobblestone. Karl felt the wagon lurch first to one side and then to the other as it shouldered onto the paved road. He thought of the phonograph records being tossed back and forth in the driver's rough satchel. He had traded most of those that he had salvaged from the apartment in exchange for a ride across the border, keeping only the few that meant the most to him and to Anna. On the way back into Germany, the false bottom of the wagon would conceal hundreds of pounds of contraband — cigarettes, beer, burlap bags of dried pork and beef, gallon cans of precious petrol, perhaps even a few guns. The records Karl had bartered would be used to purchase some of these goods from Allied supply officers, or from middlemen with American connections. He didn't care. He made no judgment of the man sitting directly above him, or of the Americans with whom that man dealt. He just wanted to cross the border and be on his way.

After a while, the stony jangle of metal shoes became as hypnotic as the soft-dirt trot had been. Karl let his eyes close and his body relax. His thoughts wandered. Before him stretched a road that he had not imagined, a future for which he had not planned. In his dreams, he had walked into the apartment and seen a changed Anna — a humble, chastened version of the woman he had married. No less beautiful, but gentler, more docile. Separation and war would have worn away the edge that had always kept him at a slight remove. She would smile, embrace him, take comfort in the safety he could provide. She would ask about Africa, but instead he would tell her about America, the place she had always idealized and that he had been the first to see. At long last, he would possess knowledge and information that she did not. He would smile, grow still, and look at her with mischief in his eyes. When she asked, he would tell her about Werner and the foundry and the job that Werner had arranged for him. New York City. Yes, he would say, as her joy brought the tears. We're really going to America.

He opened his eyes again. Above him, the hay blotted out most of the light that might have peeked in from between the boards. He drew his hand across his body and up to his face, then pressed his palm against the underside of the rough board, just inches from his nose. A few more miles, he thought. She'll be there. She's got to be. So what if it's not just like the dream? She'll still smile, maybe even cry a little. It will be like it was, like when they were kids. He'll stand tall again, free of the garish swastika and the malignancy of National Socialism. The gold will dance in her eyes. She'll regain her innocence and lose the darkness. He felt the vibrations in the wood as the wagon rumbled along. His imagination reached as far as the air above the hay, past the limits of his physical confinement, but not beyond the borders of his earthly bondage. He would not have recognized the irony of his posture, death letter in his pocket, life passing by outside of the box that contained him. He was built for struggle, not salvation. In a way, I envy that about him. He was prepared to live and to die only once; his life was a finite, definite thing. If at the very end there was only death, his heart would not be broken.

"You there!" snapped a British officer. "Right, stop then. You, in the wagon."

The driver reined in. Karl tensed at the officer's crisp enunciation and arch tone. He had learned English from southern Americans: rounded, comfortable vowels, and consonants that melted on the tongue. To him, the King's English seemed to reside in the stilted noses of those who used words as if they were demitasse — as delicate finery with which one might identify and quickly dismiss the unclassed and midlothian. There is nothing so pathetic as ignorance posing in the clothes of esteem. Although Karl didn't know it then, his aversion to pretense would serve him well in America.

There was a brief exchange, a passing of papers back and forth, a groping for common language. Karl listened as the hay above him was tossed and probed with the butt of a rifle. After what seemed like an hour, the horses pulled forward and labored up the gradual incline of a bridge. When the ground tilted forward again, they picked up the tempo until finally, on the level sanctuary of the Belgian side, they found a normal rhythm and trotted once again. He had kept his hand pressed to the board the entire time. When the wagon stopped and the driver rapped his knuckles against the side panel, Karl pushed through the floorboards and emerged from the hay with his duffel bag. Gulping drafts of cool air, he quickly settled the floor back into place and sat up on the sideboard as the wagon moved on. Around them, fields carved from dense forest stretched away to mature stands of timber. Karl unfolded the handwritten map that Anna had left behind and tried to locate some of the landmarks. Seeing none, he concluded that his best chance of finding the Ludwig farm would be to ride with the driver to the outskirts of Liege and work his way back.

A day and a half after he had jumped down from the wagon and waved his thanks to the driver, Karl found himself standing with one hand on the neck of an iron water pump, staring into the defiant glare of a Belgian woman every bit as stubborn as he was.

"I am Karl Eisenstark."

Haike Ludwig's eyes widened with astonished fear, but as the dead man kept talking she realized that there must have been some horrible mistake, that the letter Anna described must have been sent in error. The rumor was true — he was alive. Patiently, Karl outlined the trail of clues that had led him to her door. Haike had never met a German soldier who spoke with such humility. She noticed the hat in his hands, the gentle bow of his head. Her fingers found the strands of hair hanging across her face and smoothed them back. She recalled how happy Anna had been with the American, and how unconcerned Anna had seemed with the fact that her husband had been killed. Haike was twice widowed — once by the war, and again by the careless habits of the old farmer whom she had married more out of boredom than love. She was familiar with the cycles of grief. She understood Anna's instinct to renew herself, to reach out for love after a period of mourning. Anna is gone, Haike rationalized. Off to America. She does not miss this man.

Haike touched Karl's sleeve and gently led him to her door. She nodded absently at his questions, imagining the meal she would prepare, the long bath he would take, the way the bed would creak as he settled into it. Karl was struggling to pronounce the words he had written on a small piece of paper.

"Mah-teo Albe... Al-ber..." He skipped ahead. "New-ark?" He grinned with recognition. "Ach so, *New York*."

Distracted, Haike nodded. "Yes, yes," she answered in German. "Mateo. The American. Yes. 'New York?' Sure, that sounds right. Yes. New York."

She opened the door and blushed slightly as Karl walked through. Such a big man, she thought. Such a very big man.

Fourteen

Blairstown, NJ and Bronx, New York
November, 1946

Played properly, football is meditation. One afternoon
in Nineteen Forty-six, I realized that while I was on the
field there was no room in my mind for anything but the
game. We were huddled near a goal line painted on a
windswept horse pasture in western Jersey. Around us
were valleys of green grass that swept up hillsides fired
with the orange and yellow of autumn. Here and there,
the Pennsylvania horizon was dotted with little white
houses and red barns. There were maybe five little clouds
in the sky. At least two hundred people ringed the field.
And once the game started, I saw none of it.

It was our fifth game in a season of ten. We had won
four and lost one, which was more a testament to the
disorganization of the new league than to any stellar play
on our part. Out there on that open hilltop, with clean air
filling my lungs and my cleats in grass more lush than any
I had ever seen, I smiled. We were close to the end, late
fourth quarter. The square-headed farmboys on the other

side had kicked our butts up and down the field, but still only managed to score one touchdown. I looked across at their huddle and grinned at the defensive tackle whose aggressive hitting had brutalized our runners all afternoon. We would score on the next play, I knew it. I knew we would go for two and the win on the play after that. I knew what plays I would call, and who from their side would over-pursue the ball, and who on ours would take advantage of that. And at that moment in my life, that was all I knew or cared to know.

It happened as I thought it would. Izzo snapped me the ball. Mack pulled from his position at right end and sprinted for the left side. I pitched the ball to our halfback, Manny Castro, who swung wide left and then cut right as Mack blindsided the overaggressive defensive tackle. No one touched Castro as he trotted into the end zone. I lined us up for the two-point conversion, snuck the ball across the goal line behind Izzo's textbook drive block and called it a day. We had become that sort of a team, one for which every man played with the knowledge that no game was lost, no opponent too tough. But we didn't start out that way. That feeling develops gradually, with repetition. One win, two, then three. You start to realize that every practice, every drill, every play is reinforcing a collective belief. *We are winners.* You get that edge — that feeling of never wanting to be the weak link, never letting up for one second because when your hands relax the magic begins to slip away.

In time, you also get confidence. That's why I was smiling. I knew the men in our huddle were better than the men in theirs, despite the fact that we had played a sloppy game, one that at times had made me furious. I was beaten up, hit hard again and again by a bunch of

169

yokels who had no business leading by a touchdown in the fourth quarter. Our reputation had begun to travel. They were ready for us. We were looking ahead to a tough stretch of games against three New York teams, and we figured those soft country folk would lay down for a team from the city. It was a lesson I vowed not to forget. After the game, we shook hands and piled back onto the school bus that Joe Tupo, one of our linemen, had "borrowed" from the Essex County school district. Tupo was a driver. His depot chief had agreed to look the other way on Sunday mornings in exchange for free drinks at the Pelican Club on Saturday nights. Pay in advance. That was the rule of the street in Newark. That was the rule we forgot for most of that game.

I sat down in one of the cramped bench seats and looked around at my teammates. There were a lot of sober faces. Despite the fact that we had won, no one seemed particularly happy about the way we had played. Mack took the seat across the aisle from me and shook his head. I nodded. That was it. We knew what we had to do in practice the following week. Mack was our defensive captain; I led the offense. We had no coaches, so it fell to us to design the plays and the systems. Mack had emerged as the leader of the defense on an August morning choked with dust and tension. We were running a tackling drill, a one-on-one showdown between two linemen in a three yard box. A ball carrier followed the offensive lineman's block, and the defensive lineman had to stop him. Mack was on defense. Almost everybody was rooting for the young Irish tackle who had lined up against him. Mack decked the kid with a forearm to the chin and then leveled the runner. Two other Irish guys jumped in and grabbed Mack, but he fought them off, too. When the next set of linemen started toward the box, Mack shoved the defensive player out of the way. He stayed in that box and took on every lineman on the team, breaking them one by one. He never said a word, but from that day on everybody knew he was in charge.

My own stature was more a result of the position I played than of any show of dominance. I already knew several offensive schemes, so as the quarterback I had the privilege of implementing them. Although I'll admit there were times when I lost my temper, generally I didn't play the game with the ginned-up rage that a lot of guys had. For me, it was more than just a brawl. The field was a place where I put that stuff aside, where the hits and the pain were simply an obstacle and not a cause for personal retribution. There was enough of that in life — I didn't need it in games. I played for moments like the one on that hilltop, when life outside the boundaries of the game faded to a blur and the only consequences were points scored and missed, victories secured or denied. Those were stakes I could live with. That was a world I could master. Out there on the field, I could just smile.

Toward the front of the bus, Izzo began to sing in that goofy tone he had. His were simple pleasures. I thought again of his bakery box, and of what it implied about the Pelican Club and my brother. Once you walk off the field, life has an infuriating way of blurring the boundaries between the places in your life so that nothing stays clean. It all flows together, sin and sacrament. It works its way into your bloodstream, into your heart. You give up a little equilibrium, maybe, but if you're lucky the poison doesn't kill you. I stared up at the fires of autumn, leaves pulsing like orange flames against the cold blue sky. The peace that had stilled my mind was beginning to ripple again with real life concerns. Desperate to preserve the blessed amnesia of the game, I leaned against the bus window and drifted off to sleep.

Four weeks later I opened my eyes and looked out that same window, but this time at the blustered gray of late November. Around me, my teammates were singing once again. Everyone had taken up Izzo's tune. Even Mack was grinning like a new father, cigar clutched between his bright white teeth.

"Hey!" Mack shouted. "Look who woke up."

The side of my skull seemed to compress slightly and then bow outward with an agonizing surge of pressure. My white shirt was spattered with dried blood. I looked at Mack, wondering what had happened.

"Damn, look at your eyes," he said, shaking his head. "You still on Queasy Street? You took one hell of a shot when you threw that last pass. Course I didn't see it 'cause I was too busy catching the ball and running across the *goal line*!" This was easily the most emotion I had ever seen Mack display. "We did it, Pops. Eight and two. We're playin' for the championship in two weeks."

I smiled feebly, struggling to piece together the previous three hours. The singing in the bus throbbed at my eardrums. A football lay in my lap. Behind my battered head, someone had bunched a towel and padded the window for me. I tried to sit up, but dizziness and nausea chased me back down. I closed my eyes and hugged the pigskin like a teddy bear. It was a game ball, I knew that. Izzo had probably been the one to make the speech. Smiling broadly, he was standing and leading songs at the front of the bus. Images started to come back to me. Pebbled dirt field, framed on two sides by an elevated train. Loud, ugly crowd. Maroon jerseys, bunch of tough Italians. Here comes Eighty-eight again, over our right tackle. Mack's open! Throw it as far as you can. Impact. Darkness. Touchdown. I smiled and opened my eyes again.

"You caught that duck?" I asked Mack.

"Wobbled a long way, Pops," Mack grinned. "But I got there."

At home, I pressed a bag of ice to my head and dug through the papers in my dresser drawer. There was someone I needed to tell about this win. Although I heard from friends that Charlie Shapiro was playing professionally someplace, I had not tracked him down. The most recent address I had for him was his parents' home in Baltimore. I sat at the dining room table and started to write a few triumphant lines, then backtracked and asked how he was doing. At my darkest hour, back from England and sick with grief at having left Anna behind, Chiz had convinced me to play football again. I believe it saved my life. When I realized that I was writing this all down, I dropped the pencil and slapped my palm against the page, ready to crush the embarrassing words. But my hand lifted. I let it be. It might be a little too candid, but it was the truth. I signed the page, sealed it in an envelope and mailed it the next day.

Two weeks later, head healed, I arrived with my teammates at Yankee Stadium. Two gleaming coaches with "Albany Express" painted on the side were already parked at the curb. Tupo nosed our battered school bus up against the front bumper of the first one. He knew he would get a ticket for parking in the wrong direction, but

the contrast between our teams' accommodations had
amused him. Mack had smiled at the prank and I didn't
care, so he left it that way. We clattered down from the
bus in our cleats. There were few visitors' locker rooms
on our circuit, so we generally dressed for games before
we got on the bus. Several of the Yankees' representatives
seemed amused by the sight of our scarred leather
helmets, patched jerseys and mismatched pants. I glanced
over at the Albany buses. Our opponents had probably
arrived in coat and tie. Inside the stadium, we walked en
masse through the hallway the Yankees had curtained off
as a locker room for us and headed straight for the
entrance to the field. With the advent of offensive and
defensive platoons, it had become fashionable for teams
to split into groups before the game. But since there were
so few of us, and since we all played on both sides of the
ball, we just walked out as a team.

Clambering up the dugout steps, I was struck by the
sheer height of the stadium decks that seemed to
disappear into the November mist. I could barely make
out the famous arcs of the façade at the very top. Past the
outfield wall, the Longines clock and the scoreboard were
nested in a row of advertisements. A set of goalposts
stood at either end of a field drawn like a sacrilege across
the hallowed diamond. My childhood friends would have
been outraged to see an end zone in DiMaggio's
centerfield, but I decided I liked the field better with
goalposts on it. The team gathered and formed the same
two lines as always, Izzo at the head and Mack and I
bringing up the rear. Izzo started the familiar Lionel
Hampton tune, and we all answered his call as we
shuffled onto the field. For me, this was always the
beginning of the meditation, the first step in turning away

from external distraction and inward to the game. I was never one for singing in public, but belting out "Hey! Ba-Ba-Re-Bop" as I jogged past gaping spectators never bothered me. Their opinion of me was not important. All that mattered was the team.

We wore white jerseys. The Albany team wore red. High in the stands, wreathed in fog and cigar smoke, one man adjusted a pair of binoculars. He let them fall to the end of their strap each time he jotted in a small notebook, then picked them up and looked again. He focused on each man lined up for the opening kickoff, then looked up from his lenses as Tupo's leg swung forward and the ball flew out of the frame. Arcing high in the air, the brand new football came to rest in the arms of an Albany player. I chuffed through the cold air, arms pumping and eyes scanning for blockers as I angled toward the kick return man. Red jersey to my right; a forearm to fend him off. A blur of jerseys around the ball. Work closer. There he is. Go! Someone knifed in and grabbed his knees. I drove a shoulder through his chest and felt the soft impact of grassy turf that had not yet frozen solid. First contact. Relief. A hundred feet up, pencil met paper. Names and jersey numbers. Albero, Three, Newark.

What surprised me most about the Albany players was not their size or physicality, but their speed and precision. We had played tougher teams, but we had never seen one so disciplined and professional. In a way, it was good that I started out on defense so I could get a sense of how well-drilled they were. A lot of the misdirection we used on offense probably would not work against players like this. While I was covering receivers and chasing running plays from my position at defensive halfback, I revised my plan for our first offensive series. I would call plays that went straight at them. When we finally stopped them and got the ball back, I did just that. And we got nowhere.

Our league was comprised of fifteen semi-pro teams, all located in the northeast. Some of the teams, such as Albany, were better equipped and more organized than others. They had been playing together since before the war, and were famous from Maine to Delaware. We were the most recent addition, and the least well-known. Albany's player-coach, a tough Irish veteran named Tom Whalen, was the one who had arranged for the championship game to be played in Yankee Stadium. He had done this in July, confident that his boys would be there in November. Despite the fact that we were much closer to the Bronx than they were, an equal number of people had turned out to root for each side. The loud little contingents from our respective cities barely covered the first ten rows, but as the game went on the lower deck began to fill. Word must have gotten out to the local neighborhoods, or maybe they just opened the gates to non-paying customers. By the middle of the second quarter, the game was tied at zero and the noise level had risen significantly.

Just before halftime, on a play that haunted me for years, Mack knocked their quarterback out of the game. I watched as he lined up wide right and broke for the passer at the snap of the ball. The man had no idea what was bearing down on him. Mack hit him with such force that he bent backward, nearly in half. The ball popped loose and Izzo fell on it. I learned later that the quarterback's abdominal muscles had torn, but at the time it looked like Mack had snapped his spine. After I saw that play, I was always just a little more aware of my blind side when I dropped back to pass. We took over on their eleven yard line. I got lucky on the first play I called, a pass to the right corner of the end zone. The defensive halfback slipped and fell, and my easy lob dropped into Mack's hands for six points. Tupo kicked it through and we went into halftime with a seven point lead.

We traded touchdowns in the third quarter, and they tied the score in the fourth. I had finally found some plays that worked against their speedy defense, mostly fakes to the running back that lured their linebackers up and then short passes to the spots that they had vacated. When they adjusted to that, I handed the ball off for consistent three or four yard gains. We were moving the ball, but so were they. As darkness settled, the stadium light towers clanged to life, casting everything into that stark, unforgiving, last-call kind of glare, like when the bartender throws the switch and your new love's blush turns to painted rouge. The fog had cleared. I noticed their defensive backs squinting up at the lights with awestruck curiosity. We held them on a tough third and one, and they punted. There were less than two minutes left in the game, and we needed a score to win. In the huddle, I tapped Mack on the shoulder.

"Hey," I said, "what position did you play for the Eagles?"

"Whassat, Pops?" Mack looked confused.

"Outfield, right?"

"*Center*field," he corrected me.

"So you're used to the lights, no?" I nodded up at the beacons shining down from the home plate side of the field. They were at our backs.

"No problem," Mack said with a quick sideways nod.

I called a deep post pattern and winked at Mack as we broke the huddle. At the snap, I jogged slowly to my right and bought a little time for him to get up the field. Their halfback kept stride with him, and a safety drifted over to help. Despite the double coverage, I decided to take a chance. I set my feet and threw the pass as high and as far as I could. When the ball disappeared into the black sky above the lights, the defenders slowed down and hunched their shoulders as if they were nervous about where it might land. Mack kept stride and easily spotted the large circle as it descended into view. Too late, the defensive backs jabbed at the air. Mack looked the ball into his hands and sprinted the last fifteen yards to the end zone. I raised a fist and jogged up the field to meet him. Tupo's extra point sailed home as the clock ticked down to just over a minute left to play.

Our own safeties took a lesson from their counterparts' mistake and played a half step deeper than usual. It wasn't necessary. Albany's backup quarterback was not as accurate as their starter. I intercepted one of his quackers on second down. Our side of the stands erupted with cheers, drawing the indifferent locals into the celebration with their sheer exuberance. Newark didn't have too many champions back then. To send its sons into Yankee Stadium and come away with a win was a big deal, especially since we were supposed to be an afterthought, a sideshow at the coronation of the upstate kings. I walked toward the dugout and saw my sisters in the first row of seats. Little Mickey was pie-eyed. He touched a grass stain on my shoulder as if it was somehow connected to the soles of DiMaggio's shoes. I lifted him over the railing and down to the field, where he stood for a second on wobbling knees before running to the plate to take a home run swing and circle the bases. Staring at Mickey, Carmela gave me a hug. When she let go and stood back, there were tears in her eyes. Someone called my name. I turned to see a man with a pair of binoculars around his neck climbing the dugout steps toward me. He was holding a clipboard that bristled with dog-eared pages. The short cigar he chewed was barely lit.

"Albero?" He shifted his papers to his left hand and extended his right.

"Sure," I said, accepting the handshake. "Who's askin'?"

"You know Charlie Shapiro, right? I'm a friend of his."

"Reporter or something?" I asked.

The man smiled and shook his head, gesturing at the field. "The New York Times ain't exactly gonna write this one up."

"How do you know Charlie?" I asked. He had pronounced the name correctly, Shap-EYE-row, so I believed him.

"He plays for the Yankees, and I—"

"Baseball? Get outta—"

"Football." I listened as the man explained that a new professional league had been formed. It was called the All-American Football Conference. New York had a franchise named the Yankees.

"I heard Chiz was in the N.F.L.," I interrupted.

"Coulda been," the man said. "But we got him first." He puffed at his dead cigar, appraised both ends and tossed it onto the grass by the on-deck circle. Leaning against a railing, he explained that he worked in the Yankees' front office. When my letter arrived, Shapiro had asked him to say hello because the Yankees were playing in Cleveland that weekend. "I'm always lookin' for good prospects, so I figured I'd work the game," the man continued. "Maybe see if any of you pikers had half a chance."

I laughed. "Well?"

"Coupla guys," he said, scanning the field. "Him..." — he pointed at Mack, who was sitting in the dugout with his wife, Penny — "...and you."

My jaw dropped. I was suddenly aware of the fact that I had been watched. My mind raced back over the game, trying to identify something I had done that seemed noteworthy. It had been a tough win, close at the end but not spectacular. I fumbled for something to say and settled on the obvious question.

"Me?"

"Charlie told me you could take a hit," the man said as he reached into his pocket and took out a business card. "He also said you had the best field sense he had ever seen. I don't know if I'd go that far, but I liked what I saw." He handed me the card. "Frank Dante. Give me a call and we'll set something up."

He shook my hand again and walked back into the dugout. Still stunned, I looked over at Mack again. He was still talking to Penny, and holding a little white card of his own. I looked at mine. *Francis J. Dante, New York Yankees Football Club.* My hand trembled. Could I compete on that level? And what about our nameless bunch of amateurs? We had just won the league championship. What would happen to the team if Mack and I abandoned them? So much of what we had built was based on selflessness. That concept had helped me survive without Anna. I believed in something greater than myself — the team. I drew strength from it, and found strength within myself to give back to it. Greed and selfishness had taken one brother away from me, but by turning away from those values I had gained twenty-seven others. Where would I be if I left them now? I looked up at Carmela. She had a huge smile on her face, but she seemed to be looking past me. When I felt Mickey jump onto my back, I understood. He climbed up and hugged my neck. I tucked the business card into my sock, held his legs and piggybacked him one more time around the bases. Mickey and I were grinning from ear to ear when I handed him back to Carmela. I kissed her cheek and walked through the stadium to the place where the team was gathering to leave.

The bus ride back to Newark was as raucous as any we had ever had. At home, I showered quickly, eager to head out for the celebration. Mama and Pop had no interest in American football, and never would have understood the idea of being paid to play it, so I limited my comments to two words: "We won." Pop nodded gravely and shook my hand. I kissed Mama's cheek and bounded down the front stoop, eager for the night. The game had not been a physical war, so my legs felt fresh as I walked to the corner of South Orange Avenue. Inside, Izzo was already sitting on the bar with a bottle of rye and regaling a circle of onlookers with his recap of the game. Braying at me with a boozy salutation, he patted the space next to him and poured another drink. I jumped up, clinked my glass against his bottle and drank the first of many toasts to our championship season. The night blurred through a series of tall tales and random dances with neighborhood girls. At one point I looked at the stage and saw Jeremiah Walker nod and smile with satisfaction at the door. There, nearly as tall as the frame, stood John Mack. His eyes crinkled with amusement as he saluted Jeremiah. I walked over and shook his hand, then leaned in and spoke quietly.

"You talk to Frank Dante?"

"Yeah, Pops."

"Well? Whattaya think?"

"We'll see, man," Mack chuckled. "Pro game ain't like this here. You put money in the middle of it, well..." He looked at the room full of happy players. "Just enjoy this, man. Let that other business sit for now."

I nodded.

"For now," he added with a wink.

Izzo hailed Mack loudly from his perch on the bar, prompting the rest of the white crowd to relax and welcome him. We drank and sang into the night. Eventually Mack went home to Penny, but most of us stayed until closing. At the end of the evening, I found myself dancing slowly with Rosemarie to Jeremiah's sleepy rendition of a Coleman Hawkins tune. Rica stood by the bar, talking to Mary Izzo and trying not to giggle at my romantic moment. When the song ended, we decided to call it a night. I put my arm around Rosemarie's waist and we walked out with a group that was headed down Tenth Street. It had been one of the most triumphant days of my life. I tried to share it with Rosemarie, but the conversation felt empty and forced. She glowed in that drunken way, but she didn't seem to understand what I was saying or to feel anything in particular about it. I looked at her face, struggling to see only the pretty surface and not the vacuum within. A small, sober voice whispered in my ear. *This is not Anna.* I fought the word, the name, but it began to echo in my mind. Anna. My mechanical grin revealed nothing to Rosemarie, but I could feel myself beginning to hollow out again. There was an emptiness in me, a feeling that seemed like it would never go away. *Anna.*

Rica shushed the group as we approached our flat. Inside, a dim light burned in the living room. She stepped up onto the porch and peeked in the window as Mary clapped a hand across Izzo's mouth. The other women giggled. Rica looked back at me with a troubled brow and waved me up, motioning to Rosemarie to stay where she was. I looked in the window and saw Pop asleep in his chair. Across from him, a woman sat on the couch with her back to the window. She was leaning against the corner and seemed also to be sleeping. My chest tightened; the bottom fell out of my gut. Suddenly oblivious to the people around me, I grabbed the screen door and ripped it open, then shoved the interior door and barely caught it before it banged into the wall. Sprinting three steps to the living room, I stopped in my tracks and stared, swaying slightly from alcohol and shock. Rica walked in behind me. The woman on the couch gazed up at us with striking eyes flecked with gold. She was running her fingers through the hair of a young boy asleep with his head on her lap. Hair that was much darker than hers. His brow line and nose looked familiar, as if I had seen them many times before. As I looked at them, my vision began to swim in a haze of tears. She smiled, and I was not hollow anymore.

Fifteen

Newark
November, 1946

"Why not?" I asked.

"You are drunk."

"I know," I slurred, "but still, why? Give me one reason." I wobbled slightly. The hardwood was beginning to numb my kneecap. Anna smiled feebly and laid her palm against my cheek. She had always been slender, but her hand felt as light as a bird's wing.

"That is not why I came here."

I rose from where I knelt and sank down beside her on the couch, struggling to comprehend her refusal of my marriage proposal. I knew I wasn't thinking clearly, but that wasn't how it was supposed to go. The woman who sat beside me was not the same person who had haunted my sleep for two years. Time and distance had softened the gauzy portrait in my memory, against which her reality stood in jarring contrast. Her voice was huskier than I remembered. The angle of her neck, the curves of her jaw and cheekbone and the line of her nose all seemed somehow more severe, as if chiseled by the privations of war. But in her eyes, I could still see the light that I recalled. Life had changed her physically, but her soul was the same. She looked away, as if she could sense what I had seen. When her glance found my bedroom door, her expression warmed with real joy. The boy asleep on the other side was almost a year and a half old. It was my complexion that colored his olive skin, my forehead that rose from his angled brows. While his mother was carrying him from the couch to the bed, my own blue eyes had opened briefly and looked back at me.

Anna had not commented to my parents about the boy's paternity. Nor had she needed to. Mama took one look at him and walked out of the room. Pop had been more polite with his suspicions, burying them beneath the rough gallantry that he extended to all women outside of the family. He sat with Anna and listened to the radio, nodding with rumbled acknowledgement as she tried to make small talk. She found the pastries and the coffee pot, and he pretended to enjoy the thin espresso she brewed. This was as far as a European male could extend himself, which Anna understood perhaps even better than Pop himself. She had not mentioned that the boy's name was Antonio, or that he had been named for his grandfather. Pop had not thought to ask. When Pop finally dozed off in his chair, she had relaxed and lost herself in the quiet rhythms of the nighttime jazz review. After a while, she had slept.

Sometimes I think about those hours between her arrival and my own, what she must have been thinking, how very strange it must have been to see my home without me in it. In a way, I'm grateful that she had that time to sit quietly in the place that had shaped many of my own thoughts. It wouldn't have been possible to describe to her the details that she could absorb simply by occupying my space, by sensing the distance to the walls that had bounded my life and by feeling the footing that had been my foundation. She might have smiled at the pressed tin ceiling, or perhaps frowned at the memories of Mönchengladbach that it might summon. She might have winced at the aromas of spiced food — garlic and tomatoes, beef and pork — or maybe she was comforted, as I had always been. One block away, the raucous blood of victory was pounding through my gin-soaked heart. The memory of a few thousand people cheering our winning touchdown had already grown into a dream of sellout crowds that roared from every corner of Yankee Stadium. I was nearly violent with joy, buzzing with an electric optimism that even my brother Vin, skulking in the corner of the bar, could not dampen.

And then we had collided again, Anna and I, thousands of miles away from our last memory of one another. I had offered a knee-jerk proposal of marriage that she was right to refuse. Instinct had propelled me through the day, through the biggest game of my life and into a new state of being. In this new existence, it was possible for me to throw that pass in Yankee Stadium and have Mack catch it. It was conceivable that a representative of a professional football team might want to talk to me. Gravity had finally loosened its grip. I was reading and reacting, moving with the flow. It all seemed easy, blessed almost. Anna was here — of course — so I asked her to marry me. It was like one of those great dreams, where you are just awake enough to know that the usual rules of life do not apply to you. But as the liquor and adrenaline started to fade, my hair-trigger mind began to clear. I realized the enormity of what she had done. Anna was *here*. I should have dropped to my knees with awe. She smiled as she looked at my bedroom door, not because of me, but because of the life she had brought into the world, had nurtured and protected for more than a year, and had delivered to a better future. So I won a football game and took a few hits. Big deal. *She* was tough, that little woman who stretched her arms wide and arched her back to yawn with every inch of herself. My heart jumped when I realized that the last place I had seen her yawn like that was in a barn in Belgium. A lump tightened my throat. I had let myself believe that I would never see her do that again.

She stood and took my hand. I walked with her to the bedroom and held her waist as I stared down into her eyes. We both knew that I would be sleeping on the couch, so we lingered over our goodnight. She let her fingertips hover near the bruise on my left cheekbone, then she kissed it lightly. The scent of her hair drifted up, charging every fiber of me with the memory of her body next to mine. My passion rose, but with all of the energy left in me, I fought back my desire. In her eyes, in her breathing, I could see she was doing the same. We would get to that later. She had shrunk the forces of time and distance to the space between our pounding hearts. I closed the rest of the gap, pulling her close and holding her as I had prayed I could. Her hair brushed my cheek. Her warm hands found my neck, then the black ribbon, then the shard I had fashioned into a ring. She recognized both objects and smiled. My arms closed around her. I laid aside the questions, the doubts, the unspeakable vanity that had made me wonder if she ever loved me. We held one another as we had through long nights of fear and desperation in that fugitive autumn of Forty-four. Standing there together, we relaxed for the first time since those days, each sensing the completion of something that had not been whole in years.

Sometimes dreams feel like they will last forever, but morning has a different idea. For me, the first moments of waking are always filled with uncomfortable clarity, as if a small, acute part of my consciousness has awakened before the slumping bulk of assumption that makes me believe I am the man I ought to be. As a child, I would dream of skimming across a world without gravity, only to wake inside my own skin and shudder at the reality of a flightless life. But when I woke up on the morning after Anna had arrived, it was hard to separate fantasy from reality. In my pocket, a business card from the New York Yankees football club felt like a ticket to a new life. On the other side of my bedroom door lay an even greater promise, a woman who had ruled my imagination, a son I had never dared to imagine at all. For a long time, I lay there on the couch and tried to comprehend it. I could summon no acuity, no sharp sense of how I might be fooling myself. It was like waking in a strange place and expecting to see my own walls around me, but sensing instead that things had somehow been rearranged. Part of me wanted to reach out and hold onto those fresh blessings, to hoard them close and hide them from the brutal whim of fate. But a wiser part of me realized that it was that very whim that had brought them to me. I prayed my thanks, and then stood to take my first steps in a world with just a little less gravity than it had the day before.

At the door to my bedroom, my certainty began to waver. What if it *was* a dream? What if she isn't in there? The knob always squeaked a little; I turned it slowly. My eyes had adjusted to the morning light, so it was hard to see anything inside the dark room. I heard a rustle under the covers, a tiny gurgle. After a long heartbeat, I sensed a larger movement and heard Anna murmur in German. Antonio settled down. I closed the door.

My family. I closed my eyes and thanked God for bringing them to me. For the first time in my life, I felt that strange self-awareness that only a father can know. It's as if you are at once as strong as you will ever be — as if no matter who or what the world might throw at you, you just *know* that you will defend your child from it — and yet also as weak as you have ever been, staggering under the magnificent burden of the young life entrusted to you. Later, I would learn that as a father you are confronted with absolute vulnerability, yet you are also denied the luxury of fear. You are asked to stand outside the door, to venture out into the world. Responsibility draws you away from home and then tosses you back again, each time testing you, reminding you of the limits of your own free will. The vibration of the world shakes you with enough force to let you feel every shred of what you're made of, not as a person but as a barrier between the vulgarity of life and the pure soul of that baby. To be human is to mingle the profane with the divine, but you tend to forget that when it comes to your children.

It didn't take long for vulgarity to intrude on my life with Anna. Less than a day, in fact. We were sitting at a table at the bar that afternoon, trying to escape the judgmental claustrophobia of Mama's living room, when Anna caught a glint of brass on the darkened stage just before the air came alive with a lightning run through a set of saxophone scales. Drawn by Jeremiah's obvious skill, Anna got up and ambled toward the sound. Eyes closed, shoulders beginning to loosen up, he leaned into his horn and segued into the first subtle phrases of "Cherokee." I had to smile when he squinted one eye to check out Anna. The man had radar. Anna turned around and looked at me with genuine surprise when Jeremiah's music took flight. He was working hard to cram as many notes into each space as Charlie Parker himself might do. I grinned broadly and shook my head at the preening musical courtship my friend was working on her. She had no idea.

Behind me, the heavy front door chunked closed. I had not heard it open. Two patrolmen sauntered into the empty room, nodding at Gio Pietro behind the bar as they made their way back to us. Jeremiah kept playing, but I could tell from his phrasing and his wide-open eyes that he was no longer focused on the music. I leaned back and looked at the cops.

"He ain't here," I said with a casual smile. "You're looking for Vin, right? Maybe he left something for you fellas at the bar."

The taller of the two was a severely-shaved young screw whose face looked like the map of Ireland. When it dawned on him that I was talking about a payment from my gangster brother, the pudge above his collar flushed red. His partner, an older guy with a poker face, didn't seem upset at all. He actually glanced back at Pietro, who raised two empty hands and shook his head.

"That him, Sarge?" The Irish rookie pointed at Jeremiah and the older cop nodded. I noticed that Jeremiah had stopped playing. The young cop drew his gun and strode toward the stage, where Jeremiah was carefully taking his horn apart and setting the sections into the velvet cutouts in its case. The rookie grabbed Jeremiah by the collar and started to pull him away from the horn. Jeremiah struggled to set his mouthpiece into its spot, but with a violent heave the rookie tossed him to the boards. Anna gasped. I stood up, but the older cop was ready and stopped me with a tight hand on my shoulder.

"Your boy's goin' down for vagrancy," he said.

"Are you kidding me?" I exclaimed. "Do you know who he is?"

"Might be a dope charge in it, too, you keep talkin'," he growled.

The young cop looked down and saw Jeremiah reaching again with the black tip of the reed. Panicked, he ripped my crippled friend around, tearing his shirt open as he slammed him down on his back. The rookie cocked his pistol and pressed it up under Jeremiah's nose. Anna tensed visibly and looked as if she might cry.

"Drop it!" he screamed.

"It's part of the horn," Jeremiah said calmly, holding up the reed. "See?"

"Horn, huh?" the rookie snarled. He shook my friend so violently that the reed fell and skittered across the floor toward the feet of the older cop. "Here! You wanna blow on something?" He forced the end of the gun barrel to my friend's lips. "Go on, Satchmo. Play us a song."

From under the table, I heard a frightened little voice, speaking German. In the confusion, Anna and I had forgotten about Antonio. When the young cop saw the boy, he pulled back and let the gun spin on his finger so that the barrel pointed at the ceiling. He holstered it as Anna lifted our son. Yanking Jeremiah to a standing position, he squeezed handcuffs onto his thin brown wrists. Most of the buttons on Jeremiah's shirt had been ripped off; it hung open, exposing his thin chest. He glanced down at his reed, and then looked at me.

"You got that, General?" Jeremiah asked softly.

I nodded and bent to pick it up, but the older cop stepped to the side and covered it with a heavy black shoe. The sound of crunching plastic and wood went through Jeremiah like a steel blade. He stared back at the shattered reed and struggled against the hands pulling him through the door, his brown skin tight and ashy in the cold air. As the door started to close, he lifted his eyes from the black shards and gave me a look that chills me to this day. There was no anger in his eyes, but rather a deep curiosity, as if he was looking for a clue in me to explain the cruelty of other white men. He seemed to take it for granted that I, too, was capable of such bigotry — that we all were. I stared for a long time at the closed door, wondering if he saw something in me that I myself had not even considered, if perhaps there was truth to what his eyes had said. When I looked at Anna, she looked away from me and closed her eyes. She was holding Antonio close, burying his face in her bosom to keep him from seeing what was happening. She kissed the top of his head as her tears ran down into his hair. My face flushed with shame. I wanted to protest, to explain. They're the cops, for Christ's sake! What am I supposed to do?

Jeremiah's eyes still burned in my mind. I stood there, hands limp at my sides, staring down at the shattered reed. No, I thought. Not me, pal. You got me wrong. Damn it, you got me wrong.

Sixteen

Long Island City, New York
December, 1946

From a distant rooftop, red neon letters blinked through the warped bars of the iron grill. The first four letters of a longer word — "S-I-L-V" — were legible in reverse at the leftmost side of the window. The bottom three panes of heavy glass were leaded together and pivoted as a unit. They had been open all night to the December chill. The wind stirred. In one corner, a dog lay shivering from the cold and from her animal apprehension of what lay on the bare cot at the far side of the room. Earlier that day, there had been a knock at the foundry door. The dog's master had commanded her in German to stop barking and move away from the door, an order that she had ignored until the heavy panel of tin-clad wood slid open to reveal a giant of a man. When the man's scent had reached the dog's nostrils, her tail curled down between her legs. In silence, she had backed to the corner. Master and newcomer had embraced warmly and engaged in friendly German banter for the rest of the

194

afternoon, but the dog did not budge. At the end of the day, she had curled into a tight ball and whimpered softly as her master slid the heavy bolt and padlocked the shop. When the large man lay down on the thin mattress, the springs had creaked and screamed until they reached to within a few inches of the ground. Still, the dog had not moved.

Before sunrise, the man rolled to a seated position and rose from the cot. The springs squealed again. In the corner, the dog kept a wary eye on him as he crossed to the bathroom. When the man relieved himself, another more threatening scent wafted to the dog and raised a whole new layer of hackles on her neck. The sink ran for a minute or so, and then the man emerged wiping his hands on his pants. He stopped on his way back across the shop floor to appraise the heavy chains that suspended a massive iron cauldron above the casting pit. The acrid tang of scorched sand made him smile. Here, he could do an honest day's work.

"Karl!" First the dog lifted her ears, then her head. Her master's voice was a comfort after the long night alone with so threatening a visitor.

"Ja, Werner, I am here."

"She has a big ass, no?" Werner grinned, slapping the huge pot with his callused hand as he walked up.

"She is beautiful," Karl replied. "It is a good shop. Tidy."

"Well, what do you expect? We are not a bunch of Italians here."

Werner walked over to a steel countertop and opened a can of coffee. He puttered for a few minutes, walking back and forth from the sink to the Silex. Emboldened by

195

the warm aroma, the dog stood up slowly and slinked over to her master, keeping well away from Karl.

"Hey Karl," Werner asked with amusement. "What the hell did you do to my dog?"

"Dogs don't like me much," he said softly. "And maybe I don't like them, either."

"Well, this is no SS dog," Werner said, glancing at Karl's forearm. "This is Lily Marlene."

"Like the song?" Karl smiled.

He remembered the long caravans of troops that had rumbled out across the desert singing that song at full voice. It had been a time of optimism for him. The boisterous camaraderie of the Afrika Korps had almost persuaded him that his nation's armies were not completely without virtue. Werner began to sing it as he poured two cups of coffee and brought one to Karl. Behind him, the door pounded open and a stout little man with a florid complexion stomped in.

"Hey!" he shouted. "Hey, Sauerkraut! Knock it off! None o' that Nazi shit in here!"

"Sauer*brun*," Werner corrected. "You empty little Irish sock," he added in German. His whistle went from high to low as he made a deflating gesture below his beltline. Lily growled when the angry man took a few steps toward Werner. When O'Malley saw Karl, he froze, wide-eyed.

"What is the matter, O'Malley?" Werner chided. "You never saw a full-grown German before? We are all seven feet tall. Karl here takes shits bigger than you."

"Didn't stop ya from losin' the war, though, did it Boy-O?" O'Malley smirked as he lifted a cup of coffee and turned to Karl. "Aliceville, right?" he asked. "I remember you. Unfriendly bastard, you were."

Karl grunted without smiling.

"Haven't changed any either, eh?" O'Malley waited a beat, then walked away when he realized that Karl had nothing to say.

Several other men filed in, some heading straight for the coffee and others for their respective work areas. Cigarettes were stubbed out as the rhythm of the morning picked up. Karl found his place in the flow, hauling iron ingots from the truck bay and stacking them by the blast furnace. He lifted the fifty pound blocks three at a time with almost no evident strain. Falling in naturally with the men who did the most menial, physically demanding tasks, Karl toiled in silence all morning. He smiled occasionally when Werner whistled Lily Marlene just to tweak O'Malley. Karl had known Werner for more than three years, ever since Aliceville. An easygoing Bavarian with a taste for good beer and heavy food, Werner somehow managed to remain slim despite an appetite that rivaled Karl's. Early in their prison term, they had bonded over a shared distaste for the Nazi regime and for its stiff-necked devotees among the P.O.W. population. On more than one occasion, it had proven beneficial for each to have watched the other's back. Several close calls with vicious Nazi tactics had cemented both their opinions and their friendship.

At midday break, Karl found Werner. Werner's wife had prepared an extra meat loaf sandwich for Karl, so the two sat together and unwrapped the dense little bundles. Karl asked Werner how he had managed to rise from prisoner of war to co-owner of an American business, but Werner politely declined to answer and instead asked Karl how his own time had been. Karl described the destruction of his apartment, the somber fact of his wife's absence, and the huge block of stone that he had thrown

197

to the street. He talked about the clues he had pieced together that led him to Belgium and eventually to the United States. Werner shook his head.

"You come a long way for spite."

"How so?" Karl countered.

"Well," Werner said, "you were together less than a year. Once you told me that she was never happy to be a German wife. She had the wanderlust, you said." He rapped his knuckles against his own skull. "America on the brain."

"But you have not seen her." Karl's voice was quiet, but his face was beginning to flush with emotion. "If nothing else, she is still my wife."

"Ja, as much as she ever was," Werner nodded. His statement had sounded like an affirmation, yet Karl knew it was not. Before he could respond, Werner stood and walked toward O'Malley, who was approaching with a determined stride. Karl ate the last bite of his sandwich, crumpled the brown paper and stood up, tensing for conflict. But instead of continuing their earlier confrontation, the two men huddled quietly and then Werner followed O'Malley back across the room. Curious, Karl followed. At the far end of the shop floor, three men stood looking at a cast iron manifold. Although it was more than four feet square, its walls were less than a half inch thick. The complicated structure that fanned out from its top was still burred and gated. A hand-held grinder and a few cutting tools lay on the floor next to it. Someone had started the process of cutting off the gates and grinding down the burrs, but the structure had failed right at the point of the highest chisel blow. Amazed, Karl walked over and pinched the narrow gauge of one of its walls. He laid his hand on the surface of the metal, as if trying to divine the secret of its tensile strength.

Karl spoke softly, in German: "How do you make such a thing? So light, but clearly still so strong." He turned to Werner. "This is a new technique?"

Werner and O'Malley were still conferring a few feet away, muttering together and pointing at the crack. The rest of the men stood behind them, as if waiting for a verdict. Karl was suddenly aware of the esteem in which the men held O'Malley and Werner. Neither one of them had made any pretense of authority; in fact, both had taken on some of the most grueling and dirty tasks in the shop. They worked beside the other men as if they too were part of the labor force. Based on their interaction with one another, Karl had assumed that they were anything but friends. Yet having seen the humor with which they were addressing what was clearly a major disappointment, and the seriousness with which their workers listened, Karl concluded that he had much to learn about how effective leaders operated in his new country.

"They are calling it 'ductile iron,'" Werner answered Karl at last, in English. "A man in Bayonne, over in Jersey, invented the formula. We are using it. This was our biggest piece yet, but it looks like the baker needs to mix a new batch of pie crust. Hey, O'Malley?"

"Gotta break a few eggs to make an omelet," O'Malley rumbled. He grinned and waved at the piece as he turned to go. "This one's scrap. Toss it."

Karl nodded. He crouched down and wrapped his arms around the huge manifold, then hefted it to waist height and started to walk toward the wide bay doors at the far end of the shop. O'Malley stopped and slowly turned around, clearly unable to believe what he was seeing. The rest of the men reacted the same way. Werner smiled. He had seen Karl's feats of strength before, but he was always amazed at the casual way he lifted items that would have strained the limits of two men's capacity. O'Malley walked back to where Werner was standing and slapped a hand on his shoulder. They watched as Karl shrugged the piece up to his chest and launched it from the receiving dock. It gonged like a giant bell as it crashed to the ground. Buzzing with reaction, the men dispersed. A few of them walked over to Karl. The two owners stood where they were.

"That's gotta be three hundred pounds," O'Malley said softly.

"No, more like four, five," Werner grinned, "maybe six."

"Come on, seriously," O'Malley said. "That's a hell of a load. He just walked thirty yards like he was going for a piss."

"He is," Werner said. "Look." He pointed as Karl shook the last man's hand and crossed to the bathroom door.

"We gotta get this guy on a football field," O'Malley said, still shaking his head. Werner started to shake his head along with his partner, who realized he was being mimicked and swatted at Werner's head. The latter ducked backward, still smiling.

"Never happen," Werner said. "They tried in Alabama. He just laughed. He said it was too much like the military bullshit. He will not march in anybody's line again."

"Hell, he would *be* the line!" O'Malley laughed as he started across the floor. "Leave it to me, Boy-O. I'll sell him on it."

"You should try selling cracked manifolds instead," Werner called after him. "We could have the market cornered on those in no time."

O'Malley lifted one finger over his shoulder as he walked away. Werner snickered as he crossed to the garage bay. He looked out. On the scrap heap lay three hundred and seven pounds of failed manifold, and one man's anonymity. By the end of the day Karl would be a legend in Queens; by the end of the week, people in Brooklyn and Staten Island would know about him. O'Malley had a network of friends and associates that could rival that of any Tammany Hall fat cat. They had proven invaluable to the foundry's sales efforts, and they would spread the word of Karl's physical prowess all the way to the corner of One Hundred Sixty-first Street and River Avenue in the Bronx, to the ears of a cigar-chewing football man who was always on the hunt for another good prospect.

Seventeen

Newark
December, 1946

Everything felt small. The flat seemed cramped and tense, as if Mama had decided not to exhale just so she could take up more space and make everybody anxious. Anna could barely breathe. I was working double shifts, in part to make up for income lost during football season, but also just to get out of the house. In time, Anna discovered a refuge on the sidewalks of Newark. In the West Ward, she found peace in the friendly faces and the low silhouettes of the row houses. Our small corner of Newark reminded her just a little of Mönchengladbach, if not in its architecture then at least in its intimacy. Curiosity drew her even further afield. She gaped upward from the shadows of the tall buildings on Market Street. She wandered the parks and gardens as if they were green and in bloom, not threadbare and frozen. Every shop window told her a story; each cathedral played her a song. She immersed our son in the tempo of the city, the vibrant bustle of life among the living, the pulse of the

202

anonymous crowd. It was from those moments that I drew hope for our relationship. She was teaching Antonio who he was, and she was also rediscovering her own identity — in all of the same places that had defined me.

Sometimes we went out together and walked the neighborhood like a regular family. I would hold Antonio's hand or carry him in my arms, trying to rebuild a bond that had never existed. Mostly he just stared at his new world as his mother and I tried to reconstruct the years that the war had burned away. One cold morning, we left him with Carmela and walked alone. I asked Anna why she had not answered my letters. It had been a confusing time, she explained. First there was the pregnancy, and then a rumor that her husband had survived the war — a story that she was never able to substantiate. Haike Ludwig's farm had needed work. And always, all around them, was the war. Everywhere, the war. A series of massive battles were fought in that region of Belgium, displacing them at times and merely frightening them at others. I listened and said nothing, even though just one written reply from her would have spared me years of pain.

"I did write a letter to you," she said, almost as an afterthought. "But I signed the name of Haike Ludwig to it."

I stared at her as a whirlwind of memory tossed me back to the empty Texas prairie and one of the darkest moments in my life. It took me a few minutes to speak again.

"You wrote that?"

"Yes." She looked at the ground. "You did not think Haike could write English, did you?"

Of course I didn't. In my gut, I knew it had to have been Anna. When I asked her why she had never written to me about Antonio, she grew quiet. We walked in silence until at last she looked up.

"I did not want you to feel as if you were — *was ist?* — obliged."

"Are you kidding me?!" I clenched my jaw to fight back a shout, once again waiting for civility to reclaim my pounding heart. It took a block and a half. When I spoke again, I could barely whisper. "How could you think...? How...?" I grappled for the right words, but gave up. After a moment, another question came to mind: "How did you even get here?"

She smiled again in the same neutral way that she had when I proposed to her, and then she began to talk. She spoke of money scrounged from friends and past debtors, of a voyage booked, of weeks at sea. She described the rising hope offered by the Manhattan skyline and by the statue that held its beacon high in the harbor. She was vague on the details of her passage through Ellis Island, jumping quickly to mention that she and Antonio had endured a ferry ride, a train, a long walk and (another smile) a strange living room. I listened, but did not really hear. There was just something odd in her manner. Distance? Uncertainty? — maybe that's what it was. Even at her most vulnerable, at that shattered moment in the park in Mönchengladbach, Anna had retained an air of assurance. But she seemed to have lost that. I had seen her fear, and doubt, and even panic, but I had never seen her waver. It was strange. It was... false.

I stopped walking and looked at her. She turned to face me, but she did not look up right away. When she did, she could not hold my gaze.

"What is it, Anna?" I asked. "What aren't you telling me?"

"Nothing," she blurted.

She tried to hold that actress smile, but it cracked. Her brows furrowed with pain, then anger. She scowled, frustrated, as her chest heaved with sobbing rage. She balled her fists and raised one at me, turned and took a few steps away, then turned back. But as I watched, her fury shattered just as quickly as her false neutrality had, leaving in its place a frightened girl. She shivered with tears, standing stiff and alone as the core of her true emotion revealed itself to me. I slowly walked over and embraced her, gently hugging her rigid arms to her sides and resting my cheek on the top of her head. Somewhere deep inside the body I was holding, the woman I loved had retreated to a place I could not reach. For a while she was palpably absent, and yet I had the sense that I had never been closer to the truth of her. There was pain buried in her heart. To trust, to reveal, to love — all of those might leave her open to feeling that pain again. Instead, she had grown stronger and more distant. She had taken control of her pain by taking control of the men in her life, and it had worked. None of them had ever confronted her with the truth, or had even seen deeply enough to know that there was more to her than what she chose to show them. At the time, I didn't know how her father had died, or about the horrifying things she had seen in the days before we fled Germany. I just sensed the void those things had created, the place she worked so hard to defend. All at once, her strange combination of sweetness and steel made sense to me. I knew then why she had been so quick to trust me on that day in September of Forty-four, the day we met. She saw that look on my face, that smitten pliability that must have signaled the start of a familiar routine to her. She would let me fall in love with her, but she herself would never lose control. She would smooth me into the jagged void in her life, but it would end there. I would be contained within the limits of her prior loss. She would lose nothing herself when we parted, no more than she had already lost. Our goodbye was inevitable. She was planning on it.

So why did she come back to me? As we stood in the night air the question screamed in my mind, but I had sense enough not to ask. Who knows, I thought. Maybe she did it for Antonio. Or maybe for something else. It could have been that she sensed that I understood her, that I was listening to something that no one else could hear. Or perhaps she just wanted her own little slice of Big Time America, and I was her ticket in. But so what? Even if that was it, I didn't care. I loved her honestly and always had, even when I believed she was gone for good. I had already made my peace with that. She might have thought she was in control of things, but out there on that sidewalk, holding her close, I knew I was the stronger one. I had already proven that I could love her completely, without holding anything back, and that I could survive no matter what happened. As I stood there breathing the scent of her hair and feeling her gradually recover herself, I had to smile just a little. There was nothing left for me to fear.

One December afternoon, Anna was walking with Rica and Antonio by the corner of Broad and Market

Streets. I had just started a shift at the bar. Antonio had never seen a city decorated for Christmas. He was running back and forth on the wide sidewalk trying to take it all in. Rica waved a mitten at the lights and colors and asked Anna what it must have been like to "grow up Jewish and miss out on all of this." It was a moment of innocent candor, but one that opened up volumes of perception to Anna. She told me later that her first instinct had been to correct Rica and let her know that she was raised a Catholic, but that she had resisted the urge to deny her Jewish heritage because she refused to believe that, by coming to America, she had simply traded one form of intolerance for another. As they walked, Anna found herself opening up. In Rica's wide eyes and gentle smile, Anna discovered both an admirer and a confidante, a younger sister she had never had. Perhaps there is a basic human need to trust, and to relate. Or maybe it was just Rica's naiveté. Whatever the reason, Anna told her about something she had never mentioned to anyone, not to me, not even to Karl. Especially not to Karl.

"My father was a carpenter," Anna began. "This was eight years ago. November, Nineteen and Thirty-eight. There were at that time certain things happening, attacks..." She paused, gauging Rica's maturity, and decided to continue. "Against Jews. In the town, they called it '*Kristallnacht*,' the night of the broken glass. Some of the men who did these things worked at the carpenter job with my father. He said nothing to them, not at first. But in the night I heard him whispering to Mother. He was so angry. One day he was up high on the frame of a roof. Daddy loved to be up high."

Anna stopped again, this time because her voice had failed her. Antonio saw that she was crying and hugged her leg. Anna scooped him up and dried her tears against his woolen hat.

"Mother told him not to say anything," Anna continued, "but the men would laugh at the attacks. Every day, they would laugh. So one day, he said something." Antonio did not understand much English, but he could tell that his mother was not telling a happy story. Anna decided to end it there. "They told me it was an accident. For twenty-five years, my father was on these rooftops. He does not fall by accident."

Rica stared at Anna, horrified, and yet moved that she had chosen to share this with her. I always thought of Rica as one of those people who walked between the raindrops — who couldn't stand to hear anything sad. But she wasn't a little girl anymore. She squeezed Anna's hand and shifted her eyes toward Antonio.

"We'll talk later," Rica whispered to Anna. "But thank you. I know how hard it must be to think about that."

Anna stopped and locked Rica into her gaze. "My father was a Catholic. It was the family of my mother that was Jewish. Those men did not know about that." Anna hugged her son close so he could not see the dark rage in her eyes. "With cowards like that, never believe you are on the safe side."

"Hey!" a man called to them. His voice was familiar to Rica, although somewhat deeper and more muffled than it once had been. "La bella bambina! Hey, Rica! Baby sister!"

Arms wide, shirt slightly untucked, Vin lumbered toward the women with the sodden glow of one whose afternoon had been washed down a gutter of gin. There had been a time when all Vin had to do was walk through a room to charm half the women in it, but crime and gluttony had buried his dark good looks under a layer of toxic obesity. After he crossed into the world of the mob, his spirit had withered and his body had begun to swell and decay. What walked toward Rica was not a man she had watched grow wealthy and powerful, but a boy whose passing she had long since mourned. But Vin saw none of this. He was myopic in that way unique to the emerging rich, blind to all that did not shine of Mammon. He could no more appreciate the joy of Christmas or the smile of his nephew than he could the top side of a bird flying over his head. Likewise, Antonio was only briefly amused by Vin. A young boy not yet steeped in the poison of materialism could not understand why Vin felt special. To him, Vin was simply a large clown pulling faces, a mountain of shiny blue silk that stunk of alcohol and cigars. The label on his suit, the flash of his watch — even the butt of his gun — did not make any difference to a toddler whose mother was crying, and whose daddy was still a new idea.

"Pop was asking for you," Rica offered. Vin sneered his disbelief. "No, he was," she insisted. With one eye on Anna, she brushed her knuckles up and down Vin's lapel. "Nice."

"Silk," he mumbled, softening. He kept both eyes on Anna.

"Pop was saying Mr. Ballantino might need a couple of guys to help lay a foundation over on High Street. He said you —"

"Ballantino? Hire *me*?" Vin's voice nearly cracked with indignation.

"Didn't you work weekends for him back in—"

"High school," Vin cut in. "I was fourteen. I could buy and sell that guy now." Vin's face darkened. "What's he think, I need his help or somethin'?"

Rica caught a glimpse of how dangerous Vin's insecurity could be. She shook her head vigorously. "No, no," she whispered. "Pop was just asking, is all. He just wants to get you away from the..." She darted a look at Anna. "The life."

"Pop should keep his big friggin' mouth shut," Vin muttered.

He flinched over one shoulder as if he expected our father to be standing there. Filial anxiety dies hard with a guy like Pop. Vin let his eyelids drop slightly. As the gangster mask settled back onto his face, Anna felt chilled. Although she did not know why, at that moment she was certain that the man standing before her was capable of murder, and that he had already committed it. There was something in the way the human warmth just drained from his eyes. Anna shivered when his cold focus rolled back to her.

"Who's the dish?" he asked Rica.

"I'm sorry, Anna," Rica blushed. "This is my brother Vin." She looked back at him. "Vin, this is Anna."

"Anna who?"

"Mateo's..." Rica paused, realizing that she was unsure of how to characterize our relationship.

"Anna Eisenstark," Anna cut in, holding out her hand. Vin shook it roughly, suddenly aware that she was not just another 'broad' on the street. He glanced down at the little boy in her arms.

"This my nephew, then?"

"This is Antonio," Anna said evenly.

Vin smirked when he heard his father's name. "Whose idea was that? Mateo's?"

"Mine."

Anna looked directly into his eyes without betraying a hint of fear. He turned away uneasily, swaying slightly. Rica was surprised that he had not slurred his words more, until she realized that his normal speech had taken on an almost permanent mushiness. She struggled to recall the last time she had seen him sober.

"Ya know," he said as he turned away, "I could buy and sell him, too. Mateo."

"Don't be too sure of that!" Rica snapped back. Vin smiled easily, as if a child had punched his heavy chest.

"I already own a piece of his boy Izzo," he smirked. "Just a matter of time." He started to walk away, but turned back and locked Anna with a glare. "How's that shine horn player, by the way? Still shivering?"

Shock registered on Anna's face — the reaction Vin had been waiting for. He bit the end of a fat cigar and puffed at a match until a flame danced between his hands. He sucked the flame down, flicked the match into the street and waved back over his shoulder as he shuffled away. Rica laughed at his braggadocio, but Anna's face was still pursed with concern. She was not familiar with Vin's brand of street posturing. Antonio stared after his uncle. Rica touched Anna's elbow and motioned for her to follow in the opposite direction. Christmas lights blinked all around them, their sharp little bulbs outlined even more precisely by the clear night air. Shops were open late. People bustled around with parcels wrapped in the colors of the season, their faces warm with post-war optimism. Everyone was ready to believe that a season of lasting peace had finally arrived. Anna closed her eyes. She tried to feel what they felt, but she could not.

She looked back at the corner where Vin had disappeared. Something insidious had floated around him: a dispassionate resignation, an almost gravitational emptiness. He seemed to be verging on lifelessness, as if he had defined for himself an existence that had nothing to do with his own biology — as if he could fill his blood with things like approval, or praise, or deference, and thus survive. Anna had known men like Vin, or had known of them. Men whose lives were populated only with enemies and allies, who saw threats to their own fragile power in every smile they did not recognize, and in every hand that opened without coercion. These were not men who could stand alone with courage. They were the sort who with two friends became bullies, and with four, tyrants. There was evil in them, but it was the whispering kind, the kind that did not take a side until the outcome was certain. She believed that men like Vin had pushed her father to his death, and had broken down her Jewish cousins' doors in the middle of the night. Their laughter was hollow, fearful. Inside they were small and frail, desperate for the artificial potency of a mob or a gun to lend them the appearance of strength.

Put enough of these men together, and you have a holocaust. Anna knew that, too. She knew that the only way to fight their brand of evil was to stand for something good. In the shadowland of hysterical blindness, where power lies with those whose righteousness is a stolen thing, enemies can begin to look like friends. She knew the danger of chasing every flitting demon, and the ease with which one can lose the way when the only goal is to oppose what is wrong — and not to serve what is right. She may have despised what she saw in the hate-filled eyes of Nazi thugs, but she would not let it turn her own heart to darkness. She knew that her husband had been compelled to serve. She did not hate him for it. Instead, she reaffirmed her love for the goodness that his masters had opposed. Moving sideways through the holiday throng, Anna recalled the crowds that had gathered in Mönchengladbach. She had heard them raise their voices first in hope, then in anger, and finally in blasphemy. They had worshipped Hitler as a false god. What troubled Anna most about those memories was not the snickering arrogance of the bloodthirsty, but the voluntary ignorance of the meek.

She took a deep, relieved breath as they stepped through to a clear patch of sidewalk. Hugging Antonio, she fell into stride beside Rica and smiled with forced kindness at my sister's banter, all the while trying to shake the feeling that something dark was stalking them. This is America, she told herself. The war is over. We are safe. But Vin's dead eyes haunted her. She had not expected to see that look again so soon. A bus pulled up. Rica paid the fare and motioned for them to board, so Anna carried Antonio up the steps and sat with him on her lap. She stared out the window as the bus rolled uphill and west and then onto South Orange Avenue, a route she would normally walk. In time it slowed to a stop on Tenth Street. They made their way to the door and alighted just outside of the bar where I was working. Rica knocked on the window. I waved and smiled at them, and mugged for Antonio. His expression was equal parts confusion and happiness, as if he was beginning to solve the riddle of my identity but did not yet trust his conclusions. Anna forced a smile, but I could see that she was not at peace.

213

If only she stays, I told myself. If only she does not quit, or run. We can work it all out in time. Still, I knew there was a darkness in her that I might not ever reach.

At the door of the flat, Mama lifted her grandson from his mother's arms as the warmth of supper wafted out into the crisp air. By the time Anna and Rica made their way to the dining room, Antonio was bibbed to the chin and working on his second forkful of macaroni. Mama sat next to him, beaming with rekindled maternity. She never once looked up at Anna. Dinner was quiet, polite. Pop chewed in silence as Rica tiptoed around the subject of Vin and mentioned only those items of gossip that were completely safe. Anna understood that there was some controversy over Vin's involvement in what Rica had referred to as "the life." She knew it had estranged him from the family, but that was all. After the plates were cleared, Pop shook his head at a second cup of coffee and groaned into his easy chair with the newspaper. Anna trundled the groggy boy to the bedroom and tucked him in, then returned to the table where Rica was answering a hushed question from Mama. For the first time all night, Mama made eye contact with Anna.

"This is true?" Mama's mouth was a hard line of repressed anger. "He ask you to marry him, and you say no?" Feeling betrayed, Anna flashed Rica a look. "No," Mama said, "she no tell me. I ask."

Anna considered simply walking away, but decided instead to make a stand. "Yes. It is true."

"Then what is this?" Mama lifted a parchment from her apron pocket and spread it out on the table. Anna gasped, then reached for the paper. Mama pulled it away.

"How dare you!" Anna hissed. She glared at Mama, who neither blinked nor replied.

It was at that moment that I walked in. I was on dinner break and had just enough time to for a quick bowl of macaroni before I had to run back to the bar. Rica told me later that she was sorry I came in when I did, because she had never seen Mama speechless before. In the world of Italian family politics, girlfriends and daughters-in-law did not square off with the matriarch unless they were prepared for a significant loss of blood. Yet there was something in Anna's tone that had rocked Mama to her heels. As I blundered into the dining room and peppered Anna's cheeks with kisses, Rica wondered if I was completely oblivious to the tension in the room. Quite to the contrary, it was a scene I had been anticipating for years, ever since I first felt my heart slipping into Anna's grasp. It was almost a relief to me that the confrontation had begun. I danced into the kitchen singing one of Izzo's silly songs and intentionally making a ruckus of plates and pots as I ladled out my dinner. When I finally emerged with tomato gravy smeared on my chin, all three women shook their heads. I grinned as I sat to wolf down my macaroni. No one smiled back.

If a man is going to keep the peace between the women in his life, he must be prepared to make a fool of himself. He also must know when — and how — to lie. When Mama spread the marriage certificate out in front of me and I saw my own name on it, I nearly gagged on a mouthful of food, but I knew well enough not to show her that I was surprised. I held a finger in the air and chewed slowly, buying myself time and trying to read Anna's expression. There was an apology in her eyes, but also a plea. I thought back to our conversation on the sidewalk, to her breezy recollection of having crossed through U.S. Immigration without incident. It made sense to me now. I had heard of the War Brides Act, which allowed the foreign spouses of U.S. servicemen to more or less walk right into the country. Evidently so had she. Part of me was furious. But I also knew that any chance I had for a life with her depended on my reaction to the document in front of me. I swallowed hard and looked up at Mama with a blank smile.

"So?" I asked.

Predictably, my irreverence launched her into a vicious tirade about how disrespectful it was for me to have gotten married overseas without telling anyone, to lie about it when my wife came to our home, to let my own family believe that my son was a bastard, on and on. I ducked under her slaps and took the abuse, sneaking a quick wink at Anna to let her know she owed me one. After a few minutes, a grumble from the living room was followed by three loud slaps against the wall. In the ensuing silence, I could hear the crucifix above Pop's head clicking back and forth against the wall. I stood up, shrugged a sheepish apology and tried to kiss Mama on the forehead. She blocked me with a hard slap to the face. I blew her a kiss instead, pressed my hand to Anna's cheek and bolted for the door. Obviously, I knew I was not really Anna's husband, but as I returned to work, I walked just a little taller for having seen my name next to hers on a certificate of marriage.

Eighteen

Brooklyn, New York
December, 1946

Still panting from the five-flight climb, Karl brushed aside a Christmas wreath, checked the apartment number against a note that said "Albero, 5B" and knocked on the heavy wooden door. After an exceedingly long wait, a tiny old woman opened the door and nearly fainted at the size of him. Hands clasped behind his back, he bowed and greeted her politely. She stared up at him, still shocked.

"Is there here a man named Mateo?" he asked firmly. When she cupped a hand to her ear, he repeated my name again, then twice. Finally, she shook her head vigorously and waved him away with the handkerchief bunched in her hand. He was galled at having walked all the way down Flatbush Avenue from the bus stop and up those stairs only to reach yet another dead end. He shook his head at the woman and asked her in German how she managed to climb those stairs every day. She smiled and

nodded back at him, but quickly slammed the door
before he had a chance to bow again.

Nineteen

Newark, New Jersey/Bronx, New York
January, 1947

For the third time, I undid my tie and started over. It didn't matter so much whether it fell just to my belt line or not since I planned to keep my jacket buttoned, but still, I would know. I wanted to look like a professional. Once again I worked the material across my chest, looping, tucking, cinching. Damn! Tearing at the knot, my hands shook with frustration. Or was it fear? I leaned over the sink, staring at the face in the mirror. You don't deserve this, I said to myself. Other people, *they* meet with professional teams. They sign contracts. You, you wake up every day and go to work just like every other guy in Newark. You even get to keep your hands clean. It's a good life. What do you want with more? I looked at my hands again. They had stopped shaking. It *is* a good life, I thought. And it'll be here if I don't make it. So what do I have to lose?

I don't remember tying the tie that last time. All I saw was the point right where I wanted it, a half-inch down on my belt. I don't remember pomading and combing my hair, but when I looked again it was clean and in place. Coat on. Pocket square tucked. My shoes crunched grit against the bathroom tile and then out into the hallway. Anna looked up from Antonio's breakfast and stared at me. My God, I would tie a thousand ties to see that look every day. A smile played across her face. Sensing an opportunity, Antonio closed his little fist around the spoonful of oatmeal that hovered before him, squishing it between his fingers and flashing me an evil little grin. When Anna yanked the spoon away, warm cereal flew across the table. A blob landed on the gleaming crown of Pop's head. Rica sniffed back a laugh. Pop looked up with murder in his eyes, but when his grandson started to giggle he let his brow relax. His cheeks creased with amusement as he thumbed his head clean and tasted what was there.

"Cinnamon?" he called into the kitchen. "Why I no get the cinnamon too?" Mama's reply, in Italian, is not something I will translate here.

I grabbed a towel from the kitchen, kissed Mama's forehead as I passed through, and wiped Antonio's hand. Anna took the towel and dabbed the spatters from the front of Pop's shirt. He smiled patiently. Rica raised her eyebrows at my suit.

"Who died?" she asked. I smiled and ignored her question. "No seriously, what's with the monkey suit?" she pressed.

"I got a meeting," I mumbled.

"Where?" she asked.

"Yankee Stadium."

"Come on, Mateo!" For all of her poise, Rica could still sound like a teenager when she wanted to. "I'm just curious, that's all. What're you meeting one of those wiseguys that Vin—" She caught herself too late. Pop flashed her a look that almost made Antonio cry.

"I told you, it's at Yankee Stadium," I said evenly. "After that game we played there, a scout said he wanted to talk to me about a tryout."

Pop looked up. "Scout? What is?"

"He looks for players to hire," I tried to explain. "Like a foreman on a work crew. He's kind of like the boss."

After a beat, my father stood up so quickly I thought his chair might topple over. He rushed up and embraced me, then held me at arm's length and looked me up and down like a child. He turned to everyone and gestured back with pride.

"My son!" he beamed. "He gonna play with DiMaggio! My son gonna be a Yankee!"

"No Pop, wait," I said. "Not baseball. Football. There's also a football team called the Yankees."

I watched Pop's joyful expression freeze and then begin to melt. Slowly, he walked back to his place at the table and sat down. He stared at me for a long time before speaking again.

"Football?"

"Yeah, Pop."

I pinched a piece of toast from Anna's plate and took a bite. Mama steered me to a chair and pointed back at the eggs sizzling on a pan in the kitchen. I glanced at my watch. Izzo's balloon-tired Chevrolet would not make the trip to the Bronx in any kind of hurry, if at all.

"It's a professional team," I continued. "Just not baseball."

"Football?" he scoffed. "Is what? Buncha guys in a big fight all afternoon? This is a sport?"

"What would you know about it?" I muttered under my breath.

"Huh?" Pop jutted his jaw at me.

"It's not like you ever came to a game."

Mama slapped a plate of ham and eggs down in front of me with emphasis. Starved, I paid no attention to her reproach and instead loaded my fork and shoveled it in, letting my mouth hang open slightly to accommodate the scalding eggs. Rica stared at her plate in deep contrition. Anna looked on, silently thankful that she was not involved. Mama took refuge in her kitchen. I knew full well that Pop's embarrassment over his emotional display — and not my tone — was stoking his rage. I checked my watch again. I had maybe five minutes.

"The Irishman," Pop grumbled. "Sullivan..."

Christ, I thought. Not that again.

"He want to hire you back," Pop continued. "But you say no?" Pop's curiosity was calculated, theatrical. "Tell me again, why? Why the fireman job not good enough for you now?"

I held my wrist up where he could see it and looked at my watch. With regret, I pushed away a perfectly good plate of eggs and stood to go. Pop steamed. I kissed Anna's cheek and mussed my son's hair. Rica looked up in time to catch my nod of forgiveness. After a brief apology to Mama for not eating, I crossed to the coat rack and lifted my ratty winter corduroy. It was in such bad shape that I would have to leave it in the car when I got to the stadium. Behind me, Pop boiled over.

"Is my house!" he roared. "You no walk away when I ask the question!" Antonio whimpered until Pop slammed his hand down on the table. Then he cried. "Where the rent money?" Pop shouted. "Who pay for the food? You got three people under my roof. And you what, a bartender? A football player?"

Maybe it was the disdain with which he spat out the last two words. I don't know. Eyes locked on his, I practically sprinted back across the floor.

"Who do you think bought these eggs?" I shouted. "And the milk? And ham? Who? Me! That's who!" I dug in my pocket for the fat wad of singles that Izzo had handed me the night before — my pay for the week. "Here!" I growled, throwing the money at his chest. "Take it. Take it all!"

I waved the back of my hand at the scattered greenbacks and walked toward the door. His chair scraped. Steps pounded behind me. One hand spun me around, and the other punched my face. I felt the blood begin to run from my nose, but I didn't flinch. He punched me again, in the mouth. Blood spattered the wall. I stared at him, unmoved. Snorting deep breaths of rage, he raised his fist once more, then lowered it and shoved me toward the door.

"Out!" he commanded. "Don't come back."

Inside, the echo of his voice faded to an eerie stillness. The emotional implosion of Mama's household had begun anew. She could not afford to lose another son, yet she would not side against the man she had married. I looked back at Anna, letting my gaze linger on her as I decided what to do. I had a family now, and nothing Pop said or did could take them away from me, but I also had a dream. If there was any chance of making it come true, I had to get on the road immediately. I thought for a few seconds, then went back to her, pressed my mouth into her thick curls and whispered rapidly. She nodded several times as I was speaking to confirm that she understood the plan. She wiped the blood from my nose and mouth. I kissed her cheek and the top of Antonio's head, then walked past Pop to the door.

"We'll need a few hours," I said as I pulled the door closed behind me.

At the bar, Izzo loaned me five dollars and his keys. I wanted to ask him about the apartment at the back of the top floor, but there was no time. Shouting thanks over my shoulder, I sprinted out to the car, fired it up and checked my watch at least forty times as it warmed up. There were a few tiny drops of blood on my collar, but I had no time to change. Even though the bleeding had mostly stopped, I tore a bar napkin in half and plugged each nostril. My lip was fat, but not split. Hopefully Dante would not notice. I shifted into gear, eased into the avenue and started to drive. The wheel felt cold in my hands. A tangle of wires hung from the place where Izzo's radio should have been. St. Christopher smiled down from the visor. Izzo's front and back seats were strewn with the flotsam of his life; an empty beer bottle, a pair of cleats, unmatched gym socks, several sections of last week's Evening News, a Racing Form. The latter was marked with odd pencil notations, as if he had bet on almost every horse in each race. I looked closer. The notes were not in his hand. There were squiggled lines and numbers, totals of bets placed and payments owed. I tossed the paper onto the seat and focused on the sun-dappled road ahead. Something glinted in the wheel well. I glanced down. It was a fat little brass cartridge, a spent shell from a heavy-caliber pistol.

"Goddamn it, Iz!" I shouted, pounding the wheel with the heels of my hands. I wanted to grab him and shake him. "Idiot!"

I had a feeling I knew the handwriting on the Racing Form, and I was right: it was Vin's. The car began to feel somehow unclean, as if I should pull off the highway and empty it of evidence even though I had no idea what the crime had been. Ahead of me, Route One looked like a parking lot. Even in winter, the stench from the Secaucus pig farms hung in the air above the swampy land that sprawled away from the highway. I tried to forget about Vin and Pop and that damn fool Izzo and focus on what I might say to Dante, but in about five seconds my mind worked its way back to the stinging in my lip. I looked down at the shell casing again. Vin was always a wild kid, but why this? Maybe it had been that feeling of the door closing at his back, or Pop's knuckles across his mouth. Or maybe it was the idea that all things would be forgiven as long as you were tough, took no crap and brought home enough money for your family. Even Pop, hating wiseguys like he did, never spoke against their needless brutality. He was just pissed because they cheated. They didn't play by the rules that were killing him. They had figured out a way to avoid the labor with which he scourged himself like a lunatic monk. Nevermind "Thou shalt not kill." To him, their cardinal sin was sloth.

And now this. Another son gone, this time to play games. At least Vin made decent money. To Pop, I was lazy *and* poor. I chewed at the swollen part of my lip. What if it had been the baseball Yankees? Maybe then when I got home he'd be killing the fatted calf instead of tossing his grandson out in the street. But even then, in time he'd figure out that my hands were not as callused as they might have been on a steam press or a fire axe. He'd see that my work didn't leave me drained and lifeless on an easy chair. The same bitterness would eventually creep in, maybe after the novelty of the pinstripes wore off, or when his friends stopped smiling about my proximity to DiMaggio and started comparing our batting averages. Out the window, I saw a sign for the George Washington Bridge. We weren't moving very fast, but the task of driving pulled my thoughts away from Pop. I thought about the speech I had just read in the paper, Governor Driscoll's inaugural address. He said something about building a new highway called "Corridor 100" or something. The word "Turnpike" had not yet entered his imagination, but the traffic outside my window certainly had.

This is what you think about if you're from New Jersey: traffic. You might dream about the lights across the river and even get there one day, but you never let go of that feeling that somehow, even with the best of intentions, your trip could get screwed up because there are either too many cars on the road or the wrong people are driving them. I sat there wishing Izzo had not ripped his radio out, and wondering what the hell I would say to Frank Dante. What does a guy from New Jersey know about professional football? That was a New York thing. The big time. Wood paneled offices and swanky ballrooms. I belonged on this side of the river, in the swamps and factories and little bars that only heard music from people like Lester Young and Zoot Sims if they got derailed on their way to Manhattan. Now Mack, *he* belonged over there. He was hitting home runs in front of thousands of people when I was still chasing schoolgirls. He was an *athlete*. I was just a kid from Newark with sense enough to throw high when the lights were at my back. Who couldn't do that?

I nosed into the bridge lane and watched as the miracle of progress propelled me up a bowed incline and onto the span. Far below, the river rolled black with glints of bronze. From that angle, Manhattan looked like it went on forever, like the river just curled around a small part of it and the rest of it sprawled south and east until it hit Spain or something. I tightened my jaw, suddenly annoyed at my own self-doubt. There must be a million people in that city, maybe more. Not all of them were better than me. Hell, maybe none of them were. There were only a couple of professional quarterback jobs in New York, and I was interviewing for one of them. That's gotta count for something. Maybe my name isn't Rockefeller, but it's mine. If I don't believe in it, who will?

I worked my way uptown to Yankee Stadium, checking for the landmarks that Dante had given me and at last rolling to a stop in front of the gate he had specified. He was standing outside, puffing a new cigar and looking at his watch. I shrugged out of my overcoat and walked as fast as I could toward him, remembering halfway there to take the paper wads out of my nostrils. When he saw me, he glanced at my suit, scowled and looked at his watch again.

"What he hell is this?" Dante growled.

"I know, I'm sorry," I stammered. "Lotta cars on Route One."

"Not the time, you stupid guinea, the *clothes*. Whattaya think this is, dinner at Sardi's? It's a friggin' *football tryout*, for chrissakes."

"But I thought—"

"Thought nothin'," Dante said as he turned toward the stadium entrance. "You're here to run and throw. If you can't do that dressed like Fred Astaire, go back to

Brooklyn and keep flippin' pizzas or whatever the hell it is you do."

"Newark," I said, suddenly angry.

"What?" Dante clenched his teeth on the cigar.

"I'm from Newark, not Brooklyn."

"Son," Dante spat through a mouthful of smoke, "I don't care if you're from Timbuktu. If you're not on that outfield in two minutes ready to run, the only way you'll see the inside of this stadium again is with a ticket to the goddamn bleacher seats!"

He grabbed the handle of the door, threw it open and stalked inside. I stood there in shocked silence for a few seconds, then remembered Izzo's trash heap of a car. Sprinting back to the passenger side, I dove in and rooted through the backseat. Cleats! I threw my street shoes in the car and pulled on the spikes. They were two sizes too big, so I stuffed each toe with a wadded half-page from the Racing Form. Izzo's old gray sweatshirt was stained with a dipstick streak of motor oil. I pulled off my suit coat, shirt and tie and put it on. He didn't have any shorts or sweatpants, so I rolled my suit pants up to my knees. I clacked back across the parking lot and hustled inside the stadium. Seeing no signs for field access, I bounded into one of the tunnels leading to the seats and ran down the stairs. In one jump, I vaulted the last railing and landed on the dirt track beside third base. Dante stood at the far end of the field with one of the coaches and a huddle of young prospects. They had marked off a narrow fifty-yard rectangle with four white towels. At the opposite end of the lane, two more coaches stood holding stopwatches. One at a time, the players lined up and sprinted through. Aware of how silly I looked in black socks and cleats, I jogged over to them and started to stretch.

"Hey, check this out," said one of the college kids. I looked up and saw that the entire group was staring at me. The one who first noticed my strange clothing was still pointing with his thumb.

"Somebody oughta go," I replied, nodding at the impatient coaches.

Two of the players broke for the starting line at the same time, creating a moment of confusion that drew attention away from me. I sat on the dry grass and reached for my toes, fuming at my assumption that Dante would just hand me a contract without so much as a jog around the parking lot. I stood up, ran in place for a few seconds and then took a spot in line. Izzo's cleats were so broken in that the extra space didn't really bother me. I felt good. The field was familiar, yet the stark sunlight revealed much about the stadium that fog, darkness and the extreme focus of game day had hidden from me. Like a fan, I wanted to read every billboard and memorize every detail.

"Rough night, huh pal?" The guy who spoke was the only other player my age. "No time to change this morning?"

"Actually," I replied, "I just run faster in a cotton-wool blend."

He grinned. "Name's Pioli. Alfonso Pioli."

"Mateo Albero." We shook. I was two places from the front of the line. "Lemme guess," I said. "Army infantry. Probably European Theater, right?"

"Eighty-eighth," he said. "They called us the 'Blue Devils.' I was there when we took Rome. But how'd you know that?"

"Dunno," I said as I moved to the head of the line. "I was Eighth Air Force. Europe just leaves a reek on you, I guess."

I stepped up and called out my name so the coaches could mark it on their clipboards. After settling into a three-point stance, I took one deep breath, coiled and burst out low. Arms tight to my sides, knees pumping, I held that breath all the way to the finish line and a few yards beyond it. With my chest heaving to recoup the sudden oxygen loss, I turned and trotted back. The two coaches with watches were huddled together. One shook his head as they watched me jog back to the line. They took their places again as Pioli identified himself. He chuffed down the stretch, upright and laboring like most bulky linemen. He circled back and we chatted through another round, sharing war stories and slowly winning the respect of players whose college careers had dwarfed anything either of us had achieved on a football field.

When the timed sprints were finished, we were put through a series of agility drills before splitting up by position. I was one of two quarterbacks. They placed us side by side and had us throw in parallel to two different sets of receivers. My younger rival had a cannon for an arm, but he was nervous and his throws were all over the place. None of my receivers had to break stride to catch anything I threw. I watched Dante circulate to each of the coaches and make notes on his clipboard, after which he walked to the center of the outfield and blew a whistle to end the session. He waved us in.

"Some of you will hear from us, and some won't," he announced without looking up from his clipboard. "Thank you. That is all."

Suddenly, I realized why I liked Dante. He was a classic sergeant, a field leader who didn't pussyfoot around. The college kids seemed put off by his brusque manner, but I found his military precision refreshing after so many months in the amorphous world of civilian life. Pioli and I lagged behind the kids as we walked out of the stadium. He was headed to the subway station for a long train ride back to Queens. I shook his hand and wished him luck, then crossed the parking lot to Izzo's car. I changed from cleats into my street shoes. A breeze chilled the perspiration on my back when I pulled off the sweatshirt. I untangled the sleeves of my dress shirt, tensing slightly as my cold shard ring bumped against my chest.

"Holy mackerel!" Dante called from behind me. "What happened to your back?"

I turned around and saw a couple of college players dogging him with questions as he walked to his car. I knew he was talking to me. Whenever I took off my shirt in public, I thought about the criss-cross of scars on my shoulder blades.

"Just a coupla burns," I said as I pulled on my shirt. "War stuff. It's no big deal," I added, perhaps a little too eagerly. "Don't slow me down any."

"Oh, I know that," he answered. "If you can run like that in street clothes, a few scars won't keep us from signing you up."

I couldn't suppress an astonished grin. He waved goodbye as he ducked in and slammed the door, oblivious to the players crowding the side of his car. Fighting the impulse to punch the air and whoop like a schoolboy, I nodded at the young All-Americans, climbed into Izzo's bomb and steered out of the parking lot. At a red light two blocks away, I let loose, hollering and bouncing with joy in the front seat. I was pumping my fists at the steering wheel and shouting "Yeah!" with each shot when I accidentally hit the horn. Sensing something in my peripheral vision, I slowly looked over to my right. Two lanes over, Dante was laughing at me through the cigar haze that filled his car. He rolled his eyes and shook his head, but he flashed me a thumbs-up before pulling away. So much for Ellington cool, I thought. But the truth is that I didn't really care. I was going to be a pro football player. Life was grand indeed.

Twenty

Bronx
January, 1947

A short blast from a car horn broke Karl's concentration. He glanced over at the traffic idling at the red light. In the lane nearest him, a driver sat laughing and flashing a thumbs-up at a car two lanes over, cigar hanging from his bottom lip. Karl could not see the driver of the other car, or the St. Christopher medallion on the car's visor, or the bullet rolling around on its floor. Instead, he scowled at a tattered page he had ripped from a local phone book, looked around at the numbers on the apartment buildings and prepared for another fruitless trudge up four flights of stairs. *What is it with these Italians? Don't any of them live on the first floor?* He had combed three New York boroughs, knocked on door after door, and still had not spoken to anyone who even *knew my name, let alone Anna's.* But still he persisted. Werner and O'Malley were beginning to think their large friend had lost his mind.

The light changed and the cars moved on. Karl started across the adjacent street in the same direction as the traffic. Halfway across, he made eye contact with a stunning blonde whose low-cut dress left a generous amount of cleavage at the mercy of the January chill. As she walked by in the opposite direction, Karl turned completely around and followed her progress, oblivious to the smallish man in a fine-cut suit who trotted beside her. When she turned to look back at Karl, he blew her a kiss. Her husband grabbed her hand and scowled over his shoulder. Karl just laughed and waved at both of them. When the light changed again, a truck driver had to blow his horn to move Karl out of the lane. Still laughing, Karl stepped onto the curb and shook his head. He crumpled the paper in his hand, tossed it into a wastebasket and looked around for the nearest stop on the bus line back to Queens.

Twenty-one

Newark
January, 1947

Manhattan receded in my rear view, suddenly smaller and less forbidding than it had ever been. For the first time in my life, I felt like a part of that city, a genuine member of the New York community and not just some chooch wandering around Fifty-Second Street listening through open doors to musicians I couldn't afford to see. Frank Dante said the New York Yankees football club wanted to sign me up. Me, a guy who just ruined the only suit I owned. A guy who only ever left Tenth Street to fight in a war and play a couple of football games, whose brother leaves bullets on the floor mats of cars, whose own son can't pronounce the "TH" in "father." A guy whose girlfriend travels halfway around the world to say No to a marriage proposal. I leaned back in the soft car seat, steering with two fingers and letting the strange whimsy of life wash over me. Whoever believes he can control this odd business of being human is a fool. I looked up at St. Christopher's tiny bronze face on Izzo's visor medallion. He was upside down, clipped there probably by Izzo's mother or maybe by young Henry himself. I smiled back at the little saint. St. Christopher gets it. He doesn't care if he's moving backwards, or upside down, or whatever. He knows he's not driving the car.

I worked my way back to Newark through the all-day, ever-present tangle of drivers going back and forth on Route One to no place at all. What a mess that used to be. God bless the New Jersey Turnpike — at least it moves you along. Back then, you were getting nowhere fast. When I finally reached the corner of Tenth Street, I backed the car into a spot and cut the engine. I knew that when I opened the door, reality would suck back into my life and chill everything down again. I stared at my fingers on the door handle and slowly relaxed my grip. There was nobody I was dying to tell about my tryout; Anna wouldn't understand it, and everybody else would just sort of smudge it all up with their opinions. One thing I learned when I came home from Texas: nobody really gives a crap. That's not me being bitter — believe me, I got all the appreciation I needed, all the backslaps and attaboys one man could possibly want. What I'm talking about is understanding. It's a rare thing when somebody stops thinking of what they're going to say long enough to actually listen to what you're telling them. Right then, I didn't want to bother with that, so I sat in Izzo's car and told the neighborhood to hang fire. This was my victory. They'd hear about it soon enough, but for the moment it was mine alone. I folded my hands behind my head and leaned back again. You and me, St. Christopher. We're okay. Behind me, the thrum of cars on South Orange Avenue began to lull me to sleep. I closed my eyes and let the morning drain away. Five, maybe ten minutes I was out. Then hell broke loose.

"...aaahhhd-damn it, Mateo!"

The words slurred into audibility, and then someone pounding on the roof of the car startled me completely awake. I opened my eyes and saw a wall of purple sharkskin in the side window. The shocking bloat of Vin's red face dropped into view, sending me into a recoil.

"I chased you halfway down South Orange Avenue," he panted. "Where the hell you been? I need my paper. It's almost one o'clock, for chrissakes!"

I reached over and lifted the Racing Form from the floor of the car, but when I turned back to the window Vin was gone. Still groggy, I wondered if maybe I was dreaming. Then for the second time in less than a minute, the sight of my brother's face in the window nearly gave me a heart attack. This time he was on the passenger side, leering into the front seat. He whipped the door open, leaned inside and snatched the paper from my hands. After a quick search through its pages, he looked up.

"What the hell is this?!" he shouted. "You tore it up?"

He ducked onto the front seat and grabbed a fistful of my shirt. Now fully awake, I slapped his hand away and shoved him backward. His bulk kept him from falling out of the car, but at least I had some breathing room. I held up one index finger to tell him to wait, and then I reached back and retrieved Izzo's cleats. From the toe cups, I pulled each half of the sheet Vin wanted. They were tightly packed and somewhat sweaty, but intact. Eyes bulging from a face as purple as his suit, Vin looked like some kind of huge, angry fish. As delicately as his chubby fingers would allow, he unfolded the first piece and smoothed it on his leg. All of his notes were perfectly legible. He repeated the process for the second one, carefully aligning the halves until he was satisfied that none of the precious information was lost. He sneered at me and shook his head as he started to back out of the car, but a flash of brass on the floor caught his eye. After a frozen second, he slowly reached down and pinched the shell casing between his thumb and forefinger. For an instant, there was real fear in his eyes. Then they lidded over in that lifeless way and he sat back down in the passenger seat. He closed the door and stared at the shell, calculating his next words.

"Benny Bells..." He paused.

"God rest his soul," I interjected.

"Huh?" Vin looked up. "He ain't dead."

"I know. But it can't hurt to dream."

Vin glared at me, but gradually his anger faded into an expression of pragmatic neutrality. He closed his fist around the shell and jammed it into his pocket, then looked at me with the glassy affection of a politician. "So Pop kicked you out too, huh?"

"He's bad news, Vin," I said quietly.

"Naw, Pop don't—"

"Benny."

Vin held his tongue for a beat, then leaned toward the door and started to pull the handle. But for the second time he changed his mind and stayed where he was. He picked up one of Izzo's cleats and turned it around slowly, as if he was examining a moon rock.

"Yankees, huh?" Vin asked. "A.A.F.C.? Ain't the N.F.L., but we bet on it all the same. Couldn't hurt to have a man on the inside."

"Forget it," I growled.

"Lotta cannoli in something like that." Vin's tone was sing-song, mocking. I looked out the window, fighting back my temper. The image of that white bakery box flashed in my mind again.

"So how far into Izzo are you guys?" The question didn't surprise Vin, although I'm not sure I really expected it to. "Couple hundred?" I pressed. "More? Because the only reason he'd let you use his car—"

"Or his bar," Vin interrupted.

Something flared in his eyes. Anna had told me she thought he was a killer, and that look made me think maybe she was right. With three words, he laid out the sum of my vulnerability — and the extent of his viciousness. He knew where the button was. The thing about people like Vin is that they always know a guy's price. They know who you owe, they know where you earn, and they even know who you might have to pay to hide a secret or two. He had me totaled up. He knew I needed that job, even more so now that Pop had shown me the door. Cunning as he was, he might have already figured out that I was hoping to rent the apartment above the bar. He probably even knew I wanted to use my first paycheck from the Yankees to become Izzo's business partner. But three words and a glance made it clear that he would not hesitate to destroy me.

What really chilled me was that I had never seen Vin conduct his business in the bar. I thought I knew all of the back rooms, all of the places to hide or meet or whatever. I knew where Henry Senior had stashed his hooch during Prohibition. I even knew where Jeremiah took the white girls who couldn't see him anyplace else. Izzo didn't even know about that. So what did Vin mean? There was no bluff in him, of that I was sure. He was a lousy poker player, and he knew it. His stock in trade was brutality and inside information, not subtlety.

"Don't bother," Vin said. "You won't figure it out. And you really don't want to."

"Get out," I muttered.

"Think about what I said," Vin answered. "You on the field, me workin' the spread. We could make a lotta money."

"Get out."

"You need some now?" Vin cracked a faint smile as he reached into his jacket pocket. He snapped the rubber band off of a fist-sized roll. "How much you need? Fifty? Hundred? 'Cause those nickel tips you make ain't gonna get it done. 'Specially if they're layin' on Pop's dining room floor."

"Get the hell out!" I wondered how much Rica had told him, but I didn't want to listen to any more.

"Here, at least take twenty," he said. "I don't need it."

He dangled the bill in front of my face and then brushed it against my nose. I snapped. My left fist caught the edge of his brow and opened a small cut. Twisting in my seat, I drove my right into his ribs. It had almost no effect. Ready to aim higher, I coiled again but froze when I heard the click of a tiny metal hammer. He brought the pistol out from behind his coat, leveled it at my face and slowly pushed it forward until it began to flatten my nose. His eyes burned black. I struggled not to blink. All of the contorted energy of our rivalry was pulled into focus across the barrel of that gun. My body was immobilized, heart pounding with fear, yet suddenly my mind felt calm. At that moment, cold iron grinding against my nose, I knew this was all he had. It's not that I would have wanted Vin to shoot me, or that I believed he was incapable of it, it's just that somehow I felt sad because I knew that he wouldn't. I found myself wishing that there was more to Vin than the ability to aim a gun, that somehow he might dig deeper and find the strength... for what? That was his life. He chose it. But in that car, that day, it failed him. And that broke my heart. I think maybe I might have preferred to die than to see him emasculated. The love of a brother is a funny thing sometimes.

I looked away. My fist dropped to my side as I relaxed and eased away from the gun. I leaned back and stared out the front window with the strangest feeling of serenity I have ever known. Vin had not moved at all; he still trained the gun on the spot where my face had been. I couldn't bring myself to look at him, but I knew that a battle between pride and love was raging in his heart, as it had in mine. On some base level, he was thinking that if he shot me, he alone would be the alpha male in our family. And if he did not, that role would be mine. What I wanted to say to him was that it didn't matter. The odd peace I felt was because of my own invulnerability. I had finally realized that none of it mattered at all. Life, death, power — none of it. What mattered most was that I had answered the moment of my own demise with love and understanding, not fear and hatred. I had glimpsed my own immortality, and it lay in the fearless certainty that whatever Vin may have ended by killing me was in no way comparable to what would live on through my forgiveness of him.

Behind me, I heard what sounded like a gunshot. In the same heartbeat, the closed silence of the car was cracked through by the real thing. I felt the air rush past my nose as the window beside me exploded outward. A tiny curl of smoke wafted from the barrel of the gun. Vin was frozen, his eyes wide with fear, but then he quickly tucked the gun into his pocket, climbed out of the car and walked away. On the sidewalk just outside the passenger door, Mickey's baseball rolled slowly past. It had struck the rear quarter panel and startled Vin into firing. I looked back over my shoulder and saw Mickey and Antonio, agape with confused guilt. Izzo opened the door to the bar, saw his shattered window and pushed past the boys to the car, where he stood and waved his arms as he hollered back at them. Both boys began to cry. Mickey shook his head, protesting through tears and pointing first at the ball and then at the far side of the car. It was then that I realized that all I could hear was a numb whistle. On the seat beside me lay the torn copy of Vin's Racing Form and Izzo's right cleat. Vin had not forgotten to take his page of notes. When Izzo reached the door, his animated face went still. Gun smoke hung in the air.

Izzo glanced up the street in the direction that Vin had taken, but saw no one. When he looked back at Mickey and Antonio, I finally realized that my son was crying. Still in a world of watery silence, I burst from the driver's side and ran to him. On one knee, I hugged him and tried to reassure him that everything was fine, although I couldn't hear my own words and he didn't really understand them anyway. I closed my eyes and kissed his soap-clean hair. Voices began to emerge from the murk. I opened my eyes. Anna and Rica were standing over me, speaking frantically and pointing at Izzo's car. I raised one hand to my ear and said — too loudly — that I could barely hear them. When Antonio saw his mother, he wriggled free and ran to her. She scooped him up. Still on one knee, I acknowledged her furious concern and tried to explain that it was an accident, that Vin's gun had discharged by mistake. Izzo looked up from his car with mild concern and scanned the small crowd of onlookers to gauge their comprehension of what I had just said.

Anna turned away in disgust. She pulled Antonio close and kissed his cheek. Tears were forming in her eyes. Behind her, a bus screeched to a stop at the corner and discharged air from its brakes. I heard that. When its doors opened, I heard the driver announce the Tenth Street stop. Izzo's faltering explanation of the gunshot grew more audible. Around me, the sounds of my neighborhood crept closer until at last they had returned completely. I stood up and smiled at Anna.

"I can hear again!" I announced. "I'm not deaf."

"Oh no?" Anna let her eyes linger on the gun-shattered glass, then she swept past Izzo and carried her son away from the scene. Rica flashed me one of those urgent little-sister looks and clicked after Anna as fast as her heels would allow.

"I made the team," I called after them. Rica stopped and looked back. "Tell her I'm gonna play pro ball."

Rica looked at me for a long moment and shook her head as if she could not fathom my stupidity. Izzo seemed genuinely excited when he heard the news, but within seconds I saw his happiness drain away to jealousy. Fanning his arms wide, he forced another big smile and walked up to give me a hug. As he slapped my back, he whispered in my ear. His tone was edged with menace, as if both caution and congratulations were in order.

"Don't forget where you came from," he said.

❖

There is something unclean about a gunshot, something foreign and obscene and impossible to live with. In war, the whole place is such a mess that you don't even notice a single shot anymore, unless maybe it's the one that sends you home, or worse. But when it's in the middle of your own street — for no good reason — that same little crack of air can stain every house. It can make every mother drop what she's doing and stare at the echo with a look that would break even the coldest heart, as if she herself had brought that pestilence to the place her children had trusted her to keep safe. When a gun goes off, most people just stand still and listen, or maybe crouch a little. Some back into doorways. But if a mother's children are out there with that sound, she will run toward it. And then after things have quieted down, after fingers have probed the bullet crater and curious eyes have traced the ricochet to a spot just inches from a window across the street, after Signs of the Cross and whispered prayers have been offered for the small miracle of an unbroken pane of glass — after all of that, a mother will ask, Who? Who brought this filth to the place where my children play? And if it's you, she will hate you for the shame you have made her feel.

But what I love about women is that they can hate part of you, and they can trust almost nothing you say, but they'll still find that little shred of goodness in you when they need it most. I'll never forget that first night in the apartment. Since I had been sleeping on the couch at Pop's, and since Anna was mad at me anyway, I had decided I should rough it in the living room for a night or two until I was welcome in her bed. Staring up at a ceiling dyed blue by the neon pelican just outside the window, I tried to forget about the angry little beauty on the other side of the bedroom door. I listened to bar conversation burble up through the floor. A drummer tapped his wrists loose on a snare. Someone blew a sax up and down a warm-up scale. My sleepless mind wondered if it was Jeremiah Walker, but once that soggy horn started in I knew it wasn't him. The band's first piece was a passable blues, workaday and solid but with its shoes nailed to the floor. Against the wall, the radiator clanked and hissed. It was January, but I was sweating. I rolled over on the couch, wide awake and uninspired.

Behind me, the bedroom door creaked open and closed. I looked back. Anna's face was shrouded in the shadow of her thick curls, but the blue light found the curves of her breasts under sheer silk. Two points formed as they bounced with each slow step she took toward the couch. The light material clung to her thighs, riding in and out with unnerving sensuality. When she stood over me, I could see the tears in her eyes. I sat up and started to ask why she was crying, but she clapped her hand over my mouth and pushed me back down. I felt her other hand small and tight on my neck. In her wide eyes, I watched a battle for emotional control. They flashed gold as she ducked close and kissed the spot where my neck met my jaw. I tensed with desire. As our lips met, I felt her tears on my face. My hands found the hem of her nightgown and lifted it free of her warm skin. Our bare flesh came together, separated only by the ring that hung around my neck. Writhing desire climaxed with each of us clawing and pulling the other closer, tighter, our bodies heaving together in mutual release and collapsing on the floor next to someone else's coffee table. After a while, I whispered her name. She lay silent. I started to apologize for what had happened that afternoon, but she pressed her finger to my lips as her eyes welled once more. She slapped my cheek, hard, and pressed her finger to my lips again. Ducking back into the darkness, she picked up her nightgown and disappeared into the bedroom.

I pulled the sheet from the couch and wrapped it around myself where I lay naked on the floor. The bedroom door looked solid and forbidding. On the other side lay a woman who revealed herself only in bursts of impulse, short fits of courage that faded when her emotions raised the specter of loss. She was haunted by the memory of a father she adored. She was struggling with motherhood, with a dread of both the past and the future, and with a new life that she was afraid to embrace lest it fall to the same fate that her old one had.

Twenty-two

Newark
Summer, 1947

In the spring and summer of Forty-seven, I wasn't
easy to live with. After years of taking orders and serving
everybody else, I felt like I finally had a chance to make
my own mark in the world. There wasn't time to wait
around. Pop wanted me gone? I stayed gone. Mama cried
a little? Well, she'd get over it. Anna was Anna, and I
didn't have any more time to figure out what that meant.
I had a season to prepare for, my first ever as a
professional. Mack and I pushed each other in brutal
running sessions every day, after which I threw passes to
him until I couldn't raise my arm. I spent a lot of time at
work, but money was still tight. Even though Anna and I
had a place of our own, she still felt caged up. She had
never experienced heat like we had that summer, that
hanging humidity that just bleaches the soul right out of
you. Izzo had offered to float me the first month's rent if
I could get him a tryout with the Yankees, and when it
didn't pan out he kind of turned on me a little. More than

a couple of times, I wondered about that cash I had thrown at Pop. Rica told me he hadn't let anyone touch it for almost a week, but then one day it was gone — right about the time his rent came due.

Every month around rent time, Vin would show up at the Pelican Club while I was working and order a bottle of anisette. He'd set himself up at a table in the corner and hold court, always with a big pile of cash next to the cigar in his ashtray. He never said a word to me about the gunshot — or anything else — but it was clear that he was there to make a point. I needed money, and he had it. What I didn't know was that he had been a daily fixture at the bar for almost a year. I worked afternoons and evenings, and he made his rounds at midday. Every day he showed up with a box of cannoli and two loaves of bread, and every day he left without them. Izzo would take the bakery packages and disappear for a few hours, leaving the bar in the shaky hands of our daytime bartender, Gio Pietro. The only reason I learned any of this was because Rica had fallen in love with Pietro. She had always been drawn to his artistic brooding, but when their relationship began she chose to hide it from everyone in the family except Anna. Anna told me only after I had sworn not to confront Pietro about it. I promised Anna that I would forget about them, and I did.

It's not that I didn't care about my sister's love life — it's just that a promise is a promise. Besides, at the time I was more concerned about Vin's arrangement with Izzo. Of course I knew there was money in the bakery boxes. Vin probably gave him that first one as a gift, and before Izzo had even decided what to spend it on the second one would have arrived, along with the marked-up heats for that day at the track. Most likely, Vin had started using Izzo as a runner to place bets and collect winnings, but it wouldn't stop there. Izzo should have sensed that it was all too easy. When he saw that Racing Form peeking out of the first bread bag, I doubt he realized that everything his father had so carefully protected was already lost. The whole thing was depressing to me, just tawdry and sad. Izzo had scraped for the same honest nickels that we all had, but at some point he looked around and decided that a business of his own, a great wife and a new family were not enough. We all know what we need, but when we let someone else tell us what we *want* then our freedom is lost. Vin whispered in Izzo's ear and made a slave out of him.

Through the spring and early summer of Forty-seven, I watched Izzo take on more and more of Vin's arrogance and callousness. It made me angrier every day. I worked most of it out in the training sessions Mack and I had each day to prepare for our first season with the Yankees, but I still brought too much of it home with me. Anna didn't understand why I cared, or why I wouldn't just leave that job and get a new one. She viewed any sort of a connection to Vin as a threat to the safety of her family. To her, Izzo was soft-headed and malleable. I couldn't argue. By the middle of July, her patience with me had worn thin. She was relieved when I packed my old service duffel and climbed into Mack's car for the drive to training camp. For the rest of the summer, I barracked in a dormitory and learned the brutalized humility of a rookie on a team of professionals while Anna made the best of things with Antonio. I told her to ignore Mama's hysterical warnings about polio and take him to the public pool. Each day, she found her way back to the leafy shade of Vailsburg Park and the lemon ice vendors who sold meager relief. Finally, August ended and with it the dual hells of city heat and training camp.

I am forever grateful for September and the start of new things. Each year the heat of the day lingers in the green canopy above the highways and roads of New Jersey, but as summer nights fade into the first hints of autumn, I am restored. September is the American month, the resumption of worthwhile endeavor, the placing aside of the frivolous and obscene. Let him who seeks mere liberation find his way to June. September is the time for true liberty, for its effort, its reward. Some will say that the American is not worthy of his freedom, that he has softened, grown vulgar. What they see are the weak among us, those who will not rise to the challenge of September and instead choose to hide in the sandy shade of July or the indoor yammer of March. Let our critics look to the ninth month of our year, when the quiet grace of achievement is earned by those who neither seek the spotlight nor dance when it comes. I have no use for the man who splits our sacred month with his shrieks of false righteousness, his hatred, his deceit. He will never take September away from us. Let it come each year to remind him of his failure.

September, Nineteen Forty-seven marked the end of six weeks away from my family — Anna and Antonio. By then, the days had blurred into one long, grueling scramble across parched dirt into yet another bone-shattering collision. The speed and size of the pros were daunting enough, but paired with the constant tension of mental adjustment it was almost too much. Days became hours, and hours days. Each segment of time lost its meaning, yielding to the primary task of survival and the almost incidental matter of making an impression on the jaded coaches who watched us. I can't point to individual moments that made any sort of a difference in my standing, but after six weeks of two-a-days and three exhibition games, I was still on the team. I think it was more about endurance; gradual progress, play after play, jumping up after a tackle that might rob another man's will, finding and hitting the toughest players on the other side, early and often, day after day. In time, they learn that you will not go away. In still more time, they wonder if perhaps you might be of some use after all.

Twenty-three

Long Island City
Summer, 1947

Above the East River, bursts of blue, green and
yellow fire colored the sky. Karl stood at the window and
watched through the bars, feeling alone and incarcerated.
He probably thought, as I did, that the fireworks looked
like flak bursts. Since the war ended, the Fourth of July
had taken on a new level of festivity for most Americans,
but for people like Karl it didn't have the same resonance.
He was happy to share in the liberties of the United
States, and even happier to be free of the Third Reich,
but his immigrant patriotism was born more of necessity
than affection. In his experience, Americans were mostly
great musicians, affable captors and undisciplined fighters.
Outside of co-workers, he had not met many people in
his seven months stateside. He kept to himself and
mostly listened to the radio, almost exclusively to jazz.
The only books he read were New York phone
directories, and only one section within those — the
"A's." Although he declined an invitation to sleep in their

252

guest bedroom, Karl had grown to cherish the home-cooked meals and the effortless German banter he shared twice a week with Werner and his wife at their house in Astoria. By February, Werner's shop dog Lily had begun to warm up to him. It took him a little longer to reciprocate, but in time they established a cordial but wary relationship.

O'Malley was another story. Ever since Karl's first day at the foundry, O'Malley had treated him like a circus geek, standing within earshot and hatching bald-faced schemes for capitalizing on his enormous strength. The idea rooted most deeply in O'Malley's imagination was professional football. He was determined to sign Karl to a contract with one of the local teams in exchange for a percentage of his salary and full access to the field for all home games. Although Karl had politely refused to meet with the Yankees, O'Malley kept after Frank Dante until at last he agreed to stop by the shop and meet the "German giant" after a family barbecue on the Fourth of July. Lily's ears perked up long before Karl smelled Dante's cigar smoke or heard O'Malley's braying tenor through the foundry door. Barking wildly, she bolted to the front of the shop and relented only when O'Malley opened the door and kicked her with his steel-toed boot. Like a museum guide, the stout Irishman waved his new friend toward Karl's living space at the far end of the floor. Dante had drunk many bottles of beer in the heat of the day, and weaved slightly as he walked. O'Malley staggered along behind him.

Karl turned away from the window. His eyes narrowed when he saw O'Malley. He had heard one too many pitches from his greedy boss. When Dante saw

Karl, his jaw fell slack and his cigar tumbled to the floor, showering his feet with orange sparks.

"You there," Dante slurred. "Sss'yah name?"

Karl remained silent.

"Speak up, Boy-O!" O'Malley sang out. "Tell Mr. Dante yer name."

Karl stood silent and unsmiling when O'Malley shouted the same command again. Dante suggested that Karl might not understand English, but O'Malley knew better. This was insubordination, which stoked his alcoholic rage. He reached for a length of iron pipe and stalked closer to where Karl stood. Growling, he repeated the order a third time, with the same result. He gripped the pipe with two hands and took his best baseball cut at Karl's ribs. Karl bunched up and leaned into the blow, receiving it across his deltoid and trapezius. O'Malley coiled for another rip, but found his backswing halted at its apex by a firm hand. Dante was drunk, but not without judgment. His new acquaintance had crossed the line.

"Y'know, pal," Dante said to Karl as he took the pipe from O'Malley's hands, "I don't know this stupid mick from Adam, but he got one thing right. You are a big son-of-a-bitch." He leaned the pipe against the wall and reached into his pocket. "Here's my card. We start practice in a coupla weeks, and if you wanna come by for a tryout, well, okay by me. If not, good luck to you." Dante tipped his hat, pivoted and strode for the door, his gait suddenly more sober. O'Malley glared back at Karl and then hurried to catch up to Dante, who waved him away like a greenfly.

For the next few days, Karl did not speak to O'Malley or to anyone else except Werner, and then only in

German. Even Werner's goofy humor was not enough to persuade Karl to stop speaking the language that antagonized the Americans in the shop. Karl had avoided removing his shirt in front of anyone, but at last the heat of the blast furnace and the oppressive humidity were more than he could stand. Across his left shoulder, a heavy red welt lay like a brand against his pale skin. Clearly visible at one end were parallel lines of pipe threading. Werner did not ask what had caused the mark, but from that day forward he no longer tried to broker the peace between Karl and O'Malley. Summer ended, but Karl's grudge remained.

At a lunch break one Saturday, the men sat around a battered old radio and listened as the first football game of the year began. It was an A.A.F.C. exhibition between New York and Brooklyn. When Karl heard the word "Yankees," he looked at O'Malley for the first time in weeks and then stood up to walk away from the group. But when the announcer described the opening kickoff, Karl froze and then spun around as if he had heard the voice of a ghost.

"What name did he say?" Karl asked. When no one replied, he roared so loudly that half the men jumped: "What name?! Did he say 'Mateo Albero'?!" Karl strode to the radio, crouched down and grasped it with both hands. He pressed his ear to the speaker, wild intensity in his eyes. "Someone tell me!" he cried out. "Was it Albero? Mateo Albero?"

"Yes." O'Malley's voice broke the tense silence. "They have a player named Albero."

Karl stood and walked to O'Malley. "You know this man?"

"I've never met him, but I heard a few things." Karl's burning look implored O'Malley to continue. The Irishman knew this was not the time to face down his subordinate, no matter how much he believed Karl deserved it. "He was on a semi-pro team from Jersey," O'Malley said. "Newark, I believe. Never went to college. Fought in the war."

Karl's eyes widened. "Where is this New-yark?"

"Newark," O'Malley corrected. "Straight west. Other side of Manhattan, in New Jersey."

Karl stared at O'Malley for a long time. The only sound was the buzzing of the football play-by-play. When Karl spoke again, there were tears in his eyes.

"Thank you," he whispered.

He turned and made a beeline for the bathroom, where he washed his face and hands. Then he crossed to his cot, pulled off his grimy denims and dug out his best suit. Combing his hair as quickly as he could, he folded the rest of his clothes and tucked them back into his duffel bag. Without looking at anyone, he marched to the heavy door, opened it in one quick motion and ducked through. Werner looked at O'Malley for a moment and then jogged after Karl, calling to him in German.

"Karl, wait! Slow down. I will drive you there."

Twenty-four

Newark
September, 1947

There was fullness to the love in Rica's heart, a saturation so complete that it left no room for anything petty or false. She would look directly at you, eyes wide with curiosity, and say that thing that most let you know that she was there with you, present and unafraid. To Anna, Rica was a Godsend. They walked together for hours, sharing thoughts and feelings, growing together as sisters. Rica was drawn to the romance of Anna's reunion with me. Out of kindness, Anna did not mention that her quest had been more for survival than love. She had accepted the fact of our separation, but she could not live with the poverty and lawlessness that threatened her son's welfare. One day Rica would understand the demands of motherhood, but for the moment Anna chose to leave intact Rica's illusions of amorous destiny.

One Saturday afternoon at the beginning of September, Anna and Rica chatted their way past the shops on South Orange Avenue and into Vailsburg Park.

Trees drew shadows across the broad lawns as evening settled in. On one of the pathways, Anna felt the sudden creeping of déjà vu, but when she looked around there was no one but Rica within a hundred feet. She walked on, smiling bravely as she fought off the memory of the blond Nazi from the park in Mönchengladbach. But still, her sense of dread would not fade. Rica kept talking, oblivious to Anna's agitation. As they strolled slowly through the angled light, Anna squinted at the trees and gasped. She began to cry.

"What is it?" Rica leaned close with concern.

Anna shook her head as if to say it was nothing, but her tears belied the depth of her emotion. Rica put an arm across her shoulders and waited quietly for her to respond. They walked on, heads inclined and touching, until Anna was composed. She sniffled with embarrassment at the question she asked Rica:

"Do you believe in ghosts?"

"Sure," Rica said quietly. "They're real. Or at least the feelings that make us see them are."

Rica paused, but Anna's only reply was a distracted nod. She was staring into the trees as if she expected someone to step from between them. As they walked, Rica studied the shadowy trunks along with Anna. Eventually, she lost interest and decided to tell Anna the story of a Sicilian fisherman who died in a storm.

"His little boat washed up on shore one day," she recounted. "It was empty, just his net and a few fish that he caught that day. But his wife wouldn't let herself believe he was gone. The next day, she did what she always did — brought him a small kettle of salted fish, spoke to him like he was still there. That night, she wrapped herself in a black shawl and went back to the waterfront to get the empty kettle. She wouldn't admit that the meal had been eaten by the birds and not by her husband. The next day she went again. Years passed, and she never missed a day."

As Rica spoke, Anna watched the spaces between the trees. There! No, it couldn't be...

"One morning," Rica continued, "the townspeople noticed that the boat was gone. They looked for the widow, but she wasn't at her house. After a few days, the boat drifted back to shore again. Inside, they found a black shawl, a fish net and a small kettle. The kettle was empty, but the net was full of fresh-caught fish."

Anna looked at Rica. There were tears in her eyes.

"I know," Rica said. "Weird, huh? They say you can still hear them out there on the water, talking and laughing. Now that's love."

Anna nodded, but she wasn't listening. The anguish on her face made Rica wonder if perhaps she had chosen the wrong thing to say.

"You know, I'm not sure I do believe in ghosts," Rica backtracked. "It's just sometimes you hear something that makes you think."

Just then, a twig snapped in the precise spot that Anna was looking. Rica strained to see, but the shadows were too thick. Terrified, she looked back at Anna. Anna was calm, but deeply sad.

"There are no such things as ghosts," Anna said quietly.

When they returned to Pop's flat, Carmela held a finger to her lips and pointed at the couch where Antonio was sleeping. Anna nodded and whispered to let him sleep. She said she would retrieve her overnight things and come back in a while to stay at Carmela's place. Rica watched her go. There was an odd tone in Anna's voice, but Rica decided to leave it alone. Anna walked to the doorway that led up to our apartment, paused and looked back at Pop's place, then kept walking around the corner to South Orange Avenue. In the shadows between the streetlights, she let go. Her chest heaved. Each time she passed into a circle of light she tried to control her tears, but after a block or so she gave up and wept openly. As she passed one recessed doorway, she heard footsteps begin to follow her. They fell heavily, at long intervals. She knew them instantly and slowed her pace. After a few more steps she stopped, but she did not turn around. Her shoulder tensed beneath Karl's large hand. When he gently tightened his grip, she pulled away suddenly and whirled around.

"You are dead!" she cried. "That letter from the army... You are... were..."

Anna was startled by Karl's appearance. His face was etched and weathered, his forehead bisected by a two-inch scar. There was something of the wolf in his posture, solitary and edgy, unsafe. Whatever light there had been in his eyes was long gone. He looked down at the hand that she had rejected, then back at her face. He seemed ready to cry as he lifted that same hand to touch her cheek, pausing just before his fingertips reached the flush of her skin.

"Anna," he whispered. "So much pain. So many tears." He was relieved to be speaking German, but the words did not come easily. "And still, you are so beautiful."

"No! You cannot!" she snapped in English. "You were dead! You do not know. You do not know..."

260

She dissolved into tears, recoiling so violently at his hand on her elbow that he did not try to comfort her again.

"I know how you are feeling," he said softly, still in German. "I—"

"You do NOT know!" she insisted in English. "You CANNOT know! They killed him! My father, they *killed* him. And you with your uniform, your hat with the little black button, your swastika. You say you know how I feel? They killed you too. All I had was your picture!" A heavy sob wracked her body. "Your picture," she choked. "Always, the bombs and your goddamn picture." Once again, she broke down.

"Anna, please," Karl said quietly, in English. "I try. I am wanting to try. To know..."

"You don't want to know!" she screamed. "You never wanted to know! This!" She tore at her forearm, scratching deeply. A red line appeared. "This is where they put the numbers on my cousins' arms! This is what they hated! This blood! Jewish blood! Here!" She held her arm up, straining to reach his face. "Here it is! The blood of a Jew! Is this what you want? You, with your hat? With your goddamn swastika hat?"

Anna faltered, struggling to breathe through her tears. She seemed to deflate with each exhalation. Yielding, she collapsed to a crouch and then sat down heavily on her gathered skirts. Karl knelt and supported her head. She lashed at him with a few weak punches, but then she allowed herself to fall into his arms.

"You were dead," she whispered, her voice fading to a spent silence. Recently, the fatigue had come to her more often. She knew what it was. The second pregnancy seemed harder, more tiresome and nauseating, especially in the morning. And now the shock of Karl. She closed her eyes and let her mind drift into a dark, peaceful haze as he lifted her into his arms. On Tenth Street just up from the corner of South Orange Avenue, a tidy black sedan sat parked, its driver asleep. Karl opened the door as quietly as he could, laid his wife onto the back seat, and nudged the door closed until the latch caught. He slid into the front seat, poked Werner's arm and motioned for him to remain silent and drive. For the first time since he had known Karl, Werner was truly afraid of him. He did as he was told.

Twenty-five

Astoria, Queens
September, 1947

"*Mutti*," Anna murmured in her half-sleep. Mother. The smell of warm *brötchen* and fresh jam and tea wafted over her. Sunlight warmed her face. She could not believe that the American planes had missed Mönchengladbach yet again. So many sorties, yet no bombs. How was it possible? She rolled over and pressed the crisp sheets to her face. She always loved the smell of the soap that mother used to clean their sheets. She had missed it all these years.

Years? Anna sat upright in bed. She was wearing a woman's nightgown. As her mind rapidly stitched together those things she could remember, she stood and ran down the short hallway toward the smell of baking bread. A stout woman stood at the oven with her back to the door. Anna stopped short in the middle of the kitchen floor, her bare feet skidding on the polished wood. The nightgown hung askew. At the table, a man with thick hands and an open smile looked up at her and winked.

"I am older than you, but I am not dead," he said, nodding at the loose neckline that barely covered her breasts. "You might want to cover up."

"Father," the woman chuckled, "you're terrible."

"Phone!" Anna cried. "Where is your telephone? I need to speak to my son!"

The man looked at his wife with a worried expression, and then frowned back at Anna. He pointed at a small table in the living room. Anna dashed over and picked up the receiver as another plane thundered overhead. She flinched at the sound, staring at the ceiling as if it might collapse. When the plane had passed, she flicked the hook on the base of the telephone and carefully enunciated the number to the operator. After a moment, she tensed with anticipation as the party on the other end spoke.

"Yes, Frau, er, Mrs. Albero," she said. "May I please speak with Antonio? ... His mother, Anna Eisenstark. ... Yes, little Antonio. ... Yes, I am okay. ... He is with Carmela? Where? ... What is her tele—? ... He is my son, Mrs. Albero! I must— ... I did think about that! I fell ill and was— ... Hello? Mrs. Albero? Hello?!"

Anna slammed down the receiver and then quickly picked it up again. "Yes, Newark, New Jersey. The party's name is Carmela..." She couldn't remember my sister's married name. "Nevermind, please try this number again." Mama answered once more and abruptly informed Anna that no one else was home. She suggested that if Anna wished to speak to Antonio, she should come back and do so in person. Anna stared at the dead receiver in disbelief. She slowly hung up the phone and looked around, realizing for the first time that she was in the home of complete strangers and wearing almost nothing. She crossed her arms in front of her breasts and went back to the kitchen for an explanation. The man introduced himself as Werner Sauerbrun, a friend of her husband. His wife's name was Helga.

"He's been looking for you for a long time," Werner continued in German. "I told him to let it go, that you weren't interested—"

"They told me he was dead," Anna said flatly in English. "For me, there was nothing in Mönchengladbach. Nothing. Mateo saved my life. He..."

Suddenly, Anna realized how desperately complicated her situation really was — and how disinclined she was to share the details with these people. Her fingers found the growing lump in her abdomen and spread out warm and flat against it. If nothing else, her children would be one true thing in which to place her faith.

"I must go back to Newark," she said. "Right now. My son is there."

"We cannot keep you here if you do not wish it," Werner sighed. "But it really would help if you wished it."

His smile was feeble. Anna did not return it. With increasing panic, she waved away Helga's offer of brötchen and tea and hurried to the bedroom to put on her dress. She stuffed her bra into her handbag, stepped into her shoes and followed Werner down a short flight of stairs. Outside, they descended the tall stoop and quickly covered the half-block to the car. From the opposite direction, a huge man in a rumpled suit strode toward them. Anna ducked into the car and slammed the door. Werner stood by the driver's side and waited for Karl to arrive.

"Where are you going?" Karl asked Werner. His German was infused more with curiosity than foreboding. Werner shrugged and nodded down at the roof of the car. "Anna," Karl said gently, "could I speak with you? Just for a minute?"

Anna faced stubbornly forward, her face pursed with anger. Werner waved at Karl and whispered one word: "Patience." When Karl shook his head, Werner spoke again. "She wants to see her son."

Karl's face drained to an ashen pallor. He could not have fathered this child.

"I'll find out what I can on the way and let you know when I get back," Werner said. "For now, go to the shop. I know it's Sunday. I'll pay you overtime. Better you have something to do."

Dazed, Karl nodded. He glanced at Anna with a wounded expression, but she didn't offer any sympathy. At that moment, he was nothing more to her than the man who had taken her away from her son. He watched as Werner put the car in gear, eased away from the curb and drove away. Werner glanced back at the solitary figure in the rearview mirror, then turned his attention to retracing the route he had taken across lower Manhattan, through the Holland Tunnel and out to the New Jersey side. Anna sat in stoic silence for most of the trip, only visibly relaxing when she saw a sign with the word "Newark" on it. Werner struggled to think of something clever to say, but gave up and opted for the plain truth:

"He really loves you, you know."

Her face was stone. The woman was inaccessible.

"Why, I have no idea," Werner cracked. "I mean, you're pretty and all, but you're no Helga."

Anna's scowl broke at the corners. Her brief glimpse at Helga's face had told her that Werner was truly a man with a heart of gold.

"And from what I've seen you're not strong, either. Really, you're a pushover."

Anna smiled. Werner steered the car through the streets of Newark until they had finished the subtle climb to the West Ward and rolled onto Tenth Street. He pressed a sheet of paper into her hand, a phone number with the words "For Emergency" written in Helga's Germanic script. Anna thanked him for the ride and closed the door. She leaned back into the open window and looked him in the eye.

"He is a good man," she said. "Remind him of that."

Werner watched Anna climb several steps to the downstairs flat and knock on the door. Rica opened it and received her with a hug. Anna was crying when she shut the door behind her. At the kitchen table, Antonio sat with Mickey eating frittata and giggling at a private joke. When he saw his mother, he dropped his fork, slipped off the chair and ran to her. She let her handbag fall to the floor and lifted him into a tight embrace, closing her eyes as she turned back and forth. From her seat in the dining room, Mama glared at the end of a bra strap dangling from Anna's bag. She raised one flat hand and bit down on her first knuckle, then swept the back of her hand across her field of vision and closed her eyes. With that gesture, she condemned the woman who she believed could run off so casually and abandon a three-year-old boy. What she did not realize was that Anna's heart had barely beaten until just a few seconds earlier, when she felt Antonio in her arms once again.

Twenty-six

Newark
September, 1947

Within the lower half of a man's leg, there is a
ropelike tendon that stretches between the gastrocnemius
muscle and the calcaneal bone. It can withstand stresses
of more than a thousand pounds, but as the half-god
Achilles knew, it is not invulnerable to the forces of irony.
On the Wednesday after our first exhibition game, our
starting quarterback learned just that. Rolling to his right
in a full-squad scrimmage, he leaped and twisted his aim
back across the field to make one of the most athletic
throws I have ever seen. I'm telling you, people gasped, it
was so beautiful. But when he landed, there was nothing
left at the back of his right ankle to support him. He
crumpled like a marionette. And just like that, I was the
starting quarterback for the season opener at Yankee
Stadium, a rematch of the previous year's championship
game against the mighty Cleveland Browns. The point
spread on Monday was five, same as the margin with
which the favored Browns had won the A.A.F.C title. By

Thursday, it was thirteen. I was an eight-point liability before I even stepped onto the field.

Truth be told, it should have been more. If the Vegas numbers guys had any idea what my home life was like, they would have set it at fifty. Small-timers like Vin and Izzo, making book on the ponies and chasing ten-dollar vig payments, saw this as the payday of a lifetime. Even without an inside deal with me, they started loading up on the Browns as early as Friday afternoon. Pietro told me that Benny Bells even stopped by the bar with a fat envelope and pinched Izzo's cheek, grinning like a cat with a mouthful of feathers. With all the weight these guys piled on thirteen, I was surprised to hear that the spread held there. Who knows, maybe if people in New York had this much faith in the Browns, just as many out in Cleveland had faith in us. You're always harder on the ones you love.

As much as I had wanted to run over to Pop's house with the New York Times and jam the page with my name on it up his nose, I stayed away. Mack and I left before sunrise every day and worked late into the night watching film on the Browns. Anna seemed distant and preoccupied, but I didn't have time to ask. When I told Izzo I would need some time off that week, he had chuckled. "Take all the time you want," he smirked, no doubt already counting his winnings. I didn't have time to set him straight. Since Friday was a light practice and Mack and I had worn out every film we had, I went home early to spend a little time with Antonio before he went to bed. Then I went down to the bar, to work. Since the Yankees were getting me practically for free, we were still short on cash. One Friday night of tips would go a long way.

I rolled the crib into our bedroom, tucked in my son and kissed his forehead. When I got back to the dinner table, Anna was sitting there pushing her food back and forth on her plate. She looked up as if she had something to say, but then just closed her mouth and glanced away. In the fading light, I noticed again how utterly breathtaking she was. There was something about melancholy that set her face just so, as if it brought forth a sweet vulnerability that she usually managed to hide. Suddenly nothing else seemed to matter, none of the defensive schemes or play lists or flickering images of men ready to administer my doom in front of fifty thousand people. All I could see was the golden sunset dancing across her eyes, trying to coax out the joy for which God had made them. It had been so long since I really looked at her. When I did, I realized that I wanted her so badly that my whole body ached.

In one impulsive motion I stood and lifted her out of the chair, grinning as I carried her over to the couch. Her eyes widened, as if the weeks apart had erased the physical memory of me and left her shocked at the image of the man before her. I laid her down gently, kneeling before her as I kissed her neck and face. In that instant, I was gripped by the love that had driven me close to her, that had consumed me in her absence and that had waned when we were distracted by the quotidian trials of life. She lay back against the cushion, her beautiful sadness framed by gleaming brown curls. I rose to one knee and took her hand.

"Anna," I began. Her eyes glistened as her lower lip puffed to a pout. "Please, will you mar—"

"No," she cut in. "Don't." She buried her face in a pillow and sobbed.

"What? What is it?"

When her breathing was steady she looked up again. I studied her expression for some indication of what had changed. She stared back, as if in my face she might find some reprieve, some reason not to say what had to come next. One deep, hitching breath. Then:

"Karl is alive."

I froze for a beat, then slumped against the coffee table, my mind racing back over images from the previous week. I had been too exhausted to notice how distant she had been. Each night when I returned, she was already asleep. Although she woke up every morning to wish me well, her kisses had lacked passion, her tone, conviction. Izzo mentioned that Rica had stopped by the bar with some important news for me, but I had not been able to get back to her. In hindsight the signs were everywhere, but that still would have been the last thing I might have guessed she'd say.

"How?" was all I could muster.

"I don't know," she whispered. Her eyes seemed to plead with me for understanding.

"What does this mean?"

"I don't know," she repeated, more audibly this time. "He is my husband."

Husband! The word echoed, condemning my heart for the second time in my life. I wanted to find that Kraut bastard, to hunt him down and rid my life of his shadow. I didn't think for a moment that it had been his wife in my arms, and not the other way around. It didn't matter to me that she was being torn in ways that I was not forced to comprehend. All I cared about was eliminating a rival, meeting a challenge, winning her love. I needed to fight that battle and resolve it once and for all. And then it hit me.

"He's here." I said it out loud because I knew she would not. "Where?" I asked her. "Newark?"

She shook her head. There was fear in her eyes, concern. Compassion. It stung when I realized what I was seeing. She was not afraid of me, but *for* me.

"Where, then?" I persisted. "New Jersey? The east coast? Where?!"

My voice echoed off the walls. In the bedroom, Antonio started to cry. Anna tightened with maternal concern, losing her passive sadness and rising to control the situation. She sat forward and pushed me out of the way, then marched quickly to the bedroom door and opened it. I heard her lift Antonio from his bed and comfort him. But my pride would not die. I followed her to the doorway.

"Where, Anna." It was not a question. I had to know.

"He will kill you," she said evenly.

"Let him try," I countered.

"No." She set her jaw and stared at me.

I knew that would be the last word she said that night. Angry and confused, I leaned back out of the bedroom and trudged to the door. I barely remember walking down the stairs, or acknowledging the greetings and calls of encouragement as I walked into the bar. I suppose people forgave me for being a little distracted that night, for mixing up gin with vermouth and for staring off into space instead of answering them promptly. They may have assumed it was because I was nervous about confronting the biggest challenge in my life, or because of my fear of failure, or of injury, or maybe even of success. Some might have known that I had been in bigger battles, but that the anxiety for this one was no less intense. They would have been right about all of it, but if they assumed the opponent that had me rattled was the Cleveland Browns, they would have been mistaken.

The night blurred into one long, boozy smile interrupted by the occasional knuckle-breaking handshake. Drunks are so sincere — and so strong. By the time we were ready to close, it seemed like half of the West Ward had stopped by to get drunk and wish me luck. Closing time can be a little dicey. People are liquored. Some may just have been jilted by the dream they were chasing all night, while others might have shown up angry and were just looking for fuel. Most of them will shuffle off to a diner or to bed, but one or two just can't let it go. Those become my problem, and maybe Izzo's too if I can't handle them. It's just part of the job. So at nearly three in the morning, two nights before my first professional game, I found myself ushering the last of these recalcitrants out of the bar. As I was flipping through the overloaded key ring for the one that fit the front door, two large men stepped from the shadows looking like they might force their way back in. When they stepped into the light, I could see their faces. Exhausted, I knew it would be a waste of breath but I tried anyway.

"We're closed."

"Yeah, whatever," Vin said as he pushed past.

"What'd you lose some weight?" I called after him as I walked back in. "You fit through on the first try."

I thought Vin's henchman had followed me in, but he stopped and held the door open for a third man I had not seen and then closed the door and guarded it after the man had entered. I looked back and saw Benny Bells walking directly at me.

"Thirteen points," Benny rasped at me. "Capice? I make it worth your while, you gimme thirteen points."

I realized that Izzo was gone. Vin was behind the bar. He lined up three shot glasses next to Benny and took down a bottle of anisette. Spilling half of what he poured, he topped them off. Benny looked at me and tilted his head toward the glasses. I glanced back at the door.

"*Aspete*, drink."

There was no mistaking the tone of command in Benny's voice, or the agreement that I would be sealing by taking the glass. I felt butterflies in my stomach. My legs were numb. But then from someplace deep in my gut, defiance rose up and roared at me. NO!

"How 'bout I go get a stepladder," I heard myself say, "so you can reach yours."

From behind me, Vin's friend grabbed both of my elbows and pulled them backward. I yanked my left one free and ripped it back across his face, then whirled in the same motion and buried a right in his cheekbone. I knew Vin would draw on me before I got in another punch, but I hadn't counted on Benny moving so quickly. He fired once into the wood above the door. Everyone froze.

"Thirteen points," Benny said again as he walked past me. He gestured with the gun at the room around him, spreading its sulfur reek like a priest tipping smoke from a censer. "I burn this piece'a shit down, you screw that up. And these two guys won't like that at all."

He aimed a thumb back over his shoulder at Vin and Izzo, the latter of whom had run out from from the back room when he heard the gunshot. The man I hit opened the door for Benny and let him pass through, then spat a mouthful of blood onto the floor and walked out of the bar. I looked back at Izzo, whose expression vacillated between pain and panic. He was in over his head, and he finally realized it. He started to apologize, but when I turned my back on him he fell silent again. He understood what was being asked of me, and it was more than his competitive heart could stand. I glanced up at the splintered bullet hole as I opened the door, but what lingered in my mind as I stepped out into the darkness were three clear shot glasses on gleaming mahogany, bulbed at the top with surface tension, still untouched.

Twenty-seven

Newark
September, 1947

I didn't go straight home that night. My body was shaking with rage and adrenaline, and I knew I would not sleep for a while. Instead, I walked a few blocks to West Side Park and sat on the bleachers. Before me lay the field where we had held our first semi-pro practice, way back when. Prior to that, there had been a hundred high school practices. Back then Izzo was so sincere, so eager. At the far end of the park, a streetlight shone on the precise spot where I had first seen John Mack. What a long time ago. There had been that glimmer of duplicity in Izzo's eyes when he greeted Mack, but I had chosen to ignore it. It was a mistake I vowed never to make again.

I stood and walked to the center of the grassy expanse. Around me, I could sense the open distance of the field, the smell of the thick lawn stretching a hundred yards in each direction, the weight of the trees at the perimeter, and beyond those the houses of the West Ward. My dreams had been formed on that field. All of my Septembers started there.

There is a feeling in the blood of an honest man, a sense that what might be spilled from his veins could never truly empty his heart. It is an ease, a sort of letting go. He is secure in the knowledge that the end of his life will carry with it the beginning of something new, something as unseen as the lines on that moonlit field, yet also as tangible. I walked through the darkness, knowing without seeing that each step would meet something solid. Out in the same air that had sustained my dreams all those years, I knew that Sunday's game would be like so many I had played in my imagination. I never sold myself out in a dream. Neither did I worry if I could do the job, or if I would win. It was enough just to be in the game, to play my best. I thought about the advice I was sometimes able to heed — to act like I had been there before. If dreams count for anything, I *had* been there before. A thousand times.

The night felt quiet, the air still. I started for home. It was the brimming of my youth, the moment perhaps in all my life when things were at their most vibrant. For a second or two I think I sensed that, and it brought me peace. So many battles, so many joys — and in all of it, *life*. I ambled slowly up the sidewalk and into the indifferent light of a streetlamp. My thoughts ranged ahead to Anna. My pace quickened. For the first time that night I prayed; for patience, for wisdom and for time. Maybe above all else, for time. I needed to see her, to be near enough to her that she could sense my contrition without my saying anything. I craved the proximity that, when tolerated, made all things right. The unspoken apology, the getting on, the normal. I wished that I had known better in April and May how precious September might be. I might have let her know how much I cared, or loved her more, or at least tried.

The smell of the apartment stairwell was like a confrontation with the mundane. Sometimes even the best of intentions die with a whiff of yesterday's news. I felt myself gather and tense, bracing for threats I had already defeated, yet thankful that the fights were familiar. But in reality they were not. Life had changed. There was no hiding from that. I turned the key and shouldered through to the dim blue light of the living room.

"Where have you been?" Anna had been crying, I could tell.

"Hey," I whispered. "No place, really. Just needed to think."

Squinting, I saw her. She was sitting on the couch, wrapped in a blanket. I sagged into the spot beside her, stretched out my legs and rubbed my eyes.

"Jesus," I sighed. "What a day."

"Tomorrow, I must go," she said.

"Anna, can we—?"

"Please," she whispered. "Enough. Downstairs, they are shooting guns. And you, your talk of fighting with Karl." She sniffled, but did not sob. "This is not a good place for Antonio."

"But where are you gonna go?" I asked. "And Antonio. When will I see him?"

"Rica told me they are threatening you," she said. "For the football betting. She told me it was your own brother."

I bowed my head in defeat. If she wanted to go, I wouldn't stop her. After a minute or so she leaned over and kissed my cheek. She walked into the bedroom and quietly closed the door. I lay down on the couch.

A few hours later, two tiny hands grabbed my cheeks. The sun had started to brighten the room, and when I opened my eyes I had to squint to let them adjust. Antonio's face was inches from mine. His mouth was covered with oatmeal, a condition that did not prevent him from kissing my forehead until I sat up and showed him that I was awake. Anna sat at the table; beside her were two large suitcases. Across from her, John Mack was dressed in his trademark white shirt and tie. He chuckled into his cup of coffee and shook his head at the cereal making its slow way down to my eyebrow.

"Five minutes, Pops," he said. "I'll be outside."

I sat up and kissed the top of Antonio's head. In three minutes, I had washed my face and brushed my teeth, pulled on pants, buttoned up a clean shirt and grabbed my jacket and tie. I sat across from Anna and started to put on socks and shoes.

"Is there even a phone number?" I asked.

"If I gave it, would you call?"

"Yes." I locked eyes with her. She looked away.

"Then no," she whispered.

I stood up. Leaning close, I kissed her cheek. "That door will never be locked," I said softly. "Never."

She turned away. I could tell from her sharp inhalation that she was crying. I gave my son a hug and a kiss, told him to look after his mommy, and walked out the door.

And the Cleveland Browns did not care.

All the way up to the Bronx, into the locker room, changing into practice sweats, walking through the offensive and defensive schemes, showering, meeting one final time with the team and driving all the way home, never once did I mention my personal affairs to Mack. And never once did he ask. He would have cut me off if I had started to talk about it. Life was life. Tough shit. The job was football, and we didn't have time to mix the two.

Mack's only comment was a cautionary nod as he dropped me off. It was early, but I went right upstairs, switched on the radio and vowed to stay put for the rest of the night. That strange hollow feeling filled my chest again. Anna's spot on the couch was empty. Antonio was not sleeping in the bedroom. After a while I dozed off, but I woke up two hours later to the sound of someone blowing a wicked horn. The guy was lightning. When I was fully awake, I realized that a completely different song was coming out of the radio; the music I heard was live. *Jeremiah Walker.* It had been nearly a year since Jeremiah had played the Pelican. I had seen him only occasionally. Our conversations had followed the same pattern: I would beg him to play at the bar, and he would smile and nod and disappear for another two months. But now, for some reason, he was back. I could tell from the noise that the room was on fire, one of those rare nights when everyone there just *got* it. Well, maybe a few minutes, I thought. Coupla songs. After all, it was Jeremiah. I got up and grabbed my shirt, but paused with my hand on the doorknob. Naw. There was too much at stake. I didn't trust the chaos of the bar. I switched off the radio, opened all the windows so I could hear better and started to flip through my playbook. Wired as I was, I must have been drained enough to nod off again. The next sound I heard was the booming kick of a heavy boot against the apartment door.

There were three of them, guys I had never seen before. One rushed me straight on, while another snuck to the side and blackjacked the base of my skull. When I woke up again, I was bumping along in the back seat of a car. They had gagged me with a strip of rag and bound my hands and feet. Each breath I took sent a shot of pain through my ribs. My face was wet; one eye felt swollen. As the brakes squeaked to a stop, the guy on the right side got out and reached back into the wheel well for a coil of rope. Below his short, sloping forehead, his face was a blank stare. The driver, a big man, opened the door nearest my head and pulled me out. When my ribs scraped against the seat, fire raged through my back. He held me up, while the bald guy who had sat in the middle grabbed my feet. Above me in the dark night sky, I could barely make out what looked like a giant bottle. The Hoffmann Soda factory? Their water tank was shaped like a soda bottle; it towered over all of the other structures in the West Ward.

A tall ladder rose from the factory roof to a catwalk at the base of the bottle. They carried me to a door, then up an interior stairway and onto the roof. The bald one looked at the slim ladder and shook his head.

"Let's just leave him here," he said. He pointed up at the ladder. "I ain't climbin' that."

"Boss said string him up," the driver said.

"No, he said slow him down," the bald one shot back. "Them ribs oughta do that." He poked my side with the toe of his shoe. I roared through the gag, wishing I could get my hands on his throat.

"Maybe it was the other one who said the string thing," the third one offered, his blank face contorted with thought. "The fat one."

The driver shoved him a half step backward and commanded him to keep quiet. After a moment, he seemed to have an inspiration. He asked how long the rope was, then took one end and tied it around my ankles. With the other end, he climbed up to the catwalk and looped it over the railing. It dropped almost to the surface of the roof. I watched him grab the rope and wind it around his wrist. Praying for him to have some sense, I shook my head vigorously as he steadied himself and dropped from the platform. With a sudden tug, I was lifted upside down. I swung out over the grass below and hurtled upward toward the railing. My feet stopped about four feet away from it. The bald guy quickly tied the end of the rope to the base of the tower. Still swinging back and forth, I tried to gauge the strength of that knot. They slowly let go of the rope. It held — for now. I snorted with panic at the thought that at any moment I might drop fifty feet and land on my head. They went downstairs and walked across the lawn. Only one of them looked back — the bald one. I squinted through stinging moisture to identify the car. It was a two-tone sedan with Jersey plates, orange letters against a black background.

Gradually, my pendulum motion slowed and stopped. The binds on my hands were fairly slack, so I worked them until I managed to free one. I raised the other hand over my head and let the short rope fall to the ground. It took a long time to land. After undoing the gag, I grabbed my pant legs and pulled myself up until I was bent double with a decent grip on the rope tied to my feet. My ribs burned, but I held on tight. It was an awkward climb to the railing, each precarious movement renewing the agony in my side. After a struggle, I grabbed the metal bar, pulled myself up and over and dropped onto the catwalk. I lay panting on the diamond plate surface for a long time, struggling to comprehend what had just happened. Rolling onto my side, I looked at the height of the tower and vomited over the edge when a dizzying wave rushed through me. After another long rest, I sat up and untied my feet, then slowly climbed back down the ladder. I took the stairs to the ground floor and walked out to South Orange Avenue.

The first people I saw on the sidewalk were a pair of old ladies who, thankfully, did not know my mother. I must have had a lot of blood on my face, because they rushed over and made a big fuss out of helping me. They drove me to St. Michael's Hospital and waited with me until a doctor was available. Two washcloths, three stitches and several painful pokes in the ribs later, I was discharged and once again found myself in their custody. It was just after ten o'clock when they dropped me off at my doorstep. I walked up to the apartment, examined the little black crosshatches that blended nicely into my swollen eyebrow and concluded that I was not much worse for wear — until I sneezed a spray of blood onto the mirror and nearly doubled over from the pain in my side. The back of my head was beginning to throb. I checked the splintered door frame; luckily the top bolt was still intact. I slid it closed, tucked the top of a chair under the doorknob and lay down to sleep. Without Anna. If not for the beating I had received — and the painkillers it yielded, which dumped me into an abyss of unconsciousness for a few hours — I doubt very much I would have slept at all that night.

Thank God for small favors.

Twenty-eight

*Bronx, New York
September, 1947*

High in the stands in Yankee Stadium, way, way back in a spot where you would never want to sit for a football game, there was a seat that had two deep little scratches on the back of it. If you're there at just the right time, which in my case was shortly after sunrise, you can almost convince yourself that they form a cross. I know it isn't much as far as omens go, but it worked for me. And the seat number started with three, which was my jersey number. I was a creature of habit, and Mack was the same way, so we felt compelled to leave for the Bronx at oh-five-hundred even on game day. We were insanely early, but I didn't mind. At four a.m., I was already showered, shaved and dressed in my suit and tie, waiting at the kitchen table and trying to meditate away the pain in my ribs and head. My eye was edged in black and green and still slightly swollen, but you could barely see the stitches. Soon adrenaline would take care of everything, but in the meantime the deliberate erasure of the temporal self would have to suffice.

Mack didn't ask about my eye, and as usual I didn't offer. As we drove through the pig-farm stink of Secaucus, I found myself thinking about Vin and Benny. The more I thought about their ignorant greed, the angrier I got. Who were they to take away my life's work for a few bucks in winnings? The angrier I got, the more determined I was to win the damn game outright. Screw the spread. Burn the goddamn bar. Hang me from the neck this time. I didn't care. If I let them run my life, it was all over anyway.

"You remember the Albany game, right before the half?" Mack asked.

"What, you breaking that guy's back? Thanks, I need *that* in my mind today." Mack's blindside shot on their quarterback was still one of the most frightening hits I had ever seen.

"No, man, the touchdown," Mack said. "The halfback fell down..."

"Yeah, I remember."

"This guy today has the same bad feet," Mack pointed out. "If we get down that dirt infield side again, I'm thinkin' I can turn him around the same way. Make him trip up." Mack glanced over to make sure I heard him. "Just keep it in mind."

I nodded, then leaned back against the seat and looked up at the visors. The image of St. Christopher hanging upside down crossed my mind. I guess I know how you feel now, pal. What were the odds that anybody else in the game had spent the previous night suspended by the feet from a giant soda bottle? I laughed out loud. Mack glanced at me again like he thought maybe the pressure was getting to me, but I just smiled. Sometimes when things are strange enough it sets you free. We crossed the river to the dim lights of Manhattan and made our way up to One Sixty-first and the stadium. Except for a few cops and some maintenance guys, we were pretty much the first ones there. Mack went inside to lay down, and I climbed up to that seat with the little cross gouged into it. As the sun angled into the ballpark and touched the goalposts down below, I thought about redemption. You can't choose the life you are born into, or the people who are there with you, but you can find those places that keep your soul clean.

At the time, all I wanted was for everything to feel normal again, but I knew there was something very special about that first game. You can get comfortable after a year or two at the same level. Then when you move up, it all gets thrown into doubt again. In the mad scramble to assimilate, what you might not realize is that you are facing one of the great opportunities in life, the chance for renaissance, and rebirth. Maybe even redemption. It might be that you are better suited to higher competition, and that you've never seen your greatest self because there was no one around who was good enough to draw it out. I think that might be the real beauty of September in America. It's when all of us have a chance to ascend just a little higher and maybe, finally, to see our better selves. I pressed my thumb against the little cross and prayed for that to be true.

From above the Hudson River valley, the wind sometimes starts as a delicate waft of clean pine and loam that floats down to the wide water, finding its direction amid the rolling bluffs above New York City and rippling the iron surface of the river as it gathers enough strength to wash through bridges and over rooftops; strength enough to lift the scent of diesel and marinara past the high walls of legend and into the privileged intimacy of championship pennants, flags of state, and the tousled hair of first one, then five, then fifty thousand spectators before fluttering through Opening Day bunting and scattering warning track cinders into the shining waves of grass that brush halfway up the scarred leather sides of a pair of football cleats. And sometimes that wind gives you a little connection to the outside world, the world where time doesn't stop and then start again, where people adhere to a reality by which you are no longer bound — at least for those three blessed hours. And sometimes that's okay.

But not that day.

Out on the field, that wind tickled my ankle and I kicked it away. I jogged to midfield to warm up with my teammates, but for me the journey was longer and more desperate. I wanted to lose myself within those predictable boundaries, to find asylum in that hundred-yard sanctuary, far from the place where brothers sold your dreams and husbands rose from the dead to steal back the women you loved. I shut out the wind, and its whispers of home. The kickoff sailed up into the dry blue and then down again, caught by a waiting runner whose white-and-orange-and-black fast blur of motion brought the supreme focus of impact, skidding shoulder-first on the too-clean turf as I breathed again and my bruised ribs lit up. Until that first tackle, it feels like you aren't even touching the ground.

Mack was one of those people who could recall most of the plays — and even the names of the opponents — from the games he'd been in. I was the opposite. Most of it faded behind a watercolor wash of images, lost to my meditative process of executing and then forgetting each play in succession. I remember shutting out the ache in my side, then getting hit and having to do it all over again. Nothing was the same as the game we had played in the November fog; this was all so vivid and so much less dreamlike, and across the line were the white leather helmets of the *Cleveland Browns*, for God's sake. Not some half-assed gang of patroons from Albany, but names I had read in the newspaper and heard on the radio. For a play or two it really stuck in my mind that those were actual professionals, guys way better than me. But once the rhythm of the game kicked in, I began to see them as patches of white and orange against green, not former N.F.L. linemen and defensive backs.

By halftime, we had played to a two-touchdown tie. I had never seen guys with skills like that before. They picked me off twice, but only one of those interceptions led directly to a score on their part. Both of our touchdowns came on running plays; our speedy veteran halfback Tillman was having a career day. Shapiro and Pioli were opening bus-sized holes on the right side of the line, so all I had to do was hand the ball off and watch those quick feet scamper through. We walked off to a general roar of approval, but through the cheers I heard my name paired more than once with words like "bum" and "amateur." One loud voice hounded me all the way off the field. When I looked up, I saw Vin's associate — the one I had punched in the face. He was standing just behind the railing in the first row, wearing a long coat. As I passed, he opened the coat slightly and flashed the butt of a gun. I forced a sarcastic smile and kept walking.

The sky had clouded when we came back for the second half. When the Browns scored a touchdown on their opening drive, everyone assumed that the rout was on. But that was all the scoring they would do until more than halfway through the fourth quarter. Mack was all over their backfield, hurrying passes and beating down the halfbacks who tried to block him. On offense, his aggressive ball-hawking helped turn some of my weaker throws into completions. There was a quiet intensity in his eyes, the look of a consummate pro. I drew confidence from it as the game wore on. We were driving out of our own end zone into a light rain when I called a pass to the sideline. At the snap, Mack ran eight yards and broke left. I released the ball just as he turned, but it slipped a little. I felt sick when I recognized my mistake. The Cleveland defender intercepted it in stride and broke for the end zone. I turned to chase him, but a blindside forearm knocked me off my feet. I landed hard, sending fresh pain through my side and back. Nobody else was close. He scored.

I lay on the ground by the ten yard line, trying to ignore the boos that rode the misty rain down from the upper decks. When I got up, I looked at the section where the gunman had been. He was there in the second row, next to Vin and Henry Izzo. Vin was laughing as he heaved back and took another deep drink from his big silver flask. He bellowed his thanks to me for letting the

Browns beat the spread. Izzo's face looked grim. When our eyes met, he looked away in disgust.

"You're bleeding," Mack said, pointing at my eyebrow.

The Browns kicked the extra point and increased their lead to fourteen. I wiped the blood from my eye, pulled my helmet on and got ready to go back in. Mack stopped me with a hand on my shoulder.

"What's going on?" he asked with chilling solemnity.

"Whattaya mean?"

"I mean, last night you get your face all busted up, then today some meatball yells at you about the point spread?" He leveled a dagger look. "I was open, man."

"The ball slipped," I said.

"You sure?"

"Goddamn it!" I roared. "The ball was wet! It slipped!" I glared at Mack. "Nobody owns me."

Mack stared as if he was waiting for something else, but that was all I had: the truth. Without breaking eye contact, he nodded and walked toward the field. I followed.

A disappointing runback gave us the ball on our own thirteen, with a little over four minutes left in the game. Four running plays brought us to the forty-five yard line, but burned almost two minutes off the clock. I threw that same sideline pass to Mack and this time completed it for another first down. Three plays later we faced fourth and two at their thirty-six yard line. I called a short rollout pattern to the halfback on the wide side of the field. Mack would run a secondary route a just little deeper. When the center snapped the ball, I broke to my right and looked for Tillman. He slipped and fell. Further downfield, Mack was covered by two defenders. I kept running. Two Cleveland linemen stood between me and the first down marker. Bracing for impact, I lowered my shoulder and drove for the gap between them. A knee came up and caught my brow, but I kept fighting for yardage until one of them gave ground and fell backward. With a final push, I ground out a half yard more.

The chain crew trotted out from the sidelines to measure the play. First down, by barely an inch. I wiped my eyebrow with my sleeve and was surprised by the amount of blood that had seeped from my broken stitches. I jogged to the huddle and called a sweep to the sideline, which gained seven more yards before Tillman hopped out of bounds. My second-down pass fell incomplete. In the huddle, Mack gestured at the dirt infield beneath our feet. I nodded and called the pass play that he had mentioned in the car. With a good break off the line and some fancy footwork, he crossed up the defensive back who was supposed to cover him. I lofted the ball on a perfect arc to Mack's right shoulder, but at the last second the defender lunged and tripped him with a desperate slap to the ankle. The ball bounced out of the end zone. The referee decided not to call a penalty on the play, so we faced fourth and three on their twenty-seven yard line.

Conventional wisdom would say that if you are losing by two touchdowns with a minute left in the game, and it's fourth down, you have nothing to lose in going for the first down. In fact, it's more or less your only move. But I desperately wanted to kick the field goal. As I stood in the huddle looking at our kicker on the sidelines and debating my options, Mack tapped my shoulder and pulled me off to the side.

"You can't do that."

"Why the hell not?" I snapped. "They don't own me, Mack. I need to prove it."

"No you don't," he said softly. "Newspapers'll eat you alive, you kick here."

"I don't care."

"Throw it again," he said. "Just one more time. Make that throw again and I'll get you six points."

I stared at Mack, then looked at the kicker. Time was running out.

"Just once more," he implored.

I leaned into the huddle, still unsure of what I would say. After a quick glance at my teammates, I decided to trust him. I called the same play again. With his first step off the line, Mack flicked his head to the inside and dug hard that way. The halfback didn't bite. He cut to the outside and shoved the defender to gain a half-step of separation, but still the man dogged him. I waited with the ball as the defense pressed in, praying for an opening for the throw. It never came. Out of desperation, I pulled the ball down and started to run, dodging left and right until a lane appeared. Through the narrowest of gaps, I snuck straight ahead for two yards and darted for the sideline. I sprinted for the first down marker with three Browns in pursuit, diving at the last moment and stretching out as far as I could. The ball crossed over the line just as one of the Browns drove his shoulder into my exposed ribs. My entire body clenched with pain. As I rolled out of bounds, the other two players landed on me. Barely able to breathe, I struggled to a sitting position and called time out. There were twenty-seven seconds left. First down.

I lurched to my feet and walked slowly down the sideline to the coach. One look at my bloody face and weak posture, and he was barking for my backup. I shook my head and motioned for the kid to sit back down. Clearly skeptical, the coach gave me two plays to call. I could tell from his tone that he had already accepted the fact of our loss. Showing as little discomfort as I could, I jogged back out to the huddle and called the first play, a deep corner pass to the right end. The throw was slightly short, but the receiver made a great play to prevent an interception. On second down, I was forced to run again and picked up four yards before going out of bounds. There were twelve seconds left. We had two downs to go twenty yards, and we got sixteen of them on one play when Mack caught another sideline pass and turned it upfield for a big gain. It was first down on their four yard line with three seconds left. I had an idea.

Each time I dropped straight back to pass, the rush came hard from either end but Pioli and Shapiro were shutting them down in the middle. I called for Mack to run a shorter version of his corner route. This time, instead of sending the halfback out for a pass I told him to stay by my side in the backfield. At the snap, I held the ball high and watched Mack run his pattern. From either side, the defensive ends bore down on me as that same lane opened in the middle again. At the last second, I jammed the ball into Tillman's gut and watched him run a perfect draw play. In the next instant I was hit simultaneously from both sides. I crumpled in agony as the crowd roared for the touchdown. Tillman ran off the field to a hero's salute, with Mack and everyone trailing behind. You'd have thought we won the game. I took off my helmet and rolled onto my hands and knees, then sat back on my heels and labored for breath. Blood dripped from my brow down onto my pants as I lingered, wondering how long I could hide in the violent oasis of the gridiron before I would again have to face reality. Fans climbed toward the exits. After a while, I looked up at the fence that lay just beyond the end zone. There, leaning against the railing in the first row, was Anna.

Twenty-nine

Newark
September, 1947

Giordano Pietro watched the two-tone sedan make one, then two, then three passes by the window. He was alone in the bar, preparing to open for the late afternoon crowd. On the fourth pass, the sedan slowed. A man with a bald head leaned halfway out of the passenger window, touched a Zippo to a rag dangling from a milk bottle and shattered the bottle against the plate glass window. Gio thought it was beautiful, a perfectly circular flower of flame against the unbroken window. But then the glass cracked and burst, and flaming gas dripped into the bar, and all that was wooden began to steam and ignite. And then, Gio told me later, he didn't think it was so beautiful anymore.

Thirty

Bronx
September, 1947

There were tears on Anna's cheeks when I reached
the railing. I had to move slowly, but I tried not to hunch
over or anything like that. There was nothing I could do
about the blood; I wiped it off, but it kept coming. She
put her hands on my face and kissed me on the lips. I
reached over the low fence and lifted her past the railing,
biting my lip to keep from crying out at the hot spasm
gripping my torso. I set her down and took a deep breath.
She smiled.

"The door was locked," she said. I stared at her,
confused. "At home," she clarified. "I went back last
night but it was locked."

"How...? Where's Antonio?"

"We went to sleep at Carmela's," Anna said softly.
"Antonio is there. I took the trains to get here."

"But Karl," I mumbled. "I thought you—"

"I did," she said quickly. "I phoned his friend Werner
for a ride. He took me to see Karl." She paused to dry her

eyes. The rain kept falling. "Mateo, I had to explain myself to him. He was my husband. I owed him that."

I smiled. "You said 'was.'"

With my arm around her waist, I walked her to the dugout where the locker room door was propped open. She climbed up on the high bench, sheltered from the rain. I kissed her cheek and ducked inside for a shower and the post-game meeting. The coach acknowledged the team's effort and singled out Mack and Tillman for game balls. I slapped Mack's shoulder as he headed to his car and told him I would need a few minutes. His wife and kids were with a group outside, so we agreed to meet in the parking lot. Weaving back through the locker room, I paused to shake hands with Frank Dante and then walked down a narrow hallway and up the steps to the dugout. Anna was not there.

My first panicked thought was that Vin had found her. I raced up to the field and looked back at the stands, shouting her name. And then I saw her. She was in the middle of the field, dancing with her arms open to the gentle rain. All around her crews were working to break down the equipment, but she didn't care. Her face was serene. I thought back to the sight of her singing in the park in Mönchengladbach, trying to smile even as the sky fell down around her. The difference now was that her joy was real, her peace complete. I knew then that she never would have left me for Karl. In a way, perhaps, the bombs had freed her. The walls that surrounded her were more than plaster and lathe and three coats of paint. They were part of a security she had never really known, a safety that she had only imagined for herself and her family. As I watched her spin around and around, I saw the little girl who had hoped for more than her grandmother's deceptions, her mother's denial and her father's sacrifice. I recalled the woman who had married to seal a wound and not a destiny, but before me danced the spirit that had been freed from that life of fear. I walked to the center of the field and winced slightly when she threw her arms around me.

"You know I am, how do you say, closed-true...?"

"Claustrophobic?" I chuckled.

"Yes, that one."

"No," I whispered, "you're beautiful."

Anna smiled and leaned close to me. I kissed the top of her rain-soaked head. We walked to the steps that led up through an exit tunnel, then found our way down to the street level and circled back toward the players' entrance. A huge man stood in the shadows next to a telephone pole, watching the doorway. As we approached the lighted walkway, Anna saw him. She grabbed my sleeve and tried to steer me away, but I was stronger. He stepped forward to confront me.

"I am Karl Eisenstark," he announced. "That is my wife."

Anna answered his assertion in rapid German, which only seemed to antagonize him. He was game for a fight. Aching and exhausted, I was not. I knew there was no way that I could beat someone as big as he was, even without two cracked ribs. I looked around for Mack, but he and everyone else had already walked to their cars. It was just me and Karl, with nothing but a hundred pounds of stubborn beauty between us. I took a step closer, hoping to negate his reach. He slipped to the side, aware of my tactic. Anna kept dancing to the middle, effectively preventing the first punch. We circled like this for a few seconds until the sound of screeching tires froze us where we stood. The gleaming Cadillac had barely come to a full stop when the passenger door swung open and my brother stumbled out. I caught a glint of silver in Vin's right hand. He reeled into the light and tilted his head forward to focus on me.

"Hey!" Vin shouted, his voice slack and muffled. "Hey, hero!"

He waved the silver object at me. Chilled, I realized it was not his flask. He stumbled closer, then stopped and tried to steady his aim. With a little sidestep, he managed to keep from falling over while squinting down the barrel and into my eyes.

"Vin, come on," I said carefully.

"No!" he blurted. "You know how much you cost me today? I gotta do this."

"You don't—"

"I gotta!" he cried.

He tried to stand up straight, but lost his aim and hunched over again, squinting hard. I realized that he was crying.

"I gotta," he said more softly. "You don't understand. You got no idea about me. You don't know how easy this is for me," he sobbed. "You don't know how easy..." His voice choked to silence.

"Hey!" the driver called. It was the guy who had shown me his gun in the stadium. Izzo was not in the car. "Quit bullshitting around!"

Vin wheeled and aimed at the car. While he was looking away, Karl took a small step backward, away from me and Anna. Vin quickly turned back to me, his gun hand shaking.

"I gotta do this." Vin's eyes were bleary. "You took everything away from me. You took it all. I gotta. I gotta take everything from you now. I gotta..." His sobs mingled with the slur of his words until they tailed off again. He started to lower the gun, but then brought it back up and aimed it at Anna.

"For you, she's everything," he mumbled. "I'll take her."

Vin's finger tightened. Karl froze. I didn't.

The bullet would have hit Anna square in the face if I hadn't jumped in time. I felt its searing impact on the right side of my chest. It spun me around and threw me backward with an almost humiliating amount of power. My body went slack, my arms and legs splayed almost at random. The embarrassing heat of urine filled my pants; I had no control. Mercifully, after a few more seconds I blacked out. Anna told me later that Vin had stood gape-mouthed, the gun drifting slowly to his side, as I lay bleeding. His friend honked the horn a few times and then pulled away without him. Karl tackled Vin and took the gun away. Vin offered no resistance. When the police finally came to arrest him, Anna swore that my brother still had not blinked.

Thirty-one

Newark
October, 1947

Henry Izzo could have been many things: a Marine, a husband, a football player, a business owner — even, in the final reckoning, a good man. In many ways he was all of those things, but none of them completely. He was a man who kept his options open, never fully committing, never closing off other avenues. He trained his mind to believe in God, even though his heart would not, because it seemed like the prudent thing to do. He started a football team so that no one could cut him from theirs. He married sincerely, but flirted without shame. He wore prominently the psychic scars of wartime loss, both to honor the dead and to mask his own deep relief at not having joined them. He had inherited an honest business, but did not defend the honor of the man who had passed it to him. He pledged allegiance to the flag, but smirked at the idea of true sacrifice. He was a modern American, but an old soul. His sophistication ended where his blood began. In the end, that was what saved him.

After three days, I regained consciousness. Henry Izzo's was the first face I saw. I thought he was Vin, and for some reason that made me happy. Izzo didn't say anything. He just smiled and woke Anna so she could be the first to greet me. It would be a while before I could stand, or even sit up, but I would make a full recovery. The bullet had glanced off my second rib, breaking it completely in the spot where it had been cracked. It had exited my back at a thirty-degree angle. The police found the slug in the wall of Yankee Stadium; they calculated that it had missed Anna by just a few inches. I never bothered to tell her about that. Aside from teammates, the only official representative from the New York Yankees Football Club who visited me in the hospital was Frank Dante. He told me that they had acquired the rights to a veteran quarterback, and that the team would be in good hands until I returned. I found out later that he had made the deal almost immediately after the starter went down — before the Cleveland game. He was kind enough to omit that detail when we spoke.

My days in the hospital were long and dull, but I reminded myself that it could have been worse. With Vin's arrest and the bar's almost complete incineration, Benny Bells declared the matter closed. He was never much of a fan of American sports, and gambling only exposed his lack of understanding, so he shut down the bookmaking operation and washed his hands of my brother. Vin was arraigned for attempted murder. After a week or so I was transferred to St. Michael's in Newark, where Anna brought me a stack of library books. Mama and Pop came by with Antonio. Although I know that in the back of her twisted Sicilian mind Mama blamed Anna for everything that had happened, she found a way to embrace the expectant mother of her fifth grandchild. When I was finally permitted to eat, my sisters spoiled me with home-cooked meals. John Mack stopped by with the New York newspapers and asked if I was happy that he hadn't allowed me to call that field goal. The papers had reported just enough of the truth to make me look pretty good. I was smiling a lot for a guy with a hole clean through him.

One night I was awakened by that strange itching on the inside of the wound. I was about to reach for a glass of water when I sensed something across the room. In the glow of the dim hall light, a tall figure loomed in the doorway. Slowly, he walked toward me. As he advanced, he reached into the pocket of his rough denim coat. Helpless and virtually paralyzed with fear, I wanted to call for the nurse but I could make no sound. When he reached the bed, he stopped and leaned over. The smell of scorched metal and burnt sand hung over him. He lifted his hand from his pocket; in it was a flat object, which he raised almost to my face. When I calmed down enough to look at it closely, I realized that it was a phonograph record in a paper sleeve.

"Here," Karl Eisenstark said quietly. "Play this when she is sad."

I took the record and nodded my thanks. Karl bowed ever so slightly and walked out of the room. His footsteps echoed in the hallway until at last a stairway door opened and closed. Only then did I begin to relax. I lifted the disk out of its sleeve and into the light, but I knew what it was before I read the label: Ella Fitzgerald, "A Tisket, A-Tasket." It was the song that Anna was singing when I first heard her voice. I studied the record, well aware of how hard it must have been for Karl to let

Anna go. Although he was already well out of earshot, I waited a long time before I moved again. When I did, it was to lean over as far as I could and toss the record into the wastebasket.

Anna wouldn't need it anymore.

Thirty-two

Newark
December, 1947

The snow gleamed brilliant white and clean in the early sunlight. On the sidewalk in front of Pop's flat, Antonio scooped up a handful, tossed it into Mickey's face and ran off down the block toward South Orange Avenue. Mickey chased after him. Bundled against the cold, Rica held the door open for Anna, who waddled through in a heavy wool sweater that was stretched across her big, round belly. She smiled up at the blue vault, the blush of pregnancy rising in her cheeks as she met the immaculate morning air. Anna followed her son's footsteps and climbed a rough plank stairway to the first floor of a newly-framed structure. Within the skeletal walls, Henry Izzo and I held each end of a long wooden beam. Although I really wasn't supposed to be straining myself, I lifted it above my head and set it on top of a framed wall as the first in a series of horizontal joists. Izzo parked his end in the same way at the other side of the room. From an upturned barrel in the center of the floor, a wireless radio blared a lightning-fast sax solo out into the morning. The style sounded familiar, but I couldn't quite place the tune.

Antonio chased Mickey in and out of the open walls and followed him to the doorway. Trying to mimic his cousin's bravado, Antonio jumped down to the ground but slipped and fell as he landed. He stood up, brushed himself off and chased Mickey down the block until he was corralled into a hug by his Auntie Rica. Anna crossed the floor and put her arms around my neck. She kissed me, but I could feel her fumbling with something just above my collar. When she pulled her hands away, I saw both ends of the black ribbon, and in the middle of it, the iron shard I had fashioned into a ring. Smiling up at me with mischief in her eyes, she let the ring fall into her palm and slipped it onto her wedding finger. The crystal air grew still around the framework I had helped to raise from the ashes of the Pelican Club. We held one another, her head on my shoulder, my face in her hair. When she leaned back again, the sunlight shimmered in her golden eyes. But as I watched, a shadow of fear and anger darkened her gaze. She buried her face in my chest, as if to hide from a horror she could not bear to see.

I felt a tap on my shoulder and turned around. Before me was a face I barely recognized, one that had been far more familiar to me in the early days of my life. It was my brother Vin, but paler and much thinner than he had been in years. Anna pulled closer to me, shaking with rage. Vin looked down at the ground.

"I just wanna say thanks for not pressing charges," he mumbled.

Anna pushed away and looked up at me, aghast. "They were not your charges to press," she said. "He tried to kill *me*."

"Anna, let it go," I said softly.

"No."

"Anna, please. He's family."

Vin started to walk away, but I stopped him with a hand on his arm. For a moment, I wondered if we would ever find words to repair what had passed between us. But then, on the radio, the first few plinking notes of "Take the 'A' Train" brought our heads around at the same time. As the song gathered steam, I smiled at my brother. He looked away. After sixty days in jail for unlawful discharge of a firearm, he looked as if stress — and perhaps penitence — had burned fifty pounds off of him. Anna was trying to contain her anger, but failing. For her, it would be a longer road to forgiveness.

"Gotta go," Vin mumbled.

"Yeah," I stalled. "Well, take care of yourself."

"Yeah, uh, you too." He shuffled toward the plank stairway.

"Listen," I started. "Where...? Uh, you okay for dinner? I mean, you're lookin' a little thin."

Behind his back, he flipped me the same finger that he had as a kid that day at the baseball game. He smiled and nodded slightly as he hopped down to the sidewalk.

"Take good care," I called after him.

At first, Anna was puzzled by the clemency I had stubbornly granted the man who had almost killed me. But as his shadow retreated down Tenth Street, her eyes brightened once again. Between the beams of the resurrected club, sunlight played across the snow. She glanced up the block, then back at me. Her expression softened to a smile. She shook her head and chuckled softly as she fiddled with the iron band on her finger. I pulled her close and kissed the top of her head, then stood with my arm around her. A light wind sprayed us with a snowy mist, washing us clean. Washing all of us clean.

Acknowledgements

Without the patient reading, candid feedback and generous advice of family and friends, this story would not exist. To my wife Julie, thank you for sharing countless hours of early dreaming, midstream frustration and bittersweet completion. You are my Anna.

My parents, Renata Bouterse and Al D'Emilio, my grandmother Helene Reinartz, and my late aunt Millie Romeo provided the kind of insight that could only be given by those who have lived in the time and locations in which this story takes place.

Thanks to trusted friends and family for reading draft after draft and always providing fresh analysis. In addition to those mentioned above, they include: Mark Shapiro, Scott Pioli, Ron Shapiro, Matt Spencer, Mary McLoughlin, Lori Thatch, Paul Zimmerman, Michael and Jeanne Romeo, Willem Bouterse, Carl D'Emilio, Brenda Gallagher and Dominick Abbruzzese.

Lastly, I would like to thank two literary agents, Richard Abate and Jill Marsal, who chose not to represent *Autumn Fool* but who did take the time to read the first draft and offer thoughtful commentary.

Made in the USA
Middletown, DE
16 July 2019